Wings of a Flying Tiger

Best wishes !

Iris Yang

Iris Yang

Open Books

Published by Open Books

Copyright © 2018 by Qing Yang

Learn more about the artist at www.flickr.com/photos/fox3nova/

ISBN-13: 978-1948598064

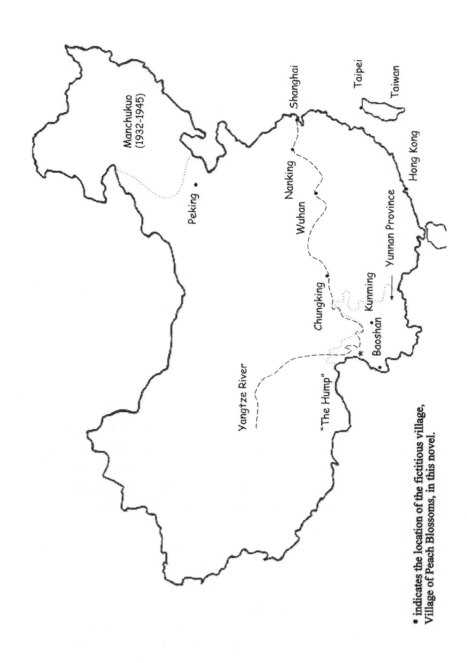

Manchukuo
(1932-1945)

Peking

Shanghai

Taipei

Taiwan

Nanking

Wuhan

Hong Kong

Chungking

Kunming

Yunnan Province

Baoshan

Yangtze River

"The Hump"

* indicates the location of the fictitious village,
Village of Peach Blossoms, in this novel.

Prologue

‒ ‒ ‒ ‒ ‒ ‒

"Get the hell out of there, Jack. Now!" Danny Hardy barked into the radio.

Through the debris that erupted from the enemy plane he'd shot down, he gazed at a flaming aircraft emblazoned with tiger's teeth. *God, please*, he silently prayed, hoping to see his wingman pop out of the airplane any second.

Danny hadn't heard Jack's voice on the radio since he'd been hit, but that didn't stop him from calling out again: "Jack, bail out!"

Minutes ago Jack Longman had sent two Japanese aircraft spinning down to earth, but now his plane was on fire. Two Zeros flanked him. He'd been hit from both sides. Fire blazed from the fuselage tank of his P-40 and roared into the cockpit. His airplane remained level for only a moment then plunged, nose down, toward the earth. Rolling back the canopy, Jack leaned left and tumbled out of the plane, which was now wreathed in smoke. When he opened his parachute, part of his body was on fire.

Danny let out a relieved breath when he saw Jack's tall figure drop out of his airplane. One corner of his lips tilted upward. But before his smile had formed completely, to his horror, a Japanese fighter dropped on Jack, firing a heartless spray of bullets.

"No!" Danny cried. His heart thundered. Waves of panic spread throughout his body. It all had happened too fast. He wasn't close enough to catch up with the Japanese. Helplessly, he watched as his best friend was strafed to death while strapped in his parachute.

"Jack!" A lump formed in the back of his throat and burned as Danny tried to choke back tears. He couldn't let the enemy get away. He roared after the Japanese. His P-40 wasn't as versatile as the enemy airplanes, but it was faster in a dive. Flying Tigers were trained to exploit that advantage. Within seconds, he caught up with one of the two fighters that had killed Jack. He brought his guns in line for a shot from the rear. Before the Japanese pilot realized his fate, Danny poured a salvo directly into his cockpit. Flames erupted from the Zero. A fireball spun earthbound.

This maneuver exposed Danny's P-40 to the other Japanese fighter, who fired at him from the left. An explosion blasted his left wing, and the plane shook. At the same time, bullets riddled his cockpit. One of them grazed his scalp; others buried themselves in the instrument panel. Blood gushed from his forehead, covering his goggles and blocking his sight. Red spots spattered the white scarf around his neck.

Pulling his stick with his right hand, and lifting his left to wipe the blood off his goggles, he realized that his left arm and leg had been injured by shrapnel. In the midst of the white-knuckled fight, the excruciating pain hadn't hit him until now.

Switching to his right hand, Danny pulled off his goggles. Once he could see, he checked his left wing. What he saw made his blood run cold. The explosion had left a hole two feet in diameter, halfway between the wingtip and the root. He was astonished the wing was still attached.

The shock didn't last long. No time to waste. He was trained as a fighter pilot, and fighting was second nature.

Ignoring the throbbing pain, Danny hauled his P-40 into a tight turn. Advancing the throttle, he flew toward the enemy fighter who had shot at him. His engine roared. The force jammed him into his seat. Bullets ricocheted through his plane, flashing like firecrackers. But nothing deterred him. Swooping toward the fighter, he thumbed on the gun switch and opened fire. His tracers strafed the front of the Zero.

The Japanese seemed startled by the American pilot's comeback. The bravery of the American Volunteer Group, the Flying Tigers, was well known by this time, the summer of 1942, but this Tiger was completely insane. The little airman flinched, yet held his course.

"If you don't ram into me, I'm going to ram you!" Danny shouted, sweating beneath his sheepskin-lined jacket. He knew he shouldn't do this—the Japanese pilots were disciplined flyers; they were not cowards. And Danny had no intention of dying. However, this Zero was the one that had shot Jack down. Revenge was the only thing on his mind. He had no plan to turn around.

Might as well take someone with me if my number is up…

Although he had lived only twenty-seven years, that was long enough to destroy twelve enemy airplanes. "Let's make this one the thirteenth!" he shouted, his hand on the trigger and death in his eyes.

The two planes were so close that Danny could see the stone-faced Japanese pilot glaring at him. For what seemed like an eternity, they stared at each other. Time slowed as their planes closed in. It was a contest of wills.

A split-second before the crash, the wide-eyed Japanese pilot lost his nerve and tried to peel away from a head-on collision, a maneuver which left him vulnerable.

Danny jumped at the chance and blazed with everything he had. His hand never left the trigger. His tracers tore the Zero to pieces.

He watched the enemy plane turn into a fireball. It streamed black and white smoke, went into a rapid spin, and plummeted to Earth.

Danny had no time to celebrate his success. Hits that he'd sustained during the death match made his plane wobble like a drunkard. He had to abandon his P-40. As he prepared to jump, he glanced down at the exotic highlands unfolding below him. Yunnan Province of China was composed of magnificent mountains and sweeping plains. He was over a mountainous region carpeted by lush green trees. Somewhere beneath the shady canopy lay his best friend's body, burned and riddled with Japanese bullets.

Suddenly, Danny changed his mind. By now, fewer and fewer of their aircraft remained intact. *God knows we need every single one.* Their air-worthy planes were already outnumbered—today four P-40s had had to fight two dozen Zeros. Now, with Jack's death, two airplanes would be gone if he bailed out.

Danny felt exhausted. He grimaced. The injuries to his head, arm, and leg were nasty, but something else was wrong. Could it be the cold he'd come down with during the past few days? No matter how tired he was, Danny refused to let his plane go down. Not without a fight. Not until he'd tried everything he could. With one last look at his damaged left wing, he took a few deep breaths and forced himself to lean back against his seat. His hand clutched the stick in a death grip, and with what seemed like a superhuman effort, he fought to stabilize the aircraft.

He didn't think about dying, he was too involved in keeping his P-40 in the air. Setting his course toward Kunming, Yunnan's capital, he tried to level the plane. But it was so crippled, he could barely maintain control.

He had managed to fly for twenty or thirty minutes, but the mental pain of losing his best friend from childhood, the physical ache of his wounds, as well as that mysterious illness—whatever it was—all crashed in on him, and before long the aircraft would not respond to his commands. The stricken P-40 snapped into a spin, and no matter how hard he tried, he couldn't recover it.

Now he had no choice. With his last ounce of strength, he slid back the canopy. The wind screeched and plastered the skin over his face. He was barely conscious when he tumbled, head over heels, into space.

Part One

Deep-seated Hatred

Chapter 1

———————

Jasmine Bai sat up straighter when she heard Mr. Peterson's proposal. For a moment her face showed only blank astonishment. *What did he say? Marry him?* She thought for sure she'd heard him wrong.

They were sitting across a white linen-covered table full of dishes. Nanking Salted Duck, Lion's Head, Lotus Root Soup, Steamed Shrimp Dumplings, Yangzhou Fried Rice, Red Bean Rice Cake… Mr. Peterson, her art teacher at the college, had invited her to a pre-Christmas celebration. Throughout this fancy restaurant in Chungking, Christmas ornaments twinkled, and red lanterns glowed. Soft light complemented the soothing music. Delicious aromas permeated the air.

"Will you marry me?" Peter Peterson raised his voice and asked again. Fair and lanky, the American was a fine-looking scholarly type. He wore a well-tailored dark blue suit with a light blue shirt and red tie.

This time Jasmine heard him clearly. They'd been talking about art all evening, and this abrupt change of topic took her aback. *What's wrong with him? Is he drunk?* Seeing his reddened face, the eighteen-year-old girl turned her gaze to a half-empty bottle of Maotai on the table. The most famous brand of liquor contained fifty percent alcohol.

"God, you're so beautiful," said Peter, eyes glowing. His left hand held the bottle while his right hand gripped a large glass.

Not knowing what to say, Jasmine bit down on her lip. She was gorgeous—silky skin, delicate features, and shiny hair cascading like a cloak of satin down to her waist. She was dressed in a carmine red cheongsam. This body-hugging dress with a side slit accentuated the curves of her frame.

"Jasmine?" Without hearing her answer, Peter sprang to his feet, dashed around the table, and dropped to one knee. "Jesus! I'm crazy about you. Can't you see? Marry me. Please!" Excitement made him look younger than his twenty-seven years. Moved by his own bold gesture, he sputtered, "I don't have a ring, but I'll buy one tomorrow—"

"Mr. Peterson—"

"Call me Peter."

"Yes, Peter. Please…stand—"

"Not until you say yes."

"Thank you for your…kind gesture," said Jasmine with all the politeness she could muster. Everyone in the crowded room was now staring at them; some were smiling, others gaped in surprise. The background music was still playing, but the room was quiet. The spectators, a mixture of Chinese and Westerners, held their breath, waiting for her answer.

Peter remained on his knee.

"Sit down. Please. Let's talk," she whispered in nearly perfect English. Unlike most Chinese females in the 1930s, she was well educated. Both her parents were professors at the prominent Nanking University. "I need time to think. I didn't expect… This is happening too fast." She twisted a strand of hair around her right index finger. Lowering her head, she kept her eyes averted.

Reluctantly Peter stood up. Disappointment was written all over his face. The onlookers let out a collective sigh. Sinking back onto his chair, he poured himself more Maotai. Sullenly, he rolled the glass in his fingers.

An awkward silence descended.

Peter raised the glass to his lips and drained it in two swallows. The strong liquor burned his mouth and tongue, causing him to cough into his fist. When he looked up, he said, "You may think I'm drunk. I'm not." He licked his lips. "I've never done anything like this. True. But I'm serious. Believe me."

Jasmine hunted for words. When none came, she continued to fiddle with her hair.

"I know it's hard to believe. Everyone thinks I'm such a cool-headed guy." Peter gave a wry chuckle. "Most of the time, yes. I used to pride myself on my even-tempered nature. But the first time I met you…"

He stared at Jasmine through steel-rimmed glasses. "God, I don't know what happened. I lost it. Your beauty, your sweetness. Then… your incredible painting. I…I fell in love…with you, with your artwork."

Another pause stretched between them.

Peter rubbed his thumb across a furrowed brow and sighed. "Anyway, will you think about it? Seriously, think about it?"

"I will."

"Promise?"

Jasmine dipped her head. She felt bad for Mr. Peterson. *Oh, he must feel let down. This is a romantic place.*

His proposal was flattering. She had to admit it. If anyone found out about tonight, she would be the envy of the school. And eighteen wasn't too young to marry. Most Chinese girls got married at this age; some already had children.

But something was wrong. Jasmine picked up a porcelain teacup with a fragile handle and gold rim. *What's missing?* She liked Mr. Peterson. The young teacher with blue eyes and curly blonde hair was a great catch: he was kind and well-mannered, his teaching was admired by his students, and his artwork was impressive. Jasmine, for one, was a big fan of his landscape paintings.

But why am I not blushing? Why isn't my heart beating faster? Her eyes didn't even glow as she'd expected at a moment like this. *Is this it?* Sipping her tea, she wished that there was more.

After the party, Peter drove Jasmine to her uncle's house where she lived.

————

It was drizzling. Chungking, a major city in Southwest China, seemed deserted at this late hour. Only vertical neon lights pulsed in the darkness.

Staring out the window, Jasmine wondered about her parents. What would they think of Mr. Peterson's proposal? Would they want her to get married so young? *Marrying a foreigner shouldn't be a problem.* Her parents were highly educated and open-minded.

As long as you're happy, Jasmine imagined her mother saying. She'd seen how fulfilled her parents were, and she craved a relationship like theirs. *But can I be happy without being madly in love with him?*

The car wound through cobblestone streets. The headlights penetrated the mist, illuminating several banners—"Down with the Japanese devils," "Fight Japan, rebuild our nation," "Japanese bandits will lose. Victory belongs to China."

The slogans reminded Jasmine that her country was in the middle of a war. *How are Mom and Dad doing? Is Nanking safe?* Even with a coat draped over her shoulders, she felt a sudden chill. Hugging herself, she rubbed her hands up and down her arms.

Noticing her discomfort, Peter turned up the heat.

Jasmine nodded in appreciation. She mustered a slight smile and folded her hands upon her lap. But the uneasy thought wouldn't go away. *Dad is too stubborn. His work is important. But who cares about school when the Japs are coming? It's too dangerous to stay in Nanking.*

As early as 1931, Japan had launched an undeclared war on China and conquered the Northeast territory. The region became a puppet state called Manchukuo, and it generated anti-Japanese sentiment throughout the country. For years, the conflicts between the two nations never ceased. A few months earlier, in the summer of 1937, Japan launched a full-scale invasion. Peking fell. Shanghai followed. Nanking, the capital of the Republic of China, soon became the primary target of the Japanese.

Jasmine's uncle, a colonel in the Air Force, had tried many times to convince her parents to leave Nanking, but to no avail. She sighed and looked outside. The rain had turned into a light snow. The bleakness matched her mood.

She turned to face Peter. "I'm leaving for Nanking tomorrow," she blurted out without knowing why. It was a secret. She hadn't told anyone.

"No!"

"Yes. My parents won't leave. I have to get them out."

"It's too dangerous. Don't you know Nanking is Japan's next target?"

"I know. That's why I have to go. They won't listen to my uncle. If they won't leave with me, I'm going to stay with them."

4

Peter shook his head.

"It may take me some time," she continued. "So if I don't show up for class after the break, don't worry about me. I'll be back when they decide to leave." A hint of a smile broke through her gloominess. "My parents are stubborn. I'm their daughter—double stubborn."

"It's not wise," Peter said. His brows knitted. "How can your uncle and aunt let you go?"

"I...I haven't told them. They would never allow me—"

"Jasmine!"

The squeal of tires interrupted their conversation. The car skidded to a stop in a secluded neighborhood on the outskirts of Chungking. A thin layer of ice shimmered on the ground.

Peter parked by the side of the street. He turned to face her. His hands tightened on the steering wheel. "Jasmine, think it through. A war zone isn't a place for anyone, let alone a beautiful girl like you. Those horrible things... You must have heard about some of them."

"That's why I have to go. I won't let Mom and Dad—"

"Don't go!"

"Thanks for your concern, Peter. But I've made up my mind."

Peter shook his head. With a sigh of frustration, he got out, walked around the car, and opened the door for Jasmine. They parted politely without even holding hands—that was the proper way.

He bowed and gave her a longing glance. The night was dark. A chilly wind whipped down the street. Pulling his coat collar up around his ears, he walked slowly back to his car. The light from the streetlamp silhouetted his lanky and slightly drooped figure. He seemed lost.

Standing by the gate guarded by two stone lions, Jasmine watched him and felt a twinge of guilt. *I bet Mom and Dad will like him. Mr. Peterson is a scholar and a gentleman.* She tossed a wave to him as he drove away. *Perhaps I should reconsider? Hey, I'll tell Mom and Dad about Mr. Peterson. Maybe they'll be curious to come here to meet him. Maybe they will persuade me to accept him.*

When his car disappeared from sight, she walked through the curved archway and into the house. *I'd better leave a letter. Sorry, Uncle and Auntie! I'll apologize in person when I come back. This letter will do for now.*

Chapter 2

Professor Bai sat in his usual spot after dinner. An evening newspaper lay open in his lap, but he couldn't concentrate. Headlines like "Japanese Troops Besiege Nanking" and "The Capital Faces Imminent Threat" disturbed him greatly.

An invasion was no surprise. The war between Japan and the Republic of China was the direct result of a Japanese imperialist policy to expand its influence and obtain raw materials, food, and cheap labor. The period after World War I and the Depression brought about a large slowdown in exports and economic stress on Japanese society, which culminated in the rise to power of a militarist fascist regime. In 1931, Japan launched an undeclared war on China and conquered the Northeast territory. For six years, small localized conflicts between the two nations never ceased. Finally in July 1937, Japan launched a full-scale invasion. After attacking Peking and Shanghai, Nanking, the capital of the Republic of China, was clearly Japan's next target. The city of one million inhabitants had endured dozens of air raids in the past four months, forcing its citizens to hide in basements, trenches, and wells.

Professor Bai and his wife could have left the city. His brother had urged him many times. Most of his colleagues and students had fled. Half the residents had escaped. As the head of the Art Department at Nanking University, he refused to leave. A graduate of the University of Tokyo, he was determined to act as liaison to negotiate with the

Japanese so that his university would not end up in ruins.

"You're so naïve," his brother had shouted over the phone.

"I know their language," Professor Bai argued. "I can help."

"You're such a fool. Have you forgotten the saying? 'A scholar is always wrong when he confronts a gunman.' Don't be so stupid. Get out of there now. For God's sake, don't keep Suying in a war zone."

At age forty-five, Professor Bai should have known better. Even from his comfortable home near the campus, he'd heard gunshots and explosions rumbling in the distance. And the frequency of bombardment increased by the hour. *How long will the Army hold the fort,* he wondered?

Four days earlier, Chiang Kai-shek, the leader of the Nationalists, and his government had fled the city, shifting the burden of defense onto his subordinate. General Tang, the Defense Commander, had vowed to live or die with Nanking. His ninety thousand troops had transformed the face of the capital. They had dug trenches in the streets, strung barbed wire over intersections, and set up machine-guns along the city wall. This charming, ancient town now resembled a battlefield.

What will the Japanese troops do once they capture the city? Professor Bai thought as he checked the date on the newspaper to remember this particular day—December 13, 1937.

I should've sent Suying away. Too bad she's as stubborn as I am.

He looked up. His wife sat on a sofa between two live-in housemaids, a book in her hand. She wore a white cheongsam, her face relaxed, her voice calm. As a professor at Ginling Women's Arts & Science College, she loved teaching the illiterate servant girls who were just a couple of years younger than their daughter Jasmine.

At least Jasmine is safe. Professor Bai sighed with relief. *Chungking is over nine hundred miles away.* He took off his wire-rim glasses and pinched the bridge of his nose to stem a headache that was developing behind his eyes. Moments later he put the glasses back on and walked to the window where heavy drapes were drawn to hide the lit room from the Japanese bombers. Lifting an edge, he peeked outside.

Daylight had taken its last breath and dusk had settled in. In the twilight, gunfire flashed like lightning over Purple Mountain to the east of the city, and the sky to the south glowed with flames. Nearby shadows slanted across the ground that was covered with patches of graying snow.

Professor Bai stared into the gloominess then pulled the drapes closed as if to shut out the danger.

"Anything wrong?" asked Mrs. Bai.

The housemaids also lifted their heads. Nowadays everyone was on edge. Chen Hong, a lanky girl with freckles, took a nervous breath. Xiao Mei chewed her lip. Two waist-length pigtails hung at each side of her heart-shaped face, and she looked younger than her sixteen years.

"No," said Professor Bai. "Just checking."

Mrs. Bai nodded and went back to her reading.

The living room was lit by porcelain lamps with white silk shades. A three-panel floor screen with bamboo stalks and birds painted on black lacquer stood at one corner. Oil paintings of landscapes and flowers, all done by Jasmine, decorated the walls. Years ago, it had been Professor Bai's ink-and-brush paintings that hung on the walls.

He stopped scanning. His gaze lingered on an image of a peony the color of pink and magenta with a center of bright yellow stamens. A proud smile flickered across his face as it had every time he looked at her artwork. Relaxed, he slid back onto the love seat, closed his eyes, and listened to his wife's voice.

She started a new story.

"There was a boy named Yue Fei in Southern Song Dynasty. His mother asked him when the northern Jin people invaded the country, 'Our homeland is under attack from the barbaric foreigners. What are you going to do?' The boy replied, '*Jing zhong bao guo*.' 'Excellent,' she said. '*Serve the country with the utmost loyalty* is exactly what you should do. I'd like to tattoo these four words on your back so that you'll always remember.' Without the slightest hesitation, the boy lifted his shirt. 'It'll hurt, Son. Aren't you afraid?' 'Of course not. If I'm afraid of a little needle, how can I fight the enemy?' The boy dropped to his knees and bowed to the heaven, the earth, and his ancestors. His mother wrote the characters with a brush on his back. She pricked his skin with an embroidery needle and smeared ink on his back so that the words would stay. It was the year 1120. Yue Fei was only sixteen. Years later he would become a military commander and a national hero."

Mrs. Bai finished the story by saying, "We'll keep reading tomorrow. His story is fascinating. The four characters—*jing zhong bao guo*—inspired countless young men to fight for our homeland." She picked up two notebooks from a coffee table and handed them to the girls. "Write the phrases related to *guo—country*. Can you think of any?"

"Protect our homes and defend our country," said Chen Hong, punching her fist in the air.

"Every man is responsible for the rise and fall of his homeland," Xiao Mei answered.

"Anything else?" Mrs. Bai asked.

Xiao Mei added, "*Guo po jia wang—when one's country falls, one's home is ruined—*"

"That's what the Japanese troops are doing to us," Professor Bai opened his eyes and said through clenched teeth.

Just then loud bangs at the front door broke the peace.

———————

Professor Bai jerked his head up. His gaze flew to his wife who turned to him in stunned disbelief. "Father John?" he asked. The American priest had tried to convince them to move into the International Safety Zone.

She shook her head.

He shot to his feet. "Wait here," he said, signaling the women not to move. *Thwack!*

The sound of the door being slammed open took the professor aback. A sense of foreboding tightened his chest, and he picked up the pace. Several steps later, he came face to face with four Japanese soldiers. They marched into the living room, bayonet blades shining upon the barrels of their rifles.

Professor Bai's shock mixed with fear and anger. He'd studied in Japan for four years, and the Japanese people he'd met were polite almost to a fault. It took him a few seconds to bring himself back under control. Adjusting the collar of his shirt, he opened his mouth.

The soldiers showed no interest in listening. One shoved him so hard that he spun, tumbled, and crashed into the wall. His vision blurred.

His ears rang. A livid bruise blossomed on the left side of his forehead, and he grunted in pain. His eyeglasses were smashed.

The soldiers kept advancing, treading upon the oil painting of peony that had fallen from the wall. They grabbed the women by their arms, hauled them to their feet, and tried to drag them out of the house.

Screams filled the room.

"Suying!" Professor Bai cried out. He stepped in front of the group with open arms. His bruised face twisted. Blood dripped from his forehead. Controlling a roar of rage, he was ready to argue with the invaders.

But he didn't get the chance. Without a word, one soldier stuck a knife into his chest.

Everyone gasped.

Professor Bai's eyes widened. His hands flew to his chest. Blood surged out, staining his blue shirt red. An exclamation of horror broke from his lips as he stumbled backward.

"Bai Wen!" Mrs. Bai uttered a sharp cry. She stretched her arms, trying to catch her husband. But hands held her back. Kicking and thrashing, she fought to extricate herself from the grasp of the soldiers.

It was too late. The genteel professor fell on his back with a thud. His body convulsed twice, then stilled. His unseeing eyes gazed into nothingness.

Screams and cries split the air.

The soldiers wasted no time. Disregarding the women's wails and protests, they pulled them again. Their hands groped their bodies as they grinned and exchanged obscenities.

Mrs. Bai paled. Panic flashed in her eyes as she understood what the men were saying. Fear and sorrow ripped her usual graceful composure. She yelled in flawless Japanese, "Take your hands off me."

No one listened.

A hand snaked under her torn cheongsam.

She shivered involuntarily. "I'll go with you. Just let me close his eyes. Please," she pleaded, louder and with even more urgency, "I beg you!"

For a split second the young soldier dragging her hesitated, seemingly wondering why the woman could speak their native tongue. As he loosened his grip, Mrs. Bai wrenched her arms free and leaned down to her husband. Instead of closing his eyes, though, she yanked the knife out of his chest.

She straightened her body, facing the enemy and the maids. An array of emotions swept across her colorless face: grief, anger, contempt, sympathy.

The soldiers let go of the girls and backed away several steps. The one who had held her slid his rifle up in a practiced motion, aiming at her.

He didn't have to fire.

Lifting her hands, Mrs. Bai thrust the dagger deeply into her own chest. Blood soaked through her clothes. Red droplets trickled along the knife handle and across her fingers, dripping down to the hardwood floor. She collapsed on top of her husband. Her eyes were open, but the film of death had settled over them.

The soldiers gaped at the two bodies. The fact that this fine-looking woman had spoken their language fluently seemed to trouble them. Was she Japanese? Had they killed one of their own? Doubtful glances flew between them before they staggered out of the house, leaving the two shaken housemaids behind.

For a moment Xiao Mei and Chen Hong stood frozen, staring at the bodies. Then, as if the earth had crumbled under her feet, the lanky girl swayed and slumped to the floor.

"Chen Hong!" Xiao Mei cried and grabbed her companion by the elbow. Barely four feet, ten inches, she slipped an arm around the taller girl's waist, steadying her. "Chen Hong, we have to go." Despite the warmth inside the house, she trembled. Worried that the soldiers would come back, she gathered her strength and urged again, "Now!"

Arm-in-arm, they fled the house. It was dark. No one was in sight. The rising moon cast eerie shadows over the empty streets. An icy wind blasted through every crevice in their thin clothing and made their teeth chatter. In the distance, heavy artillery pounded away.

"Where can we go?" asked Chen Hong. Her voice carried a trace of hysteria.

Xiao Mei shook her head and looked up. The lanky girl's eyes mirrored her own: sheer terror. The house was unsafe, but the outside hid impending danger too. "Go back." She retreated, pulling Chen Hong along. "Wait until daybreak."

They hurried back to the house. Xiao Mei dragged a few chairs to barricade the front door with the broken lock. She switched off the lights. In darkness, they scurried through the living room, trying not to look at the bodies.

Once in their bedroom, Xiao Mei closed the curtains. "Let's block the door," she said. Not knowing if it would be of any use, they moved a bed against the door.

They huddled together. A whisper of light slinked under the drapes. Periodically, screams, shouts, and gunfire sliced through the darkness, sneaking into the house, terrorizing the young women. Around midnight, the electricity went out, taking away the faint light from the streetlamps and plunging the room into total blackness.

The night was long.

They cringed, cried, and held each other for comfort. Whenever they heard a noise outside the house, they jammed their fists into their mouths to prevent themselves from crying out, but their bodies quivered uncontrollably.

Chapter 3

▬ ▬ ▬ ▬ ▬ ▬ ▬

Am I really foolish by coming back to Nanking? Jasmine wondered. They'd just passed the last train station. No one got on, and only a half dozen passengers remained in coach class, which was usually overcrowded.

It was still more than an hour to their destination. The outside looked as black as death. Leaning against her seat, Jasmine winced and turned her gaze to the inside. Most of the fellow travelers were sleeping. She could see the back of their heads nodding with the movement of the train. An old man slumped against the window, his bald head bumping onto the glass, waking him up. He dozed again in no time. One stocky young man, whom she'd seen earlier, disappeared behind his seat, only his feet in black canvas shoes sticking out. A middle-aged woman paced back and forth from one end of the cabin to the other. She was wrapped in a thick brown twill jacket. On her fourth pass, she slid onto a seat across the aisle. "Are you going to Nanking by yourself?" she asked.

Jasmine nodded. She was exhausted, but anxiety made it impossible for her to sleep.

"Why? It's dangerous there!"

"I'm worried about my parents," replied Jasmine, pulling her coat collar a little higher. "I'm going there to convince them to leave."

"Good girl." The pleasant woman patted her on the hand. "If we don't live too far away, we should share a rickshaw. It'll be safer."

"My parents live near Nanking University."

"We're close. Only three or four blocks away. I can send you home first."

Jasmine tipped her head in appreciation. "What about you? Why are you going to the city?" she asked. The nine hundred-mile, and nearly twenty-hour train ride had been long and lonely. She was glad to have someone to talk to. Their conversation broke the rhythmic, *clickety-clackety* sound and diluted an air of melancholy that surrounded them.

"My daughter-in-law is due to give birth in a few days. It's too late for her to leave and there is no one to help her."

Jasmine arched an eyebrow.

"My son is a lieutenant in the Nationalist Army. He's fighting on the front line. He took part in the battle in Shanghai. I'm not sure where he is now. Maybe he's close to Nanking." Concern made the wrinkles around her eyes more pronounced. "Their maid left. Who can blame her? No one wants to be there nowadays."

Jasmine felt a twinge of sympathy. She knew how worried her aunt had been about Birch, her much-loved cousin. Being a fighter pilot was dangerous, especially since he had to face the more powerful enemy. Thoughts of Birch tugged at her heart. She prayed for his safety for the umpteenth time.

"Maybe the Army can hold the fort for a while," Jasmine said. "My uncle is a colonel in the Air Force. He said that the Japanese leaders boasted that they could conquer us in three months, but it took them more than three months to capture Shanghai—one city. Our Army is far less advanced, but our soldiers are brave. Maybe it'll take the Japs even longer to defeat Nanking. You'll have time to take your daughter-in-law and grandchild away with you."

"Hopefully you're right. What's your name, girl?"

"Bai Moli. Call me Jasmine."

"That's a sweet name."

"Thanks. What's yours?"

"Li Suying."

Jasmine's face relaxed into a smile for the first time on the trip. "My mom's name is Bai Suying." She took a paper sack of roasted chestnuts from her book pack and shared with her new friend, who reminded her of her mother. She'd bought two bags of roasted chestnuts which were her mother's favorite. *I'll buy more, once I'm in Nanking.* She also had peanuts for her father in her pack. Those were all she had. She'd left home as if she were going to school. *Uncle and Auntie should have found the letter by now. I hope they're not too angry with me.*

A pale light appeared on the eastern horizon as the train pulled into Nanking. The platform was crammed with people. Even though the train was still moving, Jasmine could see anxiety on their faces. *What had happened here?*

The brakes let out an ear-splitting screech, and the train wrenched to a halt. As soon as the door opened, and before the passengers could exit, the crowd rushed onboard like a flood.

"Wait! Let us out first," the young man in the black canvas shoes shouted.

No one listened to him. People streamed onto the train, and the crush of humanity pressed everyone back into the cabin. A few stepped on Jasmine's toes. She winced.

"It's hopeless," said the young man. As stocky as he was, he couldn't do anything to break through the single-minded throng. He ran toward a window in the middle of the compartment and shoved it open. "Come on." He waved his arm. "We can go through here." With that, he crawled through the opening, dragged his luggage with him, and disappeared within a few seconds.

"Hurry," said Jasmine, limping and dragging the middle-aged woman along with her.

"I can't do this," mumbled Li Suying, shaking her head.

"Yes, you can. Watch how I do it." Jasmine bent her upper body and swung her right leg through the open window, holding onto the frame and bringing her left side over. As she lowered herself to the ground, she felt two strong hands catch her waist. "Thank you." She faced the young man and tipped her head.

"No problem," he said. Looking up, he urged the middle-aged woman, "Come on!"

"I can't do this." Li Suying stepped away, but she was being pushed from behind.

"You must!" Jasmine said. "Your daughter-in-law needs you!" She stood on tiptoes and grabbed the older woman's wrists. "It's not hard. You can do it. We'll catch you." She turned to the young man.

He nodded and glanced around. "Do it now!"

More and more people swarmed the platform. Several dozen Japanese soldiers in yellow uniforms and star-studded caps were among them. Their bayonets gleamed. Their Rising Sun flag fluttered in the chilly breeze.

Reluctantly, Li Suying bent her body.

Just then, a gruff voice spoke on a loudspeaker, "Attention. Attention everyone. This train is retained by the Imperial Japanese Army. All passengers must get out immediately."

Li Suying retreated. "Everyone has to leave." She wiped her forehead in relief.

No one else seemed to share her opinion, as even more struggled to get onboard, and some even climbed onto the top of the train. The loudspeaker demanded compliance several more times.

"Auntie Li, come on," said Jasmine, holding her hands up.

The middle-aged woman stuck her head out. She wasn't in any hurry, probably still hoping everyone would disembark.

Bam. Bam. Bam. Three gunshots rang out.

Screams filled the air.

By reflex, Jasmine ducked. Her hands flew to cover her head. An involuntary shudder rippled through her body. As she crouched, paralyzed by terror, she felt warm raindrops. *What's the matter?* She turned, and as she looked up, another drop fell onto her face. She brushed her cheek. Her fingers came away sticky. And red. She screamed. Her voice was drowned out by a deafening roar.

"Run!" the young man yelled. He gave her sleeve a tug.

Jasmine resisted the pull. "Auntie Li!" She stood up, trying to convince the woman. Then she saw it—Li Suying slumped lifeless over the window; blood and tissue sprayed from a dark hole above her temple. "No!" Jasmine shrieked.

Her scream was cut short by three more gunshots.

"Run!" the young man urged again. Then, without hearing Jasmine's answer, he ran.

People fled in all directions, screaming, shouting, and crying. Breathless with fear, Jasmine raced for the gate. As she ran, she heard the voice over the loudspeaker say, "Anyone remaining on the train will be killed."

How could this happen? How could Nanking fall so quickly? How will we get out, even if Mom and Dad agree to leave?

Chapter 4

The entrance of the train station was total chaos. It was like a choppy sea with waves going every direction. Some people had just escaped the platform while others still tried to get to the train. Dogs barked, horses neighed, and chickens clucked. The abandoned animals only aggravated the situation.

The sun was barely above the horizon. The morning was cold. The air smelled of manure. Jasmine shivered, and it wasn't just because of the cool air.

Her right toe seemed swollen. Every step brought pain. Normally a line of the two-wheeled carts waited outside the gate. She grimaced as she scanned the area. Luckily, she was among the first to escape the station, and soon she spotted a rickshaw around a corner. Relieved, she let a long breath pass through her teeth.

Limping, she elbowed her way through the crowd toward the rickshaw. Her right foot was already on the footstep before a man gripped her arm from behind. He yanked her hard and pulled her off the cart. Jasmine staggered sideways, crashing into another man who murmured a curse. Helplessly, she watched the rickshaw depart. Only the man's shouts to hurry were left in its wake.

Frustrated, she hobbled forward. Two blocks away, she spotted another rickshaw. "Wait!" she yelled and waved, trying to catch up. The puller had just dropped off his passenger and was ready to leave.

"Nanking University," she said breathlessly.

He shook his head. "No. I'm going home. Different direction…"

"Please!" Jasmine begged.

"Can't you see what's happening here?"

"Please," she pleaded again. Her parents' house was only a half hour away. If her toe didn't hurt, she wouldn't beg. She fished out two bills from her book pack and handed them to him. "This is twice the fare."

The man wiped his forehead with the back of his hand before dismissing her request with an impatient wave.

Jasmine took out two more bills. "Help me, please!"

Muttering a curse, he took the money.

"Thank you!" She sat upon the chair and slumped against the headrest. The hood and the semi-enclosed space provided a semblance of safety. She closed her eyes, shutting out the ugliness. The wheels squealed. The puller's rhythmic breathing and his feet thumping on the pavement put her at ease. Fatigue caught up with her, and before long she drifted into an exhausted sleep.

―――――――

A voice jolted her awake. She didn't know how long she'd dozed off. It felt like only a minute. Sitting upright, she blinked to bring the world into focus and realized the rickshaw had stopped.

"Get down," the puller said, an edge of panic in his voice.

"But…." She looked around, rubbing her eyes, confused. "But we're not there yet."

"It's only ten minutes away. I can't do it anymore." He grabbed her arm.

Jasmine resisted the pull. "What are you talking about? I've already paid. You—"

"There you have it." The man took the money out of his pocket, thrust it to her, and dragged her off the cart. Two bills slipped out of her grip, floating on the wind.

"Money is useless if one is dead," he said, picking up the handles. Before she could argue, he turned and ran, leaving her in the middle of a littered street.

Jasmine shook her head as she chased the bills. She snatched one, but the other had blown to the edge of a building and landed at the bottom of an outside basement entrance. Hissing a sigh of irritation, she trod down the steps.

The bill lay on top of a propaganda leaflet. A picture showed a smiling Japanese soldier holding a Chinese baby while giving food to her parents. A few words printed near the Rising Sun flag—"Trust the Japanese Army. We will give you rice to eat, clothes to wear, and a home to live."

As she picked up the papers, shouts erupted. Gunshots and explosions followed. Instinctively, she hunkered down. With hands over her head, she hid behind the wall, making herself as small as possible. She was afraid to even take a breath.

From her hideaway below street level, she heard a few people pass in a hurry. They were shooting and yelling in Chinese. Her hands covered her ears so she couldn't make out anything except for a couple of words like "Fire" and "Run."

Rat-tat-tat-tat. Rapid fire exchanged, and ear-splitting explosions went off. The sound of firearms mingled with yelling and screams.

Soon a much larger group rushed by, shouting in Japanese.

She recoiled. Her fear grew into a full-blown panic. Her body shook uncontrollably. The sickening stench of blood and gunpowder blended with the animal manure. With one arm shielding her head, she jammed her fist into her mouth to prevent her from crying out loud.

Time seemed to stall. To Jasmine, the fighting seemed to go on forever, but it actually lasted only a few minutes. The soldiers moved on, and the area became quiet.

She waited, listening, making sure she was alone before peering out. No one was there—at least no one was standing. Ten yards to her right lay a corpse in the blue cotton Nationalist Army uniform. He was on his face, a mat of blood on his back. Further away, two more Chinese combatants lay on the sidewalk. One man's chest was a giant red blossom, and half of the other man's head had been blown off. Stray dogs circled the bodies.

For a second, Jasmine stood frozen, immobilized by shock and grief.

But she allowed herself only a moment before she jumped to her feet.

She moved as fast as she could. In case she had to hide again, she kept running near the edge of the buildings and paid close attention to the basement entrances or any other hideouts. Rubble from artillery fire, abandoned vehicles, weapons, and Nationalist Army uniforms littered the street.

The ten-minute distance seemed longer than the Great Wall. Luckily she didn't encounter another soul before reaching the house. She was out of breath. Her chest seemed about to explode. She trembled so violently that she could hardly stand.

Leaning against the frame, she banged on the door. Huffing and puffing, she yelled at the top of her lungs, "Mom! Dad! Open the door. It's me, Jasmine. I'm home. Open up!"

Chapter 5

▬ ▬ ▬ ▬ ▬ ▬ ▬

Faint light finally shone around the edges of the windows. It had been a very long night for the two servant girls. They had waited until the sun was well up in the sky before pulling the bed away from the doorway to leave the bedroom. Keeping their eyes averted, they tiptoed through the living room as if they were afraid to disturb the dead.

The two bodies lay in a dark pool surrounded by wiggly lines of dried blood. Flies buzzed about, making a repulsive hum. One notebook lay open in their way. Blood covered most of the writing. Only a few words like *family*, *country*, and *hatred* stood out.

Xiao Mei drew up short. "Wait a second." She pivoted and ran to the master bedroom.

"Come back!" yelled Chen Hong.

"In a minute." A moment later Xiao Mei returned with a white sheet in her hands. She offered one edge to Chen Hong. But before they covered the bodies, she lifted her arm and shoved the bedsheet to the other girl.

Xiao Mei bent down. Grimacing, she took Mrs. Bai's left hand and slid the gold wedding ring off Mrs. Bai's blood-crusted finger.

"What are you doing?" cried the taller girl with palpable disgust.

Ignoring her companion, Xiao Mei walked to the other side of the bodies, stepping between the rivers of blood. The offensive odor caused her to squint in revulsion. Holding her breath, she pulled Professor

Bai's left arm from underneath his wife's dead weight. This time it took her a little longer, but when she straightened up, she was holding both blood-coated wedding bands in her palm. "Here." She thrust one ring to the lanky girl.

Chen Hong backed away two steps. "No!" she said, shaking her head, her disbelief mixed with horror and contempt. "I don't want it. I—"

"It's not for you," Xiao Mei cut her off. She grabbed the girl's arm. "It's for Miss Jasmine. We have to save these for her." She swallowed, forcing back whatever churned inside her stomach. "You take one. I keep one. If…when…we see her…" Her voice trailed off. Professor Bai's family was Xiao Mei's savior. They had rescued her from her previous owner who was going to sell her to a brothel.

Chen Hong nodded.

They put the rings on, trying a few times to find the right finger.

As the girls spread the bedsheet, they heard loud bangs at the front door. Chen Hong let out a gasp and Xiao Mei shivered. They stood frozen. Fear pinned them to the spot and robbed them of their ability to run away and hide.

After a few seconds of sheer terror, Xiao Mei grabbed the other girl's hand and turned on heel. A few steps later she stopped abruptly.

"What?" whispered Chen Hong.

"It's Miss Jasmine!"

The door opened and Jasmine stumbled into the foyer.

"Miss Jasmine!" The two housemaids exclaimed in unison and caught her in their arms. Tears trickled down their faces.

"I'm okay." She patted the girls on their backs. Her lungs seemed to burst from rapid breaths. "God, it's horrible out there. But I'm home now."

Both servants wept.

Jasmine soothed them. "Look at me. I'm fine. Don't be silly." She peeked over their shoulders and yelled, "Mom! Dad! Come here. Save me from these crying babies." She tried to sound casual and funny.

The housemaids cried even louder. Jasmine tried to walk past them, but the girls held her back.

"What's wrong?" She shook her head and jerked herself free. Several steps later, the girls grabbed her again.

"Don't!" they begged together. Their tears wet her neck and cheek.

Jasmine extricated herself from their hold. As soon as she stepped into the living room her body stiffened. Blood had leaked from underneath the sheet, and a pair of black embroidered satin slippers stuck out. Her hands flew to her mouth.

The girls caught up with her, pulling her back. Jasmine wrenched her arms free and took two huge strides toward the white cover. Crouching down, she extended a trembling hand and tried twice to grip the corner of the sheet. Finally, she swallowed her dread and flipped the cover. Her father's mouth was frozen in an anguished scream. A fly had just landed on his upper lip. Her mother stared at her with sightless eyes. A knife protruded from her chest.

Jasmine slumped in the pool of her parents' blood. A sharp pain struck her like the tip of a blade thrusting into her own chest. She couldn't move.

A moment later she found her voice and let out a mournful wail. "Mom! Dad!" Tears rolled down her face.

The two girls squatted down beside her, hugging her, whimpering.

Jasmine could barely take a breath. How could she go on without her parents? Life without them was unimaginable.

Now she was alone in the world. Weighed down by misery, Jasmine reached for the knife, but before she could grasp it, Xiao Mei clutched her hand in a death grip. "No!" Xiao Mei cried. "If your parents are looking down on you, they will be so sad."

"That's right," agreed Chen Hong.

"Think about your uncle, aunt, Cousin Birch, and Miss Daisy," Xiao Mei said. "They're your family, too. You know they'd be heartbroken if you…if you…"

Outside, gunshots and explosions had come and gone, some terribly close. At one point, tanks had rumbled through the streets, rattling the house.

Through a mist of tears, Jasmine stared at the younger girls. As scared as they were, they were trying their best to comfort her. Warmth crept into her frozen heart.

She couldn't jeopardize the housemaids' lives because of her loss. She knew that they should not remain in the house for long. Wiping tears from her face, she nodded. She backed up on her knees and bowed down. Her head knocked against the blood-stained floor three times, showing her highest reverence.

Bowing down, the girls followed her gesture.

The sight of the bodies wrenched another sob from Jasmine. *Mom, Dad, I'm sorry I can't bury you.* With shaking hands, she drew the sheet back over them.

The thought that she'd never see her parents again sliced into her like the very knife that she'd nearly plunged into her own chest. The heartache was more painful than anything she'd ever experienced. She pressed her hands against her chest, willing herself to stay strong.

Help me get out of here, she prayed. *Please let me return to Chungking and Uncle's family.* She straightened her upper body. Through trembling lips, she asked, "Where are we…going?"

"Chen Hong wants to go home," replied Xiao Mei. "We talked about it last night."

The taller housemaid confirmed it.

Xiao Mei added, "I want to go to Father John's church. My family is too far away. I'm afraid—"

"Good," interrupted Jasmine. She rose slowly to her feet. The room spun, so she clung to the girls. "Father John will help us." She turned to Chen Hong. "Go with us."

The lanky girl shook her head. "My family isn't far away," she said, moistening her lips. "I want to be with them."

"Then walk along the edge of the street. Pay attention so you notice any hideout," said Jasmine. She started to leave, but three steps later she whirled around. Digging into the book pack slung across her shoulder and chest, she took out the bags of roasted chestnuts and peanuts. With great reverence, she placed the treats on top of the sheet. Her throat ached with the effort to hold back more tears.

"Oh, I almost forgot," said Xiao Mei as she took the gold ring off her thumb.

Chen Hong did the same.

Jasmine's voice tangled in her throat, so she nodded her gratitude and accepted the rings.

Chapter 6

— — — — — — —

They made sure no one was around before they ran. Jasmine and Xiao Mei turned right while the lanky girl spun left. A few steps later, Jasmine wheeled around. "Chen Hong!" she called out and sprang back. Flinging her arms wide, she enfolded the girl in a fierce embrace. All three huddled together.

Tears formed deep pools in Jasmine's eyes and blurred her vision. "When the war is over," she said, sniffling, "when it is safe, perhaps we will meet here again."

Chen Hong nodded, tears wet upon her cheeks.

They parted with backward glances.

Hand-in-hand Jasmine and Xiao Mei dashed toward the church. The sun bathed the city in a rich golden-yellow color. In the warm light, the steeple glowed, giving the illusion of serenity.

———————

Rounding a corner, Jasmine stopped dead in her tracks. Xiao Mei walked right into her and shrieked before her hands curled over her mouth. Several dozen mangled corpses lay in the middle of the street. The men wore blue Nationalist uniforms and caps. With hands tied behind their backs, all had been shot. All shot except for one. A headless body lay at the front of the group; he was dressed in a blue cotton overcoat, apparently an officer. Nearby, his head rested on a barbed-wire barricade that the Nationalist Army had set up. His eyes were closed, his bruised face contorted. His nose and ears had been hacked off. Even in death he was humiliated—a cigarette butt wedged into his clenched mouth.

Jasmine felt sick to her stomach. *Was he forced to watch his men being slaughtered? Or was he tortured and decapitated in front of the group? These were surrendered soldiers!* She remembered that the middle-aged passenger's son was an officer. *What if he were Auntie Li's son?* She stood transfixed with horror.

Seconds later, as if she'd just awakened from a nightmare, Jasmine tugged at Xiao Mei's sleeve, and they bolted from the scene.

A block later, a female corpse lay sprawled on the blood-stained ground. She was naked from the waist down. Her coat had been ripped open, her shirt pushed up, exposing her bare breasts. Her stomach had been sliced open, and entrails bulged out of the torn flesh. Her legs were splayed open, a twig jabbed into her. Her face was frozen in the middle of a scream.

Nearby, trampled vegetables were scattered. Three paces away, a bundled-up baby lay face down. Dry blood from a stab wound on her back matted her floral clothing.

Bile rose in Jasmine's throat, and then she threw up. *Dear God! Had the mother seen her baby daughter die?* Her knees shook.

Next to her, Xiao Mei also shivered. Holding onto each other, they staggered forward.

Even with her thick coat, Jasmine was trembling as they reached the church. They'd seen nearly a hundred corpses within only a few blocks. The streets and ditches of this fallen city had turned red, as if the sky had been raining blood.

Suddenly, her emotions caught up with her—her parents' death, the exhausting train ride, the fearful escape, the sadness and grief, the panic. At the front step of the church, Jasmine collapsed, dragging Xiao Mei down with her.

Chen Hong stayed close to the edge of the street, as Jasmine had suggested. But a few blocks after she separated from the two girls, she encountered a group of Japanese soldiers. With nowhere for her to hide, they swarmed her. "*Hua gu niang—pretty girl. Hua gu niang,*" they chanted. Laughing and jeering, they hauled her into an empty house. "*Pikankan—let's see a woman open her legs.*"

She cried and begged. She kicked and squirmed. But the soldiers didn't care. They stripped off her clothes and tied her to a bed. All day, the dozen took turns raping her. At first, Chen Hong howled. Her ear-piercing screams mixed with the men's laughter. Soon her voice became raspy and pitiful, muffled by the soldiers' grunts and taunts. By the time they'd finished with her, the naïve, sixteen-year-old girl had lost her will and her senses. Tears, sweat, and body fluids glued her unruly hair to her face. She looked like a dying animal.

The soldiers scoffed at her. One brushed the strands from her cheeks, exposing her features. He took a picture of her, still bound, as a souvenir. Finally, they untied her and let her go.

But they might as well have killed her. Lacking comprehension, Chen Hong wandered the city streets naked. Blood dripped over her shaky legs. The day was frigid, and the wind had turned the late afternoon jarringly cold. She hugged her arms against her body, shivering. Through purple lips, she mumbled in a lifeless monotone, "Mom. Dad… Mom. Dad…"

"Come here," an old couple called out when she passed a noodle shop. The woman stepped outside and grabbed her elbow to pull her inside. "Get inside—quickly! It's dangerous out there."

Chen Hong jerked her arm free. She stumbled sideways, lost her footing, and fell. Using all fours, she scrambled to her feet. "I want…my mother," she said as if she were somewhere outside her body. Ignoring the couple's urging, she continued to walk down the deserted street in a trance. Her forlorn figure was lost in the twilight.

Before long she was captured by another group of Japanese. She had no will to fight, nor the strength to struggle. She was too weak to scream.

The last thing she saw in this world was a naked man straddling her, preparing to thrust a sword into her chest.

Chapter 7

▬ ▬ ▬ ▬ ▬ ▬ ▬

Strong hands caught Jasmine and Xiao Mei and pulled them to their feet. "Jasmine? What are you doing here? Your parents told me you were in Chungking." A middle-aged man in a black robe fired rapid questions in accented Chinese. At six feet tall with fair skin and blue eyes, Father John was a priest from the United States. Shaking his bald head, he asked again, "Why have you come back to Nanking now?"

"I was hoping to convince Mom and Dad to leave—"

"Yes, I understand. I tried. Your father is too stubborn. I told him he should at least move to the Safety Zone." Father John swept his hand, indicating the International Safety Zone signs. White flags lined the front of the church. A nine-foot American flag lay flat on the lawn. Banners with the Red Cross symbol were draped over the door and the windows. "He said he could handle it, stubborn fool. I know he wanted to let the poorest refugees use this place."

He pulled the girls inside the main sanctuary of the church, which was already packed with people of all ages. "Where are they? I hope he changed his mind. I—"

"Father John!" wailed Jasmine. Tears came faster than she could stop them.

"What…what happened?" he asked. His brow knotted. "Don't tell me—"

"They are both…" Her voice trailed off. Her body trembled like a leaf in a gale.

"But I just talked to them the day before yesterday." He turned to the servant girl.

"Last night, four Japanese soldiers came to the house," said Xiao Mei, nibbling her lip. Then, with barely coherent sentences and a flood of tears, she told the story.

When Xiao Mei was finished, Father John enfolded Jasmine in his arms. "I can't believe this. I'm so sorry. Your father was such a gentleman. And I never met anyone as graceful as your mother."

He wiped the tears from Jasmine's face. His own eyes watered. "I'll find a couple of men to bury them. Don't be too sad, child; they're in a better place now. They wouldn't want you to carry such grief in your heart."

He smoothed her hair. "Don't be afraid, Jasmine. You're safe here. I promise I'll do everything in my power to keep you from harm." He extended his arm and touched Xiao Mei's shoulder.

"Thank you, Father John," Jasmine choked.

"No need. Your father and I were best friends. It is my duty to protect you." Turning around he glanced at the panic-stricken crowd. Even children had fretful looks on their faces; only babies cried haphazardly. He sighed. "Sometimes I feel so powerless. I don't know if my best will be good enough."

"How can we help?" Jasmine asked.

"You can speak both Chinese and English—"

"A bit of Japanese, too."

"Yes, I'm sure you can be a great help." He rubbed a hand over his bald head. "For now I need someone to organize the soup kitchen. Feeding so many people isn't easy. There's a shortage of food. We have to keep a ration system."

"We'll do it," Jasmine said and brushed the residual tears from her cheeks. Pulling her long hair back, she twisted it into a ponytail.

"Are you sure?"

"Yes." She lifted her chin, her teary eyes lit with fortitude.

Father John nodded.

———————

Late that afternoon Jasmine ate dinner with Xiao Mei and several other girls in Father John's office. She hadn't had any food for the entire day. Her last meal had been twelve hours ago on the train—the roasted chestnuts she'd shared with the middle-aged passenger. It seemed like a lifetime ago.

In a few gulps she finished half of the rice porridge. She realized she'd forgotten her manners and forced herself to slow down, savoring the warm feeling of food in her mouth. During her eighteen years, she had never tasted anything as pleasing as this bowl of rice porridge.

The room was silent. Everyone was exhausted and anxious. Then a loud commotion erupted in the church's main sanctuary. Xiao Mei gripped Jasmine's arm and scooted closer. Fear glazed the young women's eyes. Father John jumped to his feet as six Nationalist soldiers filed inside, filling the small room. Filthy with mud and dried blood, they looked like homeless people.

The young women gasped.

"Help us, Father!" a man in his mid-twenties begged. With long gangling limbs and a hollow unshaven face, he was taller and older than the rest of the group.

"This is the International Safety Zone for civilians. Soldiers don't belong here. You'll bring danger to the noncombatants."

"Please!" the man said. "The Japs have surrounded the city. We have nowhere to go."

Jasmine set her bowl down on the wooden desk. She leaned closer to the American. "Please help them, Father John!" Every time she encountered a Nationalist combatant, she thought of her cousin Birch. "The Japanese killed the surrendered soldiers. We saw their bodies." She turned to Xiao Mei who nodded.

The priest sighed. "I'll see what I can do." He walked out of the room, still shaking his head. Minutes later he returned with a stack of civilian clothes. "Sorry, we don't have anything thicker."

"These will do. Thank you, Father," the man said.

The soldiers stripped off their uniforms and the young women turned around while the men changed clothes.

Jasmine remembered seeing the Nationalist Army uniforms on

the street and understood what had happened. When they finished dressing, she asked, "Why did Nanking fall so quickly? It lasted only four days!" The question had bothered her all day.

In an ill-fitting outfit, the tall man shrugged. "I don't know. I'm just a sergeant. One day we were told to fight to the last person. The next day we were ordered to retreat."

"I read what the Defense Commander said two weeks ago. General Tang vowed to live or die with Nanking. His speech was passionate and touching."

"He left us."

"What?"

"Yes," confirmed Father John. "I heard it, too. He was ordered to retreat."

"Why? Don't we have enough troops to fight? Shanghai lasted almost four months."

"We have troops—ninety thousand. But look at us." The sergeant swept his hand from left to right. "Tell them how old you are," he spoke to the shortest one.

In gray cotton clothes, with scruffy-looking hair, he looked like a street urchin. "Fourteen," he answered in a high-pitched voice.

"No way!" the American exclaimed.

Jasmine's eyes widened. She'd already suspected that these soldiers were young, but hearing their actual age surprised her.

"He isn't the youngest. There are boys as young as twelve."

Everyone gasped.

"Yes, there are many new recruits. Some have never fired a single shot. Some were drafted against their will from the countryside. In the battle at Shanghai thousands of soldiers were wounded."

Father John said, "I've seen them, several trainloads from Shanghai."

"We walked from Shanghai, fighting, retreating," said the sergeant.

Jasmine shook her head in disbelief. Shanghai was one hundred eighty miles southeast of Nanking.

"Have you heard the Japanese Three-Alls policy?" The lanky man paused, and without hearing an answer, continued. "Kill all, burn all, loot all."

33

An exclamation of shock and horror rose from the women and the priest.

"Yes," he went on. "We've seen ghost villages, ghost towns, even ghost cities. The Japs—"

"They're trying to intimidate the Chinese to surrender," Father John said. "Bombing is also part of the terror campaign."

The sergeant gave a sigh of frustration. "Apparently, they're successful. They must have scared the devil out of someone, otherwise we would not have been ordered to retreat."

"If you were ordered to retreat, then why are you here?" Jasmine asked.

"It was chaos. Some of us heard the order; others didn't."

"My unit never received the word," said the fourteen-year-old boy soldier. He ran his tongue around his cracked and scabbed lips. "My captain actually shot people that he thought were deserters."

"Dear God!"

The sergeant explained, "By the time I reached the gate near the river, it was blocked with thousands of troops. Trucks, cars, wagons, junks were everywhere. Even abandoned horses and donkeys! It was hopeless. No one could get through. No boats were left, anyway."

Jasmine grimaced. Without a boat, the soldiers couldn't cross the Yangtze River to safety. They had been trapped.

"So, I turned back and tried to find a different way. We—several dozen of us—even considered surrendering."

She sucked in her breath. "But you didn't…"

"We talked about it," the sergeant stuttered, ashamed. "Then we heard '*Jiu ming!* Help us!' and saw a group of Japs dragging four girls from a school. The dirty bastards stripped off their clothes and tied them to a wooden barricade in the middle of the street and…" He dropped his chin to his chest. When he spoke again, his voice cracked. "Dozens of Japs lined up…eager to take their turns. We were hiding in a nearby building. The girls cried. The bastards laughed. The sound drove us crazy. We had no choice but to try to stop them, so we fired."

"What happened? Did you save the girls?"

"No. There were too many Japs."

"How did you get away then?"

"Most of us didn't." A muscle twitched in his chin. "The place had been bombed and gutted. Three of us escaped to another building by crawling on a beam. They chased us, but then the oddest thing happened." He looked over at a teenager with acne.

"Our unit was hiding in that building," the teenager said. "We'd already decided to put down our weapons. We were cut off from retreat. We were hungry, thirsty, worn out. Some of us were sick or wounded. We thought, you know, maybe the Japs would give us food and water if we gave up. About fifty of us walked out with hands raised. I missed it—I was taking a leak."

The sergeant added, "The Japs probably thought it was everyone, so they didn't search the building." His Adam's apple slid up and down. "They surrounded the disarmed soldiers then tied their hands behind their backs. They lined them up on the street and…"

Jasmine could hear the undisguised anguish in his voice. Her heart constricted in her chest.

The lanky man took a shuddering breath before continuing. "They mowed down the entire group with machine guns. We watched… There was nothing we could do. There were only three of us. We had rifles but no bullets left."

Tears came to his eyes. "Hell! I'll never get their screams out of my head as long as I live. Afterward, the bastards kicked the bodies to make sure they were all dead and stabbed anyone who was still alive."

His face collapsed in grief. "When everything was quiet, we heard it again—the girls crying from the barricade. Apparently, while this group of Japs was killing the prisoners, another group had found the girls and…"

Jasmine paled. She felt Xiao Mei tighten her grip on her arm.

"We should have shot the girls while we had the chance. We should have put them out of their misery. They died anyway. But what they went through…" He threw back his head and released a roar of rage and frustration. His right hand balled into a fist and thumped against his thigh.

Despair descended upon everyone inside the tiny office. Outside gunshots and explosions came and went. Fire illuminated the sky.

Finally, the young man with acne said, "I saw them leaving the building several hours later." He pointed to the sergeant. "So I ran after them."

"Two more joined us along the way."

Jasmine felt sympathy for the young soldiers. Their commanders had clearly abandoned them in their hour of need. Chiang Kai-shek, the Nationalist leader, had left Nanking four days before the attack. General Tang, the Defense Commander, vowed to live or die with Nanking. But he, too, had fled as soon as the invasion started, leaving tens of thousands of soldiers behind without a way to defend themselves.

Moved by the plight of the soldiers, she picked up her half-full bowl of rice porridge and handed it to the lanky man. "What's your name?" she asked.

"Lu Ping." He nodded his thanks, took a sip, and passed it to his companions.

Xiao Mei and the other young women followed with whatever they had left in their bowls.

"Where are you from?" asked Jasmine.

"Northeast. My home is gone, though." Lu Ping's eyes were bright with tears, and he swallowed hard to hold them back. "The Japs burned our house and killed everyone in my family: Grandpa, Mom, Dad, two younger brothers, three sisters, my wife, and…my unborn child." He dragged his hand down his face as if to wipe away his pain.

Jasmine's heart ached. She understood his grief. The image of her own parents lying in a pool of blood flashed through her mind. "I'm so sorry," she croaked.

The priest sighed and placed a hand on Lu Ping's shoulder. "I'd better talk to the other members of the International Committee. I'll see what we can do to help the trapped soldiers."

Chapter 8

— — — — — — —

The next several days were relatively quiet. Jasmine could still hear gunshots from time to time, but no Japanese entered the church. More refugees rushed inside. Panicked and hungry, they had fled to the International Safety Zone with nothing but the clothes on their backs. With them came more stories of Japanese atrocities.

Hundreds of women, as young as twelve and as old as seventy-five, had been raped. "Operation Sweep," a Japanese campaign designed to round up Chinese combatants, was underway. Tens of thousands of disarmed soldiers were slaughtered—mowed down by machine guns, buried alive, burned alive, or used for bayonet practice.

Jasmine and Xiao Mei helped in the kitchen and tried to feed many hungry refugees. The food came from the Red Cross and from a few Westerners who had managed to travel outside the city to buy provisions.

Lu Ping and his companions volunteered to remove the benches in the main church sanctuary so it could accommodate more civilians and former soldiers.

On behalf of the International Committee, Father John wrote a long letter. He begged the Japanese military commander to show the disarmed combatants mercy and to treat them according to the Geneva Convention. To his great relief, an officer replied with leniency. "As long as the Chinese soldiers put down their weapons, they can enter the

Safety Zone and their lives will be spared."

On the fourth day, several dozen Japanese troops stormed the church. With bayonets fixed upon the barrels of their rifles, they herded the frightened refugees into the main sanctuary and separated the men from the women. One by one, they examined the men's hands and shoulders. After that, they bound some with ropes and shoved others to the side with the women.

Standing in the second row, Jasmine cringed. She understood what the Japanese were doing. Daily use of guns and backpacks caused calluses on certain areas of soldiers' fingers and marks on their shoulders. She remembered seeing calluses on Cousin Birch's hands.

A heavy set Japanese man walked over to the fourteen-year-old boy soldier. He towered over the teenager, grabbed his arms, and took a quick look at his fingers. Then he hauled the boy by the collar and shoved him so hard that he staggered and fell to the ground near the feet of the women. One older woman extended her arms, and the boy scrambled to his feet and stood with her.

By then, dozens of young men had been dragged outside, their hands tied behind their backs. Most of them were Nationalist soldiers, but a few were policemen or coolies who also happened to have calluses on their fingers.

The Japanese betrayal infuriated Father John. His face, neck, and bald head turned red with anger. He waved his arms and argued with an officer, trying to prevent the men's fate.

Now it was Lu Ping's turn. As a Japanese soldier twisted his hands behind his back, the lanky ex-soldier wrestled his arms free. He rammed his fist into the enemy's face. "Fight!" he yelled. Throwing kicks and punches to the Japanese around him, he roared, "Die fighting; not being slaughtered!"

A few men followed him. Chaos broke out. Screams, cries, and shouts filled the church. A Japanese officer with a mustache fired his pistol into the air.

All struggles stopped, and the men raised their hands above their heads—all except for Lu Ping.

The Nationalist sergeant was skinny, but much taller than his opponents. In the turmoil, he'd seized a short Japanese soldier by the neck. Jerking the little man from side to side, he used him as a human shield. But he didn't last long. Armed soldiers surrounded him and thrust their bayonets into him from behind and from the sides.

Groans of sorrow and shouts of rage rose from the onlookers.

Lu Ping howled. He fell, taking the short man with him. His fingers clasped the soldier's neck like iron claws. He never loosened his grip, even after he was stabbed multiple times. Lu Ping died, but not before he choked his enemy to death. They both lay in a pool of blood, eyes open wide.

Men lowered their heads. Women recoiled and wept.

Tears streamed down Jasmine's cheeks. Without a second thought, she pushed past the row before her, stepped forward, and leaned down. With great reverence, she moved her hand over Lu Ping's eyelids and closed his eyes. *May you be with your family soon*, she prayed.

As she straightened up, a Japanese man with a pockmarked face grasped her upper arm. He hauled her against him with violent speed. "*Hua gu niang—pretty girl.*" He grinned. Turning to his buddies, he added, "*Pikankan—let's see her open her legs.*" He dragged Jasmine toward the back of the church. His remark and his actions brought a round of obscene laughter from his fellow soldiers.

Terror seized Jasmine. She was too petrified to scream, but she fought her assailant.

"Father John!" shrieked Xiao Mei, throwing herself on Jasmine and encircling her thin arms around the taller girl.

"Father John!" everyone cried.

The priest had been standing by the door, trying in vain to stop the Chinese from being taken away to be executed. He rushed inside at the frantic sound of his name. "She's my...my secretary," he said, clamping his fingers on the man's forearm, his face stern.

The heavyset Japanese raised his rifle to Father John's temple.

"I'm an American," the priest said, lifting his hands. "Miss Jasmine is a U.S. citizen, too." He turned his gaze to her and urged, "Tell them. In English!"

"I'm...I'm Father John's secretary," she mumbled, her voice trembling.

"I…I came from…the United States."

The pockmarked face turned to the man in charge.

The officer with a tiny mustache assumed an aggressive stance with feet apart and shoulders braced. He bore down on Jasmine. His eyes were hard. "Miss Jasmine," he finally acknowledged in English, tipped his head in a curt bow, and dismissed his subordinate with a wave.

Grudgingly the pockmarked face let go of Jasmine. Licking his lips, he snatched Xiao Mei's forearm.

"She's my assistant!" blurted out Jasmine, and repeated it in Japanese. Her hands encircled the housemaid's shoulders. "I need her help with daily affairs. Please!" She turned to the man in charge and pleaded.

Again the officer's gaze zeroed in on her. A few seconds later he relented.

In the end, the Japanese identified all the Nationalist combatants except for the fourteen-year-old boy. They left with their captives in ropes without further harassing the women.

But Father John was worried. "I'm going to send you and Xiao Mei to Ginling Women's College," he told Jasmine. "Professor Valentine will take good care of you. She was your mother's best friend."

Jasmine nodded. At least the Japanese had no excuse to search for soldiers in a camp full of women.

Chapter 9

The International Safety Zone was an area of two-and-a-half square miles, including the American Embassy, various Chinese government buildings, a hospital, and several universities. Many Westerners were living in Nanking before the invasion, but most of them fled as the Japanese approached the city. However, a handful of Westerners—businessmen, journalists, and missionaries—chose to stay and formed the International Committee for the Safety Zone in order to protect Chinese civilians.

By the time Father John escorted Jasmine and Xiao Mei to Ginling Women's College, refugees had packed the buildings and spilled onto lawns and into open streets. Over a short distance, they walked past hundreds of dwellings and straw huts. Every tree, shrub, and fence was strewn with diapers and clothes of all kinds and colors. The area was littered and filthy, bearing no resemblance to what Jasmine remembered.

The fenced campus was no better. The once beautiful college grounds now swelled with not only female refugees, but also males.

"A few days ago Professor Valentine allowed only women and children," the priest said as they entered the front gate. "I guess she had no choice but to allow others as well."

Jasmine nodded. Several wild-eyed girls with blackened faces and short hair ran past them.

A large crowd had gathered on the quadrangle in front of the Central

Building. On the wilted lawn, the Japanese trained two machine guns on the people and had already separated the men from the women. One by one, they dragged the men before the crowd. If a woman vouched for him, he was released to his family. If no one claimed him, he was tied up with other men.

The day was chilly; a nipping wind made the bitter cold even worse.

Jasmine turned up her coat collar and watched. It took her a couple of minutes to realize the Japanese strategy. Her heart sank. Soldiers had no family in the city. As she understood it, a man in his late twenties was shoved in front of the crowd. He was tall and athletic, dressed in a drab gray suit that looked as if it belonged to someone shorter and thinner. It seemed hopeless to convince the enemy he was a civilian.

Two Japanese soldiers held his arms. A third man waited with a piece of rope in his hands. And a fourth pointed a rifle at him, the bayonet already reddened with fresh blood stains. Steps away, a body with a stab wound on its back lay face down on the ground. Half-frightened and half-pleading, the Chinese man searched the crowd for help.

No one spoke up.

The Japanese officer sitting on a chair waved a gloved hand. The two soldiers twisted the young man's arms behind his back, and the one with the rope moved closer.

"Wait!" Jasmine yelled at the top of her lungs from the back of the crowd. "Wait," she repeated. Before Father John or Xiao Mei could stop her, she elbowed her way through the throng of hundreds. Moments later she stood panting before the Japanese officer.

A sheen of perspiration clung to her forehead, even though it was cold. "He's..." She sucked in a ragged breath, forcing a calm appearance that belied the trembling inside her. "He's Bai Hua, my cousin, a teacher in the high school," she said loud enough for everyone nearby to hear and jabbed a finger at the direction of the school she'd attended.

The Japanese officer turned to the young man and asked in broken Chinese, "Name and occupation?"

"Bai Hua... I'm...a high school teacher."

The Japanese looked suspicious. "Teaching what?"

Before the man opened his mouth, Father John hurried over and answered for him. "Physical education. I've seen him lead his students in running. They came here once in a while, right?" He turned to face the young women in the crowd, his eyes pleading.

A few girls nodded.

The Japanese officer waved his hand, and the two soldiers released the young man.

Quickly "Bai Hua" slid away with Jasmine. "Thank you for saving my life," he said once they were a safe distance from the crowd. His breath rose in the raw December air. The cold sun brought no warmth. He leaned over and whispered, "My name is Li Ming, a lieutenant of the 88th Division."

Her eyes widened. In a hurry she asked, "Is Li Suying your mother?"

He shook his head.

Jasmine heaved a sigh, relieved and disappointed at the same time. The odds of meeting the son of the middle-aged train passenger were next to zero. "Well, from now on you're Bai Hua—my cousin Birch. We have to exchange some basic information in case they ask again. Hey, do you have a brother or friend here? Maybe we can save another—"

"Stop it, Jasmine." Father John rubbed his bald skull in frustration. He lowered his voice and said, "You scared me half to death. Don't go looking for trouble."

"I just want to save—"

"You can't save them all."

"Does that stop you from trying?"

Father John's mouth hung open, but no words came out. He shook his head.

Just then Xiao Mei cried, "Big Brother!"

"Oh, Lord," muttered the priest as he followed the servant girl.

Jasmine ran a few steps and then pulled on Father John's sleeve. "It's okay." She was breathless with relief. "He really is Xiao Mei's brother."

Xiao Mei's entire family huddled together and wept.

———

"I'm so sorry about your parents," Minnie Valentine said as she gathered

Jasmine in her arms. The fifty-one-year-old American headed the Education Department at Ginling Women's College. "Father John told me what happened. I can't believe it. I had dinner at your parents' home a week ago. They refused to leave. They thought they could help. I'm terribly sorry."

Jasmine nodded. Her cheeks were red in the cold. The sun had sunk below the tree line to the west. They'd been waiting outside Minnie's apartment for hours.

"Come in," said Professor Valentine, stepping into the foyer. "A Japanese colonel summoned me to his office. I didn't return to the campus until a couple of hours ago."

"What did he want? Is everything okay?" asked Jasmine. Candles on stools lit the hallway. The electricity had been off since the fall of the city. In the dim light, she noticed a faint bruise on the American's face. "Are you all right?"

The professor sighed. "It was a trick. They kept me away so they could come and search for the soldiers. I heard what happened here." She reached out and placed a hand on Li Ming's arm. "I'm so sorry. I promised I would—"

"It's not your fault. The Japs are devious."

Professor Valentine turned to Jasmine to explain: "I helped the trapped Nationalist soldiers change to civilian clothes. Our gardeners burned their uniforms and threw their weapons into the pond. I told them I would protect them." She shook her head. Turning back to Li Ming, she asked, "How did you—"

"Jasmine and Father John saved me. No one else vouched for me."

"He's now Bai Hua," Jasmine said.

"Bai Hua? Birch?" Professor Valentine stepped back and took another look at him. "Hmm…you do resemble her cousin, only you're a few years older. Tall and athletic… No wonder no one dared to vouch for you. Young man, you're lucky to get away."

"Don't start, Auntie Valentine. He's already thanked me countless times. Even thanked me on behalf of his wife and baby."

"You have a baby?"

"Two years old."

They walked into a living room with two dozen people. Briefly the professor introduced everyone. They were her servants or colleagues and their families.

"Thank you for having us," said Jasmine, indicating Li Ming, Xiao Mei, and her family.

"You're more than welcome. Your mother was my best friend. Your aunt was also a close friend before she left Nanking. How's she doing in Chungking?"

"She's fine…probably very angry with me right now, though."

"What? Why?"

"I…I left Chungking without telling her or Uncle."

"Jasmine!"

Jasmine lowered her head.

Professor Valentine said, "We'll call them as soon as the phone is working again." Then she waved everyone to the dining room and apologized, "Too bad we don't have any meat or fresh vegetables. All the shops are closed."

"No, no, no! This is great," Jasmine murmured her appreciation. She'd had only rice porridge for days. Steamed rice with a bit of pickled vegetable tasted heavenly.

As they sat around a big redwood table, eating and catching up, a sudden, shrill whistle blew outside the house. The sound sent Professor Valentine jumping to her feet and running toward the door.

Li Ming, Jasmine, and Xiao Mei followed.

"Stay! Don't come out. All of you!" the American shouted, and with that, she disappeared from the house.

"Please, sit down, Miss Jasmine," said a middle-aged servant. "Japs must have sneaked onto the campus." She sighed. "They come to search for girls. Professor Valentine tried her best. She set up a warning system. She hasn't had a meal without being interrupted for days. The Japs have snatched a number of girls, coming through the side gates or jumping over the bamboo fences."

The room grew quiet.

Li Ming plowed his fingers through his dark hair.

Jasmine lowered her head and chewed in silence. The steamed rice, which had tasted so good a moment earlier, now seemed tasteless.

An hour later, Professor Valentine returned, exhausted. "Don't leave the house," she warned Jasmine and her companions again. "You'll only get into trouble." She heaved a long sigh. "I didn't tell you everything the Japanese colonel said. They…they were coming tomorrow to take all prostitutes away from the camp."

"You didn't agree, did you?" Jasmine asked, shocked.

"He said he'd set up a brothel for his soldiers. I thought, you know, maybe then they wouldn't kidnap innocent girls anymore."

"Oh, no, Auntie Valentine! You can't trust them."

"Right," Li Ming agreed with Jasmine. "They may take innocent girls as prostitutes!"

"What could I do?" the professor asked, her voice frustrated and vulnerable. Her hand smoothed her cheek, then ran through her graying brown hair. "I argued with him. He wouldn't listen." Exasperated, she added, "They don't need my permission to do what they want to do. Like today. I never would have allowed them to come in the campus. Well, they forced their way in, killing a volunteer who wore a Safety Zone armband."

In the candlelight, a shadow of anguish passed across Jasmine's face. She lowered her head, feeling sad for the women who would become Japanese victims, and sorry for the American who had tried everything. But her everything wasn't enough to quell the Japanese madness.

Chapter 10

The next day a crowd of one thousand gathered on the quadrangle. This time they were all women; Jasmine and Xiao Mei were among them. Initially, Professor Valentine had kept them in the house. But the Japanese announced that they would kill anyone who tried to hide from them. "Not just the girl," an interpreter had said, "but everyone in the room!"

A Japanese officer sat on a chair facing the crowd, his gloved hands resting on a sword between his legs. An interpreter and a few soldiers stood next to him. One by one, the women walked in front of them for inspection. The Japanese picked out anyone with permed hair, makeup, or flashy clothes.

Jasmine was in the middle of the line. How the Japanese could tell which women were prostitutes was unclear to her. It seemed like a full-scale inspection of the most attractive candidates for rape. *I should have disguised myself.* She bit her lip and dragged her feet, dreading the process.

"Let's exchange coats," suggested Xiao Mei. She wore a dark blue overcoat and iron-gray cotton hat.

Jasmine shook her head. With long dark hair, almond eyes, a heart-shaped face and a well-tailored coat the color of an oyster, she was indeed in danger. *But how can I put Xiao Mei at risk?* "I'm too tall for your clothes."

Xiao Mei rolled her eyes in exasperation. "At least take my hat." She helped Jasmine twist and hide her hair under the hat.

By the time it was their turn, the Japanese had already taken twenty sobbing girls.

"Let me see your face," the officer demanded through the interpreter. Jasmine had no choice but to lift her head.

"Take off your hat," he said.

Her dark hair fell like a cloak of satin down to her waist. She hadn't cut her hair since she was ten. It was a sign of her femininity and her beauty. An icy wind sent chills down her spine as he subjected her to a slow inspection. She averted her gaze, hoping to God that her good looks wouldn't work against her.

The officer stared at her only a moment before waving his right hand. Immediately, two soldiers stepped up and held her by her arms. She protested, and Xiao Mei screamed as the men dragged her toward the other girls.

"No, no, no!" shouted Professor Valentine and rushed to the front of the crowd. "You're making a mistake." She stood before the officer. Taking a deep breath, she lowered her voice and said, "Colonel Yama-guchi, she's my...goddaughter. Her mother and I are best friends for twenty years. Please let her go."

"I'm in charge here," said the officer.

"You can't do this. She is not a prostitute!"

He thumped his sword on the ground. Wire-framed glasses and a tiny black mustache emphasized the roundness of his face. "If I say she is, then she is."

"You..." The American was speechless. Anger and helplessness passed over her face.

"Wait!" A young woman stepped up from the line. With permed wavy hair and heavy makeup, she appeared to be in her mid-twenties. A carmine red cheongsam, too thin for the cold day, hugged every inch of her slender body. A jet-black shawl draped her shoulders. "I'll take her place." Staring at the man in charge, she added, "I know a trick or two. I'm more useful." Slowly she ran her tongue across her painted red lips and fluttered her eyelashes.

The Japanese officer licked his lips, too. He beckoned the soldiers with one curled finger. The two men followed his order and released Jasmine.

The other woman turned to Professor Valentine. Her mouth stretched into a smile, but it didn't reach her eyes. "My brother is in the Science building. Will you take care of him?"

"Of course." The American gave a firm nod. "Of course."

The young woman smiled. This time, it was genuine. She turned around, sauntered toward the group of singled-out women, and never looked back.

The professor pulled Jasmine away in a hurry as if the Japanese officer might change his mind.

"What's going on?" asked Jasmine, her voice uneven, her body still trembling.

The American averted her eyes.

"Why did she save me?" Jasmine asked. Her face was pale. "What happened to her brother?"

Professor Valentine sighed. "She was trying to save him, but I'm afraid she can't—"

"What do you mean?"

"She came to me for help yesterday. Her teenager brother was wounded." The American swallowed hard. "So many people are wounded. We can't save them all. The hospital has only one surgeon. I have to turn some away, the helpless ones, you know."

"Dear God!"

Chapter 11

∎ ∎ ∎ ∎ ∎ ∎ ∎

Christmas Eve arrived cold and snowy. After a dinner of rice porridge and pickled vegetable, Professor Valentine, Jasmine, Li Ming, and Xiao Mei's family retreated to Professor Valentine's bedroom. The four women had been sharing the large bed by lying sideways. Xiao Mei's father had been using the recliner, and Li Ming had been sleeping on the floor.

"The Japanese just told us—the International Committee—that twenty thousand soldiers are still in the Safety Zone." The professor groaned. "They're going to hunt them down and kill them all."

"How can that be? They've already killed so many people," exclaimed Jasmine. She was sitting on the edge of the bed.

"I don't know where they got the figures. I'm afraid..."

Outside, the wind howled, sneaked through cracks in the house, and made the room frigid and the dire situation even more depressing.

Pasting a faint smile on her face, the American pulled a chocolate bar from a drawer in her nightstand. "On a brighter note, it's Christmas Eve. Let's celebrate with this last piece." She handed it to Jasmine.

"No. You save it."

"I did. It's Christmas Eve. I saved it for this moment."

Jasmine nodded, nibbled a little, and passed it to Xiao Mei. Everyone in the room took a small bite, except for Li Ming, who simply passed it back to the professor.

"Please," she insisted.

Tears welled in his eyes as he took a tiny bite. "I'm sorry." Frustration and pain laced his voice. "It's my duty to protect people. Instead…" He paused. His Adam's apple bounced a few times.

"You were ordered to retreat," Jasmine defended him.

"We knew it would be a disaster. We were in the middle of a break-neck defense. A few of us low-ranking officers tried to air our opinions. But we couldn't find any high-ranking officers—they had already fled. They left us, left the city defenseless. If we'd fought to the last man, Nanking wouldn't be like this."

Professor Valentine reached out and patted Li Ming's arm. "You'll have other chances. China will never perish. Your people will need—"

Xiao Mei shrieked, interrupting the conversation. She lifted her legs high in the air as she scooted back on the bed.

"What's—" Jasmine stopped her question before she, too, retreated.

Xiao Mei's father took off one of his shoes. Leaping to his feet, he beat his shoe on the floor in front of the girls.

Li Ming dived. His upper body disappeared under the wooden bed. Noisy moments later he reappeared. His mouth stretched into a wide grin as he held a fat rat in his hand. Its tiny eyes bulged; its gray fur was matted with blood.

Both Jasmine and Xiao Mei recoiled.

"What's the matter?" Li Ming grabbed the dead rat by the tail, swinging it. "It's meat!" He looked at the rat again. "How did it get so fat when we're starving to death?"

"Dead bodies," said Xiao Mei's father, his gaunt face grim. "Rats will eat anything, corpses included."

Li Ming's smile vanished. His arm dropped to his side as if the rat had suddenly become too heavy to hold.

"It's still meat." Xiao Mei's brother took the rat from Li Ming. "Beats the daisies and goldenrod other refugees are eating. Tomorrow's rice porridge will be tastier," he added, walking out of the bedroom.

Jasmine grimaced at the thought.

"I'm going to set some traps," Xiao Mei's father said.

Xiao Mei rolled her eyes in disgust.

Leaning against the wall, Li Ming dusted himself off. "Why do you do this, Professor Valentine?" he asked. "Why stay in Nanking? You're an American. You could have left the city long before the invasion."

Jasmine agreed. "Why suffer with us like this?"

"I've lived in China for twenty years," the American answered. "This is my home. My students and colleagues are my friends." She touched Jasmine's hand. "Your mother was my best friend. She taught me how to cook Nanking Salted Duck and how to make dumplings with pork and leek. We went shopping together. She took me to all the scenic places, and we walked many times near Purple Mountain."

Smoothing the girl's hair, she continued, "I watched you grow up, Jasmine. Your painting of a tiger is still hanging in the living room." Turning to the others, she explained, "I was born in the Year of the Tiger."

"Don't you know it's dangerous?" Li Ming was perplexed. "Even if the Japs care about your nationality, the bombs don't care."

"I know. But I can't turn my back on a service of the highest kind— saving lives!"

"No wonder people call you the living Goddess of Nanking!" Li Ming blurted out.

Time dragged on. The day seemed interminable, and all the days seemed alike. Every night Jasmine prayed. But great fires lit the sky, reminding her that the Japanese work of looting and destruction continued. The stench of blood, decay, and smoke crept into the house, permeating the air and making her cough. Each morning she wondered how she could live through another twenty-four hours. Life had lost all meaning. *Why does one live? Why does one have to suffer? How bad is death? Why not just give up?*

"It can't get any worse," Professor Valentine kept saying. She'd been spending her days walking from one end of the campus to the other trying to drive out group after group of Japanese soldiers. But each day seemed worse than the day before. Atrocious stories never stopped pouring into the refugee camp.

"A group of Japs carried heads on the ends of their rifles and walked around the town. They were talking and laughing along the way."

"Several Japanese soldiers took an old woman and placed her on top of a tree stump about ten feet high. She teetered on her tiny bound feet for a moment and fell. The soldiers put her on the stump time after time until she lay motionless on the ground."

"A woman survived ten stab wounds. She told the doctor and the nurses that she'd been kidnapped by the Japanese with five other girls. The soldiers brought them to a large house where they forced the girls to wash clothes during the day and raped them throughout the night. When she couldn't satisfy them anymore, two Japs stabbed her with a bayonet."

"Half a dozen Japs dug out a Chinese man's heart and ate it with wine!"

"The Japanese soldiers buried people alive, forcing them to dig the pit first, and left the protruding heads to terrorize others. The anguished howls could be heard from miles away."

"The Japanese troops killed a large group of captured Chinese soldiers with machine guns. They filled a big tank trap with the bodies to the brim so that their tanks could pass over. The bodies were dripping with blood. Some were still alive and moaning."

The horrors continued.

Surrounded by mountains and the Yangtze River, Nanking was once a charming capital rich in art and history, and now it was a Hell on Earth.

Chapter 12

━ ━ ━ ━ ━ ━ ━

It was almost mid-February, 1938, when the orgy of violence finally tapered off. Little by little the refugees left the camp. Professor Valentine's guests also began to return to their homes.

Xiao Mei's family had lived on the outskirts of Nanking where they made firecrackers for a living. Right before the Japanese invasion, her parents and her brother had fled into the city. From the top of the tall city wall, they watched their house being set on fire. The explosives in their workshop started a series of loud explosions and a display of spectacular fireworks. In a matter of minutes, their belongings and life savings had literally gone up in smoke. Now homeless, Xiao Mei's family decided to stay with her grandparents in a village fifty miles southwest of Nanking.

"Why don't you come with us, Miss Jasmine?" Xiao Mei suggested. "My grandpa owns a fishing boat. Mom said maybe we could convince them to move to Chungking. It can't be safe so close to Nanking."

Jasmine shook her head. She'd overheard their discussion. The boat was small, barely enough for everyone—Xiao Mei's family, her grandparents, three uncles and their families. She shouldn't add an extra burden. Besides, they might or might not end up in Chungking. Xiao Mei's grandparents had lived in the same village all their lives. They were getting old and might not want to move far away.

Unwilling to worry the servant girl, Jasmine forged a smile. "Father John said he would help me to go back to Chungking."

"How?" Xiao Mei cocked a skeptical eyebrow. "There's no transportation in or out of Nanking. How do you—?"

"I don't know." Jasmine touched the housemaid on her arm. "But you know Father John. I'm sure he can figure out a way."

"Miss Jasmine…" Xiao Mei swallowed as if there were something in her throat. "I'll miss you!"

Jasmine opened her arms and drew the servant girl into an embrace. The two young women held each other for a long time. Tears ran down Xiao Mei's cheeks when they parted. "Are you sure you'll be okay?"

Jasmine stretched her hand and wiped the housemaid's face. "Don't worry about me. Do you still remember my uncle's address and phone number?"

The servant girl gave a firm nod.

"Xiao Mei, you must stop at Uncle's home, if you end up in Chungking. Okay?"

Sniffling, the housemaid dropped to her knees and bowed down. "Oh! Don't—"

"Please let me do this." Xiao Mei looked up. "You and your parents saved me. I…I…" She knelt in front of Jasmine and knocked her forehead on the floor three times, using the traditional way to express her sincere gratitude and reverence. Then she straightened her upper body but remained on her knees. Using two fingers on each hand, she quoted an idiom, "'A drop of water shall be returned with a burst of spring.' How will I ever pay back—?"

Feeling the onset of tears, Jasmine grabbed Xiao Mei's arms and pulled her up. "You saved me, too. Remember?"

———

"I'm sorry, Jasmine," Li Ming said after Xiao Mei's family had left. They were standing alone in the empty living room.

Seeing the uneasiness on his face, Jasmine blurted out, "Don't tell me—"

He lowered his head to avoid her gaze. "I got in touch with two former soldiers hiding on campus. We've decided to join the resistance."

"The Communist guerillas?"

Li Ming nodded.

"But…but…" Jasmine didn't know what to say.

The Nationalists and the Communists were adversaries and had fought each other vigorously since 1927. It was only the Japanese attack in 1937 that brought the two sides together. Although Chiang Kai-shek, the Nationalist leader, and his government had failed the soldiers in their hour of need, he was still the head of the country and the army.

The silence lengthened between them. The room was quiet except for the thunder rolling in the distance. Finally she mumbled, "I know you're disappointed. But don't give up. Not everyone in the Nationalist party is unreliable. Great people like my uncle, Cousin Birch, and you are working for the government."

"Thanks, Jasmine." Li Ming lifted his chin and squared his shoulders. "But we need someone who will lead us to fight the Japanese to the end, who won't abandon us when danger comes."

"How do you know the Communists will lead?"

"Honestly, I don't. But I'm willing to take a chance. I know what happened here. Too many friends died in Nanking. I can't go through that again."

"How do you plan to get out of the city? The Japs guard all the gates. They won't allow you to pass. It's too dangerous."

"We talked about it. We're going to join a burial group."

"A burial group?"

"Yes. There are still a lot of bodies along the Yangtze River that need to be buried. In this way, we'll be allowed to go out of the city. We'll find a chance to get away."

Unable to argue, Jasmine nodded. "Are you going home first? You said you haven't seen your baby for over a year. Why don't you—?"

"I can't. They're in Peking. The Japs are there. I don't even know if they're still…alive. The last letter I received from my wife was six months ago."

Jasmine picked up a notebook on the coffee table, wrote down her uncle's address, tore out the page, and handed it to Li Ming. "If you end up somewhere near Chungking, please look for my uncle and Birch. I…I hope I'll get home one day. Just in case I can't, please tell them what happened here." Father John had tried to call, but the phone line was still out of service.

Li Ming tipped his head.

"If for any reason you need help, look them up. They're kind people. Tell them...mmm...I could swim a thousand meters when I was eight. In this way, they will know you're a close friend. They'll help you."

"One thousand meters? At eight?"

"See, it's something special, and easy to remember."

He nodded again and put the piece of paper in his pocket. "Jasmine..." He paused, switching his weight from one foot to another. "I...I don't know how to repay—"

She cut him off. Her face spread into a dimpled smile. "You're my *Li Ming Ge—Big Brother Li Ming*. Always... Remember?"

"That goes without saying."

"Take care of yourself, 'Cousin Birch.' Hopefully, I'll see you one day in Chungking."

The former lieutenant clicked his heels together and snapped a salute. His dark eyes filled with gratitude and longing.

Tears welled in her eyes, but Jasmine kept a smile pasted on her face until he had left. She hurried to the window. It was raining. Li Ming waved at her through the mist, straightened his spine, and turned around. She blinked a few times to get the moisture from her eyes in time to watch him disappear in a curtain of rain.

Lightning crackled, and a clap of thunder made the house shake. A great emptiness opened inside her. She'd lived with Xiao Mei and Li Ming for more than two months in this extraordinarily difficult time. Now both were gone.

Will we ever meet again? The same question she'd asked when they were separated from Chen Hong, the other servant girl, came to mind. The slim possibility made her heart squeeze. The tears she'd fought since Xiao Mei had said goodbye began to fall, as loneliness settled like a heavy blanket upon her.

Father John came in the evening. "I'm going to drive Jasmine out of Japanese occupied territory," he said to Professor Valentine. "As far as we need to go. Then she can take a train back to Chungking."

All three sat at the dining table. For the first time in two months, the house was quiet except for the storm that was still raging.

"How do you propose to pass the checkpoints?" asked the professor. "They won't allow a beautiful girl like Jasmine to leave. The Japanese have no mercy on Chinese and care little for Americans. We have limited power here. Haven't we learned that the hard way? They bombed the *Panay*. Remember?"

The priest nodded.

The USS *Panay* was a gunboat packed with American diplomats, journalists, and Western and Chinese refugees. Ignoring the American flags on the boat, the Japanese aviators had sunk it without warning. Afterward, they circled over the area, as if they planned to kill any survivors who cowered in a culvert of riverbank reeds.

"It's too dangerous. I can't allow her to take the chance," Professor Valentine continued. In the faint candle light, a shadow of pain passed across her face. "I'm sure her mother would agree."

Jasmine dipped her head. She had the same concern. The thought of being scrutinized and captured by the Japanese soldiers sent chills down her spine. The house was cold. They hadn't had electricity since the fall of the city. Everyone wore heavy jackets or coats, even inside. She shivered as the atrocities flashed through her mind.

Father John picked up a cup of hot water. A sudden gust of wind rattled the panes of the window. The entire house seemed to creak and shudder. Wincing, he took a sip. "Lord, when will winter be over?" He wrapped his hands around the cup to warm his fingers. "I've got an idea," he said nonchalantly, "but I need your students' help."

Both Professor Valentine and Jasmine arched their eyebrows.

"It's a good one, I think." He paused for effect. The corner of his mouth twitched with the need to smile. Picking up a pair of chopsticks, he said, "But let's eat first; I'm starving."

Chapter 13

▬ ▬ ▬ ▬ ▬ ▬ ▬

Several days later, Father John left Nanking with a Western woman. Dressed in a black robe and veil, she seemed in her sixties. Her pale skin had a wrinkled appearance. They drove in his sedan with an American flag painted on the hood.

The devastation was evident everywhere. Nearly everything in the city was razed. The houses and shops had been looted, burned, or smashed. Broken vehicles, carts, and rickshaws were left by the side of the rubble-strewn streets. Despite the recent storm, bloodstains were visible here and there, and a foul smell permeated the air. The only things colorful were the posters displayed on street corners of the wasteland. In bold characters, they all proclaimed: "Trust Japanese Army. We will protect you and feed you."

"The Nanking I knew is gone," Father John sighed.

The nun frowned. They drove in silence.

A massive stone wall, built several hundred years earlier during the Ming dynasty, encircled the fallen capital. To get out of the city, one had to pass through one of the dozen Japanese-guarded checkpoints where he was subjected to a search. Attractive women and young men were in danger; they were more likely to be singled out as prostitutes or ex-soldiers.

The path leading to the gate was crowded. Most people walked. Many carried their belongings in baskets suspended at the ends of a shoulder pole. Some parents carried their youngsters in the baskets. Sick people and the elderly were transported in push-carts.

"Where are they going?" asked the nun.

"Back to their homes, or to relatives' homes. Anywhere out of this war-torn city, I guess. Some will walk a long distance."

She shook her head in sympathy. Unwilling to see the misery on their faces, she lowered her head. Only when the car approached the gate did she look up. Instantly she tensed.

Father John put his right hand on her arm.

A dozen Japanese in muddy yellow uniforms guarded the gate. They blocked the path, checking for identification cards. Their rifles and bayonets glinted in the sunlight.

As the car approached, a soldier dragged a beautiful girl out of the line. An older woman, probably her mother, dropped to her knees in front of him. Ignoring her pleas, the Japanese shoved the girl into a truck where a group of helpless young women were guarded by several armed soldiers.

The nun gasped. She turned to the priest, her eyes imploring.

"Not today." Father John shook his head, his hands tightening on the steering wheel.

Just then, another Japanese picked out a young man. As he tied the captive's hands, the Chinese bolted. A few yards later, another soldier standing guard stabbed him with a bayonet from behind. Screaming, the young man fell. When he tried to crawl away, the Japanese finished him off with several more thrusts.

The nun sobbed.

"No!" Father John said sternly, "No tears."

She dabbed her eyes and cheeks carefully with a handkerchief.

They stepped out of the car when it was their turn. Two Japanese came to search the vehicle. The priest handed over their identification cards. The soldiers checked the paperwork. After looking at the International Safety Zone's armbands and the American flag painted on the hood, they exchanged a glance and waved them off.

As Father John and the nun returned to the car, a voice from behind commanded, "Stop! Wait!" The man was speaking in forced English.

"Turn around," whispered Father John. "Slowly."

Biting her lip, the nun followed his suggestion.

A short and stubby Japanese officer approached. "Photo"—he signaled the camera in his hand—"with her." He pointed to the nun.

She turned to Father John who nodded his approval. The officer handed the camera to the priest. From the viewfinder, Father John watched the grinning Japanese hold his sword in one hand and wrap his other arm around the nun's shoulders. Behind them, a Rising Sun flag flapped in the wind on top of the damaged city wall. He moved to the right. The truck with doomed women and the body on the ground came into his view. He pressed the button. Satisfied, the Japanese officer dismissed them.

Tension drained from her shoulders as they settled back in the car. "Are there more checkpoints?"

"Most likely. I don't know for sure."

"How long will my makeup last?"

"A long time if you don't cry."

She nodded. "Thank you, Father John. Without you and Professor Valentine, I—"

"No need to thank me, Jasmine. Your father was my best friend, and your mother was Minnie's. It's our job to protect you."

Tears welled in her eyes, but she blinked them away.

They drove along the Yangtze River. At almost four thousand miles, it was the longest river in Asia. For thousands of years, the Yangtze had been used for water, irrigation, and transportation; it had played a significant role in Chinese history, culture, and in China's economy. These days, though, it was a body disposal site. Countless corpses had been dumped into the river, and the water had turned red for days at the peak of the massacre.

Even now, dead bodies were scattered on the shoal or near the shore, their faces black and rotten, some covered with riverbank reeds. Unnaturally fattened dogs walked along the edge of the water, hunting and feasting on corpses. Two dozen young men wearing Red Cross armbands collected the bodies and fought off the dogs.

Jasmine searched the faces of the young men and wondered if Li

Ming had escaped the city. Once the car left the riverside road, she asked, "Father John, how many people died in the last two months?"

"I don't know."

"Thousands?"

"Hundreds of thousands! So far, the Red Cross has buried twenty thousand. I heard that the Advance Benevolence Society had buried over one hundred ten thousand. Several other burial groups are still at work. The Japanese troops also buried or burned bodies, or dumped them into the river. I'm afraid no one will ever know the exact number."

Chapter 14

The makeup artist at the college had done a good job. Jasmine's disguise held up well. She was anxious and scared whenever they passed a checkpoint, but with the American flag on the car, the International Safety Zone's armbands, and her false paperwork, they didn't run into much trouble. The sun sank below the tree line and the sky was streaked with tendrils of lilac light when they finally left Japanese-controlled territory.

The earliest train leaving for Chungking from a nearby town was scheduled to depart the next morning. Father John bought the ticket and found an inn. For the first time in two months, they had dinner with fresh meat and vegetables.

That night, Jasmine slept without worrying about bumping into Professor Valentine or Xiao Mei. A smile tugged at her lips when she tried to imagine how the innkeeper would react—an old Western woman walking into the room that evening, but a Chinese girl leaving in the morning.

The sun was just peeking over the eastern horizon as they arrived at the train station.

"Take care of yourself, Jasmine!" Standing on the platform, Father John waved his arm as the train pulled out of the station.

Jasmine pressed her forehead against the glass and fastened her gaze on the American until he was out of sight. Two months ago she'd had a loving family, and she'd been on an eastbound train to see her parents.

Now she was going west. She was in the same oyster-colored coat and had the same patchwork book pack, but she was alone, motherless, fatherless. A lifetime had passed in those few weeks. Jasmine slumped in her seat.

The train was overcrowded. All the seats were taken; the aisles were jammed with people and their baggage. Some passengers traveled with chickens or ducks. Others carried their belongings in baskets fastened to shoulder poles. Babies cried, children complained, and mothers tried to soothe them. The musty smell of unwashed humanity filled the air.

Three soldiers in bloodstained uniforms stood nearby. One man had a dirty bandage around his left eye. Another held his arm in a sling. The third balanced his weight against a crutch placed under his left arm. Other travelers looked at the soldiers with contempt. The Nationalist Army had failed to protect civilians and abandoned them in their hour of need.

Jasmine felt pity for the wounded soldiers. They were taking the blame for the wrongdoing of the leader of the Army and the government. "Come here!" Standing up, she signaled to the one with the crutch.

The soldier was so stunned that it took him a moment to understand.

"You shouldn't give your seat to him," said a middle-aged woman. She sat next to Jasmine and stretched her legs, blocking the way. "Look what they did in Nanking!"

Another traveler grunted with palpable disgust. "They deserted the city and let the Japs kill thousands and thousands of people." All within earshot nodded.

Demoralized and ashamed, the soldiers lowered their heads.

"They were ordered to retreat or surrender," said Jasmine resolutely. "They're soldiers. It's not their fault."

The woman grimaced and remained seated. "*Yang bing qian ri, yong bing yi shi—Troops are maintained in long years to be used in the nick of time.*"

"Please," Jasmine begged while trying to get out of her way.

"It's okay," said the soldier with a wounded leg. "Thank you. I'm all right."

"It's not easy for them," Jasmine reasoned with the woman. "The Japs killed so many of the surrendered soldiers. I've seen bodies—"

"You came from Nanking?"

Jasmine nodded. "Several of my friends are soldiers. I watched as one was…killed." The image of Lu Ping's blood-covered body flashed before her, and she frowned. After a beat, she added, "My Big Brother was a lieutenant of the 88th Division. He almost died." She was thinking of Li Ming and wondered where he was and if he was safe.

The passengers shook their heads and sighed. The woman pulled her legs in and moved. Jasmine scooted out of the seat and tugged the sleeve of the soldier with the crutch. "Sit down, please."

"Are you sure?"

She nodded.

Tears welled in his eyes as he sat. "Thank you."

"My name is Bai Moli. Call me Jasmine."

"I'm Song Fu. We'll take turns sitting." He pointed to the taller of his companions. "This is Big Wang." He gestured to the shorter one. "Little Wang."

The two men smiled at Jasmine.

"What happened to you?" she asked.

"We were stationed outside Nanking," Song Fu replied. "A group of us didn't want to surrender. We fought our way through." He paused, swallowing hard.

Big Wang finished for him, "Out of one hundred, only…only three of us made it."

Jasmine gasped. "I'm so sorry!"

Their fellow passengers clucked sympathetically.

"Better to die fighting than to be slaughtered," the three answered in unison.

"If everyone were like you," Jasmine said, "then the Japs wouldn't have won so easily."

"We heard what happened to those who were disarmed." Song Fu heaved a tired sigh.

"Where are you going now?"

"Chungking."

"Good. I'm going there, too." Shifting her weight from one foot to the other, Jasmine was glad to find three companions for the long journey.

Chapter 15

By noon, the train pulled into Wuhan. Located halfway between Nanking and Chungking along the Yangtze River, this large city was a major transportation hub within inland China.

Jasmine took out a few baked yams from her book pack. "Here." She handed the food to the soldiers. "Sorry, they're cold." Father John had bought them the night before on their way to the Inn. He'd been worried they wouldn't find anything early in the morning.

"Thank you, Jasmine," said Song Fu.

His companions nodded their agreement, licking their lips. They took out their water canteens.

The train was less crowded when it left Wuhan. Jasmine and Song Fu sat on one side of a small table, and Big Wang and Little Wang sat on the other side. Sunlight streamed in through the large windows. For the first time in weeks, Jasmine felt a semblance of normalcy as they shared food and the water like friends on a picnic.

A roar of airplanes overhead interrupted the peace. Enormous explosions rattled the train, and it screeched to a halt.

Whump! Bam!

The shock wave hit Jasmine. For a split second, she was so stunned that she thought she was dreaming.

"Run!" shouted Song Fu, pushing her.

Now she knew it was real. She jumped to her feet and ran after the other two soldiers. A few steps later she turned and grabbed Song Fu's arm. He was struggling with his crutch. They stumbled toward the door as more bombs hit the train.

Outside wasn't any safer. The Japanese planes swooped low. Their machine guns stuttered, and something exploded. Flame and smoke spewed into the air. The crowd screamed, their voices muffled by the ear-piercing sound of the explosions and firearms. Jasmine shrieked, but she couldn't hear her own voice.

The airplanes kept circling, dropping more bombs and peppering the area with bullets. Trees cracked and tumbled. Buildings collapsed. Dirt and bricks flew everywhere.

Jasmine and Song Fu staggered together. With his wounded leg, he couldn't walk fast enough. At one point, a plane dove at them. The bullets were perilously close.

"Get down!" Song Fu pushed Jasmine to the ground.

Lying flat on her face, her body was covered by Song Fu's. The debris from the explosions rained around them. Her hands flew over her head. Even so, she could hear the gunfire. Fear squeezed the air from her lungs. She screwed her eyes shut and lay as still as she could, blood pulsing in her ears.

Overhead noises announced the arrival of new planes. Jasmine trembled, feeling sorry for herself. *This is it.* Her life would end on this pavement in a city halfway between her two homes. None of her loved ones would know where she was or how she died.

Time seemed to slow, heightening her fear and panic. A few tense moments passed. To her surprise and delight, the noises overhead moved away. They sounded more like thunder on the distant horizon. No more artillery fire around them. *Is it because our fighter planes came? Did the Japs have to deal with our Air Force? Is Cousin Birch one of the pilots?*

Then she heard her name. "Jasmine? Song Fu?"

She lifted her head and called out, "We're here!"

Moments later she felt Song Fu's weight lift from her. Using all fours, she pushed herself up but froze instantly as she looked down.

Song Fu lay in a pool of blood. His eyes were closed and still.

"Oh, God!" she cried and bent down. She was pulled away by the two soldiers.

"He's gone," said Big Wang.

"Impossible," Jasmine argued. Her eyes scanned Song Fu's body. She couldn't detect any wounds.

"He's gone," repeated Big Wang. "Hit from behind." He leaned down, unbuttoned Song Fu's uniform, and took a few items from his chest pocket.

Jasmine caught a glimpse of an envelope covered with dark blood. "Are you sure?" she stuttered, dumbfounded.

Both men nodded.

Tears rolled down her cheeks. Another life vanished. And this man had died saving her.

"We have to go!" said Big Wang, grabbing her arm.

"Where are we going?"

"Airport. The rail track was destroyed. It'll take days or weeks to repair. We've got to go to Chungking. Now!"

Chapter 16

———————

It took Jasmine and the two soldiers several hours to reach the airport. The bombing created such chaos that they had to abandon buses and, finally, walk several miles. As part of a terror campaign, the air raid was focused on civilian targets, as it had been in Nanking. Piles of rubble and twisted bodies lay in the streets. The smell made Jasmine want to vomit.

By the time they reached the military airport on the outskirts of the city, the sun had slanted toward the western horizon, and except for a short line of vehicles, the area around the gate was quiet. A guard with acne stopped them. After identifying themselves, Big Wang handed him the envelope he'd taken from Song Fu.

The young guard opened the envelope, read the letter, and his expression turned more serious. "There's a plane leaving in twenty minutes." He signaled to the runway, and then handed the letter back to Big Wang. "Hurry! You might catch it."

The three started to move.

"Wait!" The guard stepped in front of them. "She's a civilian. I can't—"

"She's with us," Big Wang cut him off.

"Yes," Little Wang joined. "Look." He motioned Jasmine to turn and pointed to the bloodstains on the back of her coat. "This is the blood of our friend."

The young guard hesitated, stared at Jasmine, and then nodded.

The three raced toward the airplane across the field. They yelled and waved their arms to gain the attention of the man who was about to close the door.

"What is this?" An officer stepped out of the plane. "What's going on?"

Big Wang handed him the envelope.

The officer read the letter and lifted an eyebrow. He was an imposing man in his late thirties, tall and broad shouldered. "Colonel Lin Bin? I know him. How is he?"

Both men lowered their heads. "All the surrendered soldiers were killed by the Japs," Big Wang answered after a moment of silence.

Grief darkened the officer's face. "How did you two get away?"

"Before surrendering, Colonel Lin asked for volunteers to break through. He said it would be dangerous, but he needed someone to get back to Chungking."

The man looked surprised.

So did Jasmine.

"Colonel Lin told the volunteers he'd saved a Nationalist spy. The man was badly wounded and begged the colonel to send this to Chungking." Big Wang fished out a roll of film from his pocket.

The officer looked at the film and considered it for a while. "I'll escort you to the Central Intelligence Headquarters."

The two soldiers moved toward the stairs. Jasmine followed.

"No!" The officer stretched his arm. "No civilians."

Oh, no! Jasmine thought. His stern expression had given her the impression that he was a man of principle.

Big Wang and Little Wang defended her as before, but the man wouldn't budge.

"Her uncle is a colonel—"

"I don't care if her uncle is Chiang Kai-shek," the officer cut Big Wang off. "No civilians!" His mouth pressed into an uncompromising line as he checked his watch. "Wheels up in one minute." He took the stairs two at a time. At the top of the steps, he turned around, his tall figure blocking the door, "Are you coming or not?"

The two soldiers looked at each other, exchanged a nod, and turned to Jasmine.

"I'm really sorry," said Little Wang with a sympathetic look.

"Me, too," grunted Big Wang. "But we have to go to Chungking." He motioned to the film in his palm. "This is important. Too many people died for it."

———————

Jasmine watched the airplane take off. The forest green dot became smaller and smaller until it disappeared from her sight. A sudden stab of loneliness struck her. She was standing by the side of the airfield, alone. *Dad was killed. Mom is gone. Uncle, Auntie, Birch, and Daisy are so far out of reach.* A world separated her from her loved ones.

What am I going to do? With little money, she would last only a few days. There were over five hundred miles between Wuhan and Chungking. How could she reach her family?

The wind tossed fallen leaves around her and moaned on the perimeter of the field. Jasmine felt sick. She was like the leaves, tumbling, not knowing where she would end up next. Bending forward she hugged herself so she wouldn't be blown away. She wanted to cry, but she didn't dare release the floodgates for fear they might never close again. She shut her eyes. A shadow crept over her, and she felt totally exhausted from the strain and sadness of these days. She had seen too many gruesome deaths. How could she live with such memories? She had considered following her parents to the grave when she'd first seen their bodies. Only the words and actions of the two housemaids had dragged her out of that dark place.

Perhaps it's time. No one was here to help, to prevent her from self-destruction. Xiao Mei was with her family. *Chen Hong, too, hopefully.* Father John and Professor Valentine were out of reach. Li Ming had joined the Communist resistance. Lu Ping and Song Fu were dead. Big Wang and Little Wang had left her to her fate.

Jasmine opened her eyes. A nearby lake shimmered in the sunlight. It looked like a perfect place to rest. She walked toward it. The rhythmic slapping sound of water seemed so familiar.

She was a good swimmer, but she wouldn't last long in the freezing water. Fifteen minutes? Twenty? Soon she would meet her parents in the other world. Her mind whirled as she stepped closer to the water.

Then a memory emerged, catapulting her back in time. She heard a voice in her head: *Come on, Jasmine! Keep swimming. You can do it.*

It was thirteen-year-old Cousin Birch. He was standing at the edge of a tiny island in the middle of a lake, waving his arms.

I can't! Jasmine screamed in her mind. She was exhausted. Her eight-year-old limbs seemed to weigh a thousand pounds each. She couldn't lift her arms or kick her legs. As she let go, she heard a splashing sound and Birch's voice, "Turn onto your back!" She felt his hand under the small of her back. "Let yourself rest. That's right. You can do it." He swam by her side, supporting her. "Never give up. Do you hear me?"

With his encouragement, she made it to the island, and after a break, she swam back to the shore.

"Five hundred meters each way," he announced, pride in his voice.

She'd learned to swim earlier that summer.

"I told you," Birch added. A radiant smile lit up his face as he splashed and teased. "Let's go back. I know you want to swim more."

The memory had broken the spell.

The wind cleared her head and sharpened her mind. Jasmine pulled her coat collar a little higher as she reflected. Her uncle and aunt loved her. Birch adored her as much as he adored Daisy, who was like a sister to her. If she died here, they would never know where she was or what had happened to her. She turned to watch an airplane land on the grass strip. Her hands curled into fists inside her coat pockets. Every fingernail dug deep into her palms.

Never give up, as Birch had said. Walk!

Chapter 17

"Jasmine?"

She turned to the sound of her name. She saw a young man climbing down from the plane that had just landed. He walked toward her with huge strides. His tall, athletic frame was silhouetted against the pink sky. For a moment she thought it was her imagination—she missed her family so much...

The young man began to run. "Jasmine!" he shouted as he took off his flight cap and sunglasses. His dark hair glinted in the sunlight. Astonishment and concern etched on his face.

Now she saw him clearly. She ran and flung herself into Birch's arms.

"What on earth are you doing here? Mom and Dad told me you left for Nanking. What happened? How did you end up in Wuhan? Where are Uncle and Auntie?"

His rapid-fire questions opened the floodgate she'd tried so hard to keep closed. Huge teardrops rolled down her cheeks.

"Are you hurt?"

She shook her head.

"The blood..." Birch pointed to her back.

"Not mine."

He heaved a sigh of relief and pulled her into a fierce embrace.

After a moment, Jasmine spoke: "Mom and Dad..." Pain ripped

through her throat, robbing her of words. She stood clinging to his tall frame for support. Minutes later she took a ragged breath, found strength, and related the terrible story of their deaths.

Her experiences shocked Birch. His Adam's apple bobbed as if he was going to speak, but the words died on his lips. All he could do was hold her in his arms and let her release her anguish.

When he finally spoke, his face was grim, his voice thick with emotion. "I can't imagine how you survived all those horrors."

She pressed a hand to her eyes, trying to hold back the tears, but a mournful wail erupted from deep inside her. "I wanted to…follow them. They died such a painful death. I should not have left them." Her voice trailed off in whispered remorse. Her body shuddered with the pain of loss.

Jasmine had held back her sorrow. When she was with the housemaids, they'd been in a life-and-death situation. And when she was alone, she'd barely had the energy to pull herself out of deep depression. Grief had been a luxury. Now that she was in front of her Big Brother, all her bravado disappeared and her weakness surfaced. She felt like the eight-year-old girl who'd cried out that she couldn't swim.

Birch let her go. "Listen to me." He grabbed her elbows. "You won't bring them back by following them." He squeezed her arms; his eyebrows creased. "If you die, you just let the Japs kill one more innocent person without even using their guns or knives. I know it's hard; it's very painful. Being alive can be harder than dying. You've got to be strong, Jasmine."

She gave an almost imperceptible nod, eyes still glistening.

"Don't let the bastards kill you. Don't let them win so easily. Live! Do the things you love to do! Paint lots of pictures. You have such talent. Live a productive life, for Uncle and for Auntie. For all of us!"

Jasmine nodded forcefully this time. She understood. She'd just needed reinforcement. Wiping tears with her knuckles, she raised her chin. Slowly, her sorrow and her feelings of helplessness dissipated, and her mood began to lift. "Why are you here?"

"Nanking fell. Wuhan will be Japan's next target. We must protect it. We're getting ready to bring fighter planes here and transfer the bombers and training aircraft back to Chungking."

––––––––––

Birch guided Jasmine across the airfield, keeping a hand on her back and allowing her to lean on him. They entered a room filled with young airmen who were talking and smoking. A clay stove kept the area warm.

"Well, well, well," said a muscular man in his early twenties. He knocked Birch's arm with a fist. "Look who is lucky today."

Birch lifted a hand. "Cut it out, Meng Hu. She's my cousin. She has escaped from Nanking. Both her parents—"

"I'm sorry," Meng Hu mumbled. A frown creased his brow.

A thin man with a half-smoked cigarette in his mouth stood up. He shoved his chair toward Jasmine. Birch set her down. He nodded his appreciation then relayed the stories that Jasmine had told him.

"They dragged our unarmed soldiers out of the refugee camps by the thousands, even though they were in civilian clothes." His voice quivered with outrage. "They mowed them down with machine guns, buried or burned them alive, or used them for bayonet practice or killing contests!"

Groans and shouts of anger rose from the airmen.

Birch addressed all, "Fight the Japanese bandits to the death. Do you hear me?" The muscles in his jaw tightened. Every inch of his body radiated fury. "Don't put down your weapons. If we die, we die fighting, not in humiliation. Never surrender!"

"Fight the bastards to the end!" Meng Hu punched his fist high into the air.

"Fight to the last man!" A collective determination seized the group. Exclamations erupted.

After the excitement subsided, Meng Hu asked, "What do you plan to do with her? Wuhan isn't safe."

"I won't leave her here. But I need your help."

The thin man took a draw on his cigarette. "What would you like us to do?"

"A flight suit..."

"Consider it done," said a young man.

"And a cap and goggles."

"Then what?" someone asked.

Birch ran a hand over the thick stubble of his crew cut. "I'm not sure if it's possible, but I'm thinking of letting her sit on my lap—"

"Are you crazy?" interrupted Meng Hu. Almost six feet, he stood with feet planted apart, hands in his pockets. "The cockpit is already small for guys like you and me. It'll be—"

Birch cut him off, "Tight, yes. But I think it's possible." To Jasmine, he said, "It'll be uncomfortable, and maybe dangerous."

"Just get me out of here, Ge." Despite her thick coat and the warmth of the room, her voice shook. She hugged her arms to her body.

"How about letting her get on our big bird?" suggested the thin man, a bombardier. Tapping the ash off his cigarette, he looked at his bomber crew members. "We've got plenty of room."

There was nodding all around.

Birch said nothing. Jasmine's face conveyed her anxiety. After all that she'd been through, he couldn't blame her for being afraid.

His brow knitted. The bomber was scheduled to take off the next day. *What if someone blows her cover,* he thought? *What if another commander refuses to take her? I can't look after her if I leave earlier.*

The image of her standing in the empty field came to mind. He put a protective hand on her shoulder. "I won't leave her behind. She's been through enough. We have to stay together."

"I've got an idea!" Meng Hu snapped his fingers and paused for effect. "Let her take my seat. I'll find a spot on the bomber."

"Are you sure?" asked Birch. As a fighter pilot in training, Meng Hu was supposed to fly tandem with him. "You'll get into trouble if they find out—"

Meng Hu raised his broad shoulders in a devil-may-care shrug. "If she were my cousin, wouldn't you do the same?"

Birch clasped a hand on his friend's forearm and tipped his head in appreciation. To Jasmine, he said, "The cockpit is open. You'll sit behind me. Can you handle it?"

Jasmine gave a firm nod.

Chapter 18

Peter Peterson was scared. The Japanese had started bombing Chungking in February, 1938. Like their other terror campaigns, the air raids focused on civilian targets. Thousands of people died. Only a thick layer of clouds that covered the area for half of the year saved the "Fog City" from complete devastation. Everyone in Chungking was nervous.

The American art teacher was no exception.

Whenever a siren shrieked, he ran with the screaming Chinese to the nearest shelter. Once he lost one of his leather shoes. Another time he watched a boy being trampled. He tried to help, but before he reached the child, the crowd pushed and shoved him forward. He learned a hard lesson—civility barely existed when life was threatened.

The panic was contagious. It got on Peter's nerves.

The battle in Wuhan was about to begin. How long would the city last? A little over three months like Shanghai? Or four days like Nanking? Halfway up the Yangtze River, Wuhan was a major transportation hub in inland China. If it fell, Chungking was in danger.

No need to waste my life in this foreign country, Peter thought. He was lucky to have options. His homeland was safe. When the time came to renew his teaching contract for the fall semester, he politely declined. No one blamed him. If they could, they would have made the same choice.

Summer was fast approaching. Peter could catch the first boat once school was over. But he didn't want to leave without Jasmine. He loved her. He wanted to marry her and take her away. Peter had seen what the war had done to her. She'd returned from Nanking a few months earlier, and she lived with her uncle and aunt again. She never talked about what had happened in Nanking. But he had heard enough horror stories to guess what she'd been through. She was quieter now. Sadness lurked in the depths of her dark eyes.

But she'd started to paint again. Her first picture was a stunning landscape of a mountain and a meadow. On the ground sat a forlorn figure surrounded by wildflowers in full bloom. Her face was partly obscured, but her sorrow was evident.

How did she do it? Peter loved her artwork as much as he loved the girl.

Since Jasmine refused to meet him outside class, he set up a meeting with her aunt and uncle in the same restaurant where he'd proposed to her. He knew arranged marriages were common and most were decided by parents according to the families' economic and social status. Many people never met their mates before the wedding. Peter had learned the Chinese culture well.

"May I have your permission to marry Jasmine?" he asked them. "I promise I'll love her and take good care of her." He ordered a tableful of dishes. Kung Pao Chicken, Double-Cooked Pork, Nanking Salted Duck, Lion's Head, Lotus Root Soup, Steamed Shrimp Dumplings, Yangzhou Fried Rice, Red Bean Rice Cake—a combination of the spicy Sichuan cuisine and Nanking's favorites.

The Christmas decorations were long gone, but the red lanterns remained, and soft music was playing. Peter hoped they were open to the idea.

"She could go to school in the U.S.," he added. "Her artwork is shaping up so nicely. She'll be even better once she has the chance to learn from the best." His eyes blazed when he imagined their bright future together.

Bai Wu, a colonel in the Chinese Air Force, and his wife nodded in unison.

With a pair of chopsticks, Peter picked up a piece of roast duck and put it in Mrs. Bai's bowl. "Her talent will be wasted here. Who cares about oil paintings right now? Never mind that it is dangerous to stay in the country. Life-threatening, actually."

He hesitated, taking a sip of his tea before asking, "What happened in Nanking? I can tell she's sad. How are her parents? Before she left for Nanking, she told me she wanted to convince them to leave."

Briefly Colonel Bai told him the story. He ended by saying, "Thank God Birch bumped into her in Wuhan. It was pure luck. I can't imagine how she would have survived. It's over five hundred miles between Wuhan and Chungking, impossible for a girl without money or someone to help her."

Peter sucked in a sharp breath. "I can't believe what happened to her. How horrible! I told her not to go, but she was so determined to save her parents." His soft face became stern. He sat up straighter. "Well, all the more reason for her to leave. If, God forbid, Chungking should fall, she may not survive another massacre."

———————

"This is a great match," exclaimed Mrs. Bai when they returned home. They were sitting around a mahogany table in the dining room. Dressed in a high-necked lavender cheongsam, she leaned forward and placed her hand over Jasmine's. "A golden opportunity—go with him!"

Jasmine shook her head.

"What are you waiting for?" Mrs. Bai asked. "Where can you find a better husband than Mr. Peterson? He's gentle and kind. He's well educated. He's an American. Why wouldn't anyone want to leave this war-torn country?"

"Your aunt is right," agreed Colonel Bai, relaxing in his chair. "Mr. Peterson is a real gentleman. He cares about you, Jasmine. I feel good about this marriage. Your parents would have approved of this arrangement."

"Marriage," Jasmine said, "is the last thing on my mind right now." She paused, winding the hem of her blouse around her finger. "I can't forget what happened in Nanking."

"I understand. It's only been a few months." Mrs. Bai gave her a sympathetic look.

"But think ahead. Think about the future," urged Colonel Bai. "Moving to a different place will help to lift your sorrow. New people to meet; new things to learn."

"I don't want to leave. Mom and Dad are here."

"Your parents wouldn't blame you for leaving. They—"

"They would feel so much better"—Colonel Bai interrupted his wife—"if they knew you were safe." He ran a hand around his jaw and leaned closer. "In fact, they would be worried sick if you stayed here. Chungking isn't safe."

"Believe me. I'm a mother. I wouldn't give a second thought about sending Daisy away." Mrs. Bai squeezed Jasmine's hand. "What can you do for your parents now?"

"That's right. What could you do, even if you're here?"

Jasmine pulled her hand away from the table. "I may not be able to fight, but I can still help. I've painted posters. Too bad I can't handle blood. Otherwise, I'd become a nurse. I—"

Colonel Bai waved a hand. "You think you'll help to win the war by painting a few posters? Don't be naïve."

Jasmine lifted her chin. "I have to try."

Mrs. Bai sighed. Colonel Bai ran his fingers through his hair.

———————

Deep down Jasmine had another reason. She liked Mr. Peterson as a teacher, but she didn't love him. Not enough to share her life with him. From the start, she'd sensed something was missing. There was no chemistry, no romantic feelings. Highly influenced by Western culture—and unlike most Chinese women who were much more practical—she had a strong desire for romance.

"I want to find a man I'm madly in love with and can't live without," Jasmine confided to Daisy the next morning. "Someone with whom I won't hesitate a second..."

"Where will you find someone like that?" the thirteen-year-old asked.

They were sitting on a bench in their backyard with its green trees and colorful flowers. It was early June. The air was cool, dampened by a night shower. A ray of sunlight fought through the clouds. No bombing. No gunshots. No sign of the war.

They didn't notice the colonel standing behind them.

Jasmine's face was still as thin as it was four months ago, but her eyes again gleamed with undeniable willpower. "I guess I'm looking for a hero, a courageous man, one who is brave enough to avenge my parents' murders. I want someone I can look up to."

"Like our Big Tiger Brother?"

"Yes, someone like Birch."

"Why don't you ask him to introduce you to his fellow airmen? They must be very courageous." Daisy giggled, her eyes twinkled. "How about Meng Hu? He's tall and handsome, just like our Big Tiger Brother. Then we'll have another pilot in our family."

Colonel Bai could no longer keep silent. "Stop it," he scolded his daughter, stepping in front of them. "Don't be so naïve, Jasmine. Not going to the U.S. with Mr. Peterson is foolish enough. This is dangerous thinking. Give it up." Concern deepened the creases in his face.

He went on. "A hero suffers more than his share of pain. In wartime, a hero is someone who tastes too much blood and sees too much death. He has probably killed more people than he can imagine, and that can change a man."

He clamped his lips together before pressing on. "A hero faces his own death constantly. He must pay for his bravery—he pays with pain, with his body, and sometimes his life. Those pilots you girls are talking about don't even know if they'll be alive tomorrow!"

He was thinking of Birch. As a colonel, he was more than proud of the brave fighter pilot, but as a father, he worried constantly about his son's safety. "Don't romanticize the notion of falling in love with a war hero. It'll hurt you in the end."

Chapter 19

— — — — — — —

Since the start of the bombing more than three years earlier, Mrs. Bai had often suffered insomnia. On the early morning of June 5th, 1941, she was half asleep when a shrill sound jolted her awake. *Siren!* Her first instinct was to jump out of bed and hide. Only a split second later she realized that it was just the alarm clock.

Lying in a tangle of sheets, she forced herself to open her eyes. One look at the empty side of the bed, and she sighed. Colonel Bai hadn't come home. He now worked incessantly as the war deepened.

She shut off the alarm as the first glint of dawn peeked through the edges of the window where the burgundy drapes were drawn. She rolled onto her side. Feeling the onset of a headache, she plopped back onto the pillow, closed her eyes, and tried to relax.

Ten minutes later she hauled herself into the bathroom and swallowed two pain relievers. Back in bed, she tried to sleep, but her head kept throbbing. *Don't want to go to work*, she grunted.

Mrs. Bai had been running a kindergarten for over ten years. She didn't have to work. Both she and her husband came from affluent families. But she loved being with children, and Sunflower Preschool was her pride.

"Close the school," Colonel Bai had suggested. "It's dangerous."

The town center, where the kindergarten was located, was often bombed. The Japanese targeted business districts and residential areas.

82

Their house on the outskirts of the city was relatively safe. Mrs. Bai had considered his suggestion, but every time she looked at the innocent children, she was motivated to keep the school going.

"It's only a block from Jiaochangkou Tunnel," she argued, "I'm safer there than at home." She'd been right for over three years, so Colonel Bai didn't press the issue.

Should I take the day off? She debated as she pressed her temples with the heels of her palm. She had three staff members, enough to handle a dozen kids.

―――――――――

It was ten after nine when Mrs. Bai arrived at Sunflower Preschool. She wore a tailored turquoise pantsuit and jade earrings, which she received from Daisy and Jasmine on her forty-fifth birthday a week earlier. "I'm sorry," she apologized to her staff as she walked into the large open room full of books and toys. "I didn't sleep well and had a bad headache."

"No need to worry about us," a young woman replied. Deng Dandan was in her late teens, trim and petite, with a heart-shaped face and two braids to her shoulders.

"You should have stayed home," said a lanky woman. "We can handle it." Lin Ling was in her late twenties, older than the other staff members. She'd just finished braiding a girl's hair.

"I know." Mrs. Bai gave one of the girl's pigtails an affectionate tug. "But..." She trailed off, her face thoughtful.

The girl was five, short and rail-thin, with eyes too sad for her age. Her mother and grandparents had been killed during the terror campaign. Depressed and distraught, her father had no energy to take care of her. She often showed up with messy hair and dirty clothes. The little girl was bright, but she hadn't talked much since the tragedy.

Mrs. Bai moved to a skinny boy in a yellow shirt and black pants. He was sitting in the corner on the floor surrounded by toy animals. She sat down with him and picked up a stuffed tiger.

Nicknamed Fatty, the six-year-old used to be chubby. His father, an Army major, had been killed a year ago. With a poorly paid factory job, his mother struggled to support two young children. She couldn't have afforded the preschool if Mrs. Bai hadn't waived the tuition.

Sunflower Preschool had once served the needs of fifty to sixty children. Since the aerial attack, more and more parents kept their kids at home. These dozen youngsters had nowhere else to go. Either one parent had died, or both parents had to work.

Two hours later, a siren wailed.

"Get out," Mrs. Bai ordered everyone.

No matter how many times they'd heard it, the kids were terrified by the loud and piercing noise. Some held their hands over their ears. Others cried.

"Remember what we've practiced?" Mrs. Bai shouted. "Don't be afraid. Let's run together," With the help of other staff members, she herded the youngsters out of the classroom then turned to make a final check. A yellow "ball" in the corner caught her eye—surrounded by stuffed animals, the boy curled up on the floor. "Fatty!"

Mrs. Bai dashed back. As she pulled the boy to his feet, she noticed a small puddle on the hardwood floor. His pants were wet and smelly. "Let's go!" She half-dragged and half-carried him out of the room.

Outside, the sun hung directly overhead in a rare cloudless sky. Chaos had broken out in the street. People were running and screaming. On her right, the children and staff raced around the corner. The Jiaochangkou Tunnel was only a block behind the kindergarten. Mrs. Bai picked up her pace. As she caught up with the group, she watched the rail-thin girl trip on her loose shoelace and fall. She took two large strides. With one hand holding onto the boy, she picked up the girl in her other arm and hurried toward the tunnel.

Chapter 20

▬ ▬ ▬ ▬ ▬ ▬ ▬ ▬

Between the Tibetan Plateau and the Yangtze Plain, Chungking was built on mountains and surrounded by rivers. Known as the "Mountain City," it became the wartime capital after Nanking fell. Its air-raid shelters were deep and sturdy caves dug into the hillsides.

The children and staff members were the first to enter Jiaochangkou Tunnel. Thousands followed. Light bulbs dangling every few yards from the ceiling lit the area. Leaning against the dirt wall, Mrs. Bai panted to catch her breath. Perspiration dripped from her forehead despite the cool temperature. Waiting for the raid to end, she thought about her family.

Ever since the bombing had begun in 1938, she'd made it a point to say "I love you" every time she said goodbye to someone in her family. Few Chinese were outspoken when it came to affection, but highly influenced by Western culture, Mrs. Bai was open and expressive. But she hadn't had a chance to say it to anyone this morning. Daisy and Jasmine had already left for school by the time she'd risen, and Colonel Bai hadn't even come home the night before. *Have they all reached shelters in time*, she wondered? *Are they safe?* Her brow creased with concern. Nowadays in Chungking, no one knew if he or she would live through another day.

At least she didn't have to worry about Birch today. Her son was on an assignment in Yunnan. But was he safe there? His job was dangerous, and with planes and other essential equipment outdated, the Chinese Air Force was no match for the Japanese. She worried about him constantly.

"I'm hungry," complained Fatty, interrupting her thoughts.

"I know. I'm hungry too." She stretched her arm and rubbed the boy's flat-topped hair. "We'll have lunch as soon as we get out of here. It won't take long." Even as she spoke, she was afraid it might not be true. This raid seemed heavier than usual. She heard the muffled noise of bombs dropping and felt slight tremors.

"I want to go home," the rail-thin girl sobbed. "I want my daddy."

"Come here." Mrs. Bai motioned the girl closer and enfolded her tiny body in her arms. "Hey, would you like to hear a story? How about *jing zhong bao guo—serve the country with the utmost loyalty?*" she asked, trying to sound cheerful. "There was a boy named Yue Fei in Southern Song Dynasty…"

The children huddled closer and listened. Her soothing voice provided temporary relief from their fear. But then the lights flickered out, plunging the tunnel into darkness. Screams and cries filled the air.

"Don't be afraid!" called Mrs. Bai. But her voice faltered. Fighting her own terror, she repeated the phrase louder. Her hands reached out in the darkness, trying to touch the children. Seconds later the lights came back on. The crowd let out a collective sigh. Then people turned on heel and raced toward the entrance, eager to flee the shelter.

"Should we leave?" Lin Ling asked.

Mrs. Bai shook her head. "We have to wait. The kids will get lost in the crowd."

While they waited, shouts rose from each end of the tunnel. Nervously the teachers glanced at each other. What now? A sick feeling clutched Mrs. Bai's stomach. "Dandan, why don't you take a look?" She pointed to the entrance on the right. Turning to Lin Ling, she asked, "Do you mind?"

Twenty minutes later Deng Dandan returned to the group. "That entrance is damaged—completely blocked," she said, panic-stricken. Her hair was a mess, her braids untwined.

Before Mrs. Bai could think of a response, Lin Ling also came back.

One of her shoes was gone. "We can't get out." Eyes wide with fear, she pointed toward the other entrance to the tunnel. In silence, the four adults looked at each other. The implication was clear—they were buried underground.

The eighteen-year-old Deng Dandan began to sob, realizing that the last route to salvation was now closed. Several other girls' expressions mirrored the fear that was so obvious on the faces of the adults.

Fatty shrieked; he was nearly hysterical.

"Open the gate!"

"Let us out!"

"Help!"

The screams of thousands echoed throughout the tunnel. Mrs. Bai shuddered. Steeling herself, she lifted her hand and signaled everyone from her kindergarten to sit. "Don't worry." She forced the words through her trembling lips. Looking at the terror-stricken children, she swallowed twice before reassuring, "They will clear the entrances. It will take time, but we'll be fine."

Mrs. Bai did not want her life to end in this dark and stifling place. She couldn't leave her family now: Daisy was only sixteen, and Jasmine had already lost her parents. Both her husband and her son were tough men, but she so loved being a wife and a mother to them. Her maiden name had been Luo Lan—Violet. Maybe that was the reason she loved flora. She'd named their daughter Bai Chuju—White Daisy, their son Bai Hua—White Birch, and she'd suggested Jasmine's name—Bai Moli.

She had met Bai Wu only once before they were married. It had been an arranged marriage. He was a good-looking officer fresh out of college. She was the seventeen-year-old daughter of a wealthy family. They had been strangers when they bowed and vowed to live together for the rest of their lives. In time they had grown to love each other and nurtured a proud family.

The lights flickered again. Then total blackness enveloped them. The air smelled of body odor and urine.

The children and their teachers huddled into a tight circle. Tears seeped from Mrs. Bai's eyes as she braced herself for the worst. She bit her lip and stifled a cry, unwilling to scare the already petrified youngsters. As the air grew thinner, she began to feel lightheaded. In the darkness the children thrashed about. Gathering her waning strength, she tried to comfort as many as she could, but soon she began to choke. She raised her hands to her throat, but no oxygen entered her lungs. Slumping to one side, her body convulsed and twitched. Before long, death took her.

Chapter 21

Hundreds of mourners moved through the streets toward a cemetery outside Chungking. A week after the bombing, the damage was evident everywhere: the city had become an inferno after the attack. Black smoke still curled up from smoldering fires, and the offensive odor of burned flesh fouled the air.

The Japanese had flown twenty-four sorties on that day, dropping countless incendiary bombs upon the city for over three hours. The barricaded Jiaochangkou Tunnel had turned out to be a death trap, killing several thousand civilians. After the bombardment, it had taken several days to remove the bodies from the shelter turned tomb.

Birch was at the front of the line, holding a framed black-and-white picture of Mrs. Bai. He wore a white garment from head to toe, his handsome face a mixture of grief and anger. Even though he wasn't in uniform, his back remained ramrod straight. All dressed in white clothing, his family walked behind him.

Colonel Bai held a bouquet of violets, the name of his wife. A grim shadow ran over his features as he walked with fortitude and purpose.

Jasmine put her right arm around Daisy's waist. Tears trickled down her cheeks. Three and a half years after her parents had died, grief still haunted her, and now her aunt had become another victim of the war.

Daisy leaned her head against Jasmine's shoulder as she shuffled her feet. Her eyes were red and puffy, but she had no more tears to cry. At age sixteen, she looked angelic and heartbroken. If not for Jasmine's arm around her for support, she might have fallen to her knees.

Behind the family, a casket with wooden shoulder poles was carried by four young men, Birch's friends. They wore black and dark gray clothing.

The group moved in silence. No music with gong, flute, or trumpet was performed. No fake paper money was scattered. "Your mother wouldn't like loud noises or littering the street with *zhigian*," Colonel Bai had said. And his family had agreed. Now the silence seemed more powerful than loud noise. People in the street lowered their heads to pay their respects. Some followed the mourners. The line grew longer as it snaked through the city.

Once the coffin was set upon the ground, Colonel Bai placed the bouquet of violets on top of it. He caressed the casket as if touching his wife. His hands trembled. Sadness lurked in the depths of his dark eyes, but he didn't linger long before signaling to the young men.

Daisy cried when dirt fell upon the coffin.

"No tears!" ordered Colonel Bai, his haggard face hardened. He turned to face the crowd, his brow damp with sweat. The air was thick with humidity and the cloud approaching from the east was an angry gray. "The bombing is the Japanese leaders' attempt to break our resistance. They want us to be fearful. They hope we will surrender to their terror." He curled his hands into fists, his jaw set in resolve. "We will not let them break us!"

"Chase the Japanese bandits out of our country!" Birch yelled while punching his right fist high above his head. Veins on his forehead bulged. "Fight them to the death!"

Shouts of rage and determination erupted from the crowd.

"I'm going to send you both to Tao Hua Cun—Village of Peach Blossoms," Colonel Bai told Daisy and Jasmine once they were home. He did not hesitate to send his son to the front. Protecting the country was every man's duty. Although the Chinese Air Force had never been a match for the Japanese flyers and was now barely functional, he was more determined than ever to lead his regiment against the enemy.

But he could not allow the violence to reach his daughter and his niece. Delicate young ladies should not be exposed to the hideousness of warfare. He knew he could no longer take a chance.

"Yunnan is so far away," Daisy protested.

"That's the point. The war will not reach you there."

"I don't want to leave you and—" Daisy stretched her hand to clutch Birch's arm.

"It's too dangerous here," Colonel Bai said.

"But…"

"No buts!"

"I can't—" Jasmine mumbled.

Colonel Bai turned to his niece, his face stern. "Your posters won't help win the war."

Jasmine opened her mouth to argue but thought better of it.

"I should've insisted when Mr. Peterson proposed to you," Colonel Bai continued. His brow creased with thought. "It would be so much safer for you in the U.S."

"That's not altogether true," countered Daisy. "Look at Professor Valentine. She was in America when she killed herself."

Professor Valentine had left for her hometown in the U.S. a year after the Nanking Massacre and had kept in touch with Jasmine by mail. In her final letter, she'd said she couldn't stand the nightmares anymore. The living Goddess of Nanking, who had saved thousands in China, could not save herself in America.

"No argument!" Colonel Bai lifted his hand. Turning to Jasmine, he added, "You're the elder cousin. You must take care of Daisy in Yunnan."

Jasmine had no choice but to agree.

Part Two

The Wind Beneath His Wings

Chapter 22

Western Yunnan Province was shielded from the chaos of war, just as Colonel Bai had hoped, but in the summer of 1942, a year after Jasmine and Daisy had left Chungking, a loud noise overhead startled them. "Run!" Jasmine screamed at Daisy. Still disoriented by the initial shock, she dragged the younger girl by the arm and rushed toward the nearby woods. Under the safety of tall leafy trees, they knelt down, occasionally daring to peek up at the sky. Their mouths opened when they watched an airplane cross the sky above them, black smoke streaming behind it.

"What—?" Daisy cried out. Before she finished her query, the plane had spun out of control and was plunging downward. A small dot tumbled out of the aircraft, burst into a white bubble, and floated to the earth. The plane tightened its spiral and plummeted toward the ground.

Whump!

Smoke mushroomed from the explosion site as the plane crashed. Jasmine covered Daisy with her body and arms. Within minutes, the parachute fell into the meadow.

"What is that?" asked Daisy, peeping out from her elder cousin's shield, her voice low and shaky.

"An airplane," answered Jasmine, removing her arms from the younger girl.

"I know it's an airplane. Whose plane? What has happened?"

"I don't know," Jasmine said. Her eyes focused on the pile of white fabric at the far side of the meadow. Nothing was moving. "We have to investigate." She straightened up.

"No!" Daisy snatched Jasmine's arm. Her voice rose in panic. "Don't do it! It could be a Japanese plane."

"But what if it's a friendly one?"

"We can't take the risk."

Jasmine trained her eyes on the white dot. "I think I saw Tiger Teeth painted on the airplane. Remember what Birch told us—"

"I don't care. Let's leave before too late." Daisy swiveled, ready to bolt.

"We can't just leave. What if it's Big Brother Birch over there?"

"If it's him, he can take care of himself. He's the one who brought us here. We're not supposed to get involved in the war. Remember?"

Jasmine thought briefly. "No! We have to wait." Her voice was soft yet accompanied by an undertone of something much stronger.

Kneeling amidst bushes and brambles, the pair stared at the white mound in the distance. They waited, barely blinking. Seconds ticked by slowly as beads of cold sweat formed on their cheeks. It was a fine summer afternoon. The field was dotted with wildflowers in full bloom. Fresh mountain air mingled with the smoke from the crashed airplane.

No movement. The area was eerily quiet.

"Stay here," Jasmine ordered. She jerked her arm free. In spite of Daisy's protest, she started walking. After a couple of steps, she turned back. "May I have…?" She made a stabbing motion.

Reluctantly, Daisy produced a switchblade from her pocket. "Be careful!" she whispered.

With a shaky hand, Jasmine took the knife. "I will." She unfolded the blade and grimaced before clutching the handle in an iron grip.

———

Blue, orange, and red wildflowers filled the meadow. Surrounded by lush green trees and facing a mountain peak, this was a place that Jasmine and Daisy were fond of visiting. With sketch pads, a few pencils, and a bamboo water carrier, they'd often occupied themselves for hours on this pastoral hillside. But today the meadow seemed far from peaceful. Pushing through the vegetation, Jasmine moved toward the white parachute as quietly as she could.

What if Daisy is right? What if it is a Japanese pilot? Anxiety glazed her eyes; her heart beat out a frantic rhythm. She wiped her moist palm on her skirt to better wield the knife.

A mountain breeze blew a lock of hair in front of her face, momentarily blocking her view. She brushed the hair off her cheek and continued to move forward. A carmine red scarf flapped in the wind behind her neck.

A few yards away, she could see what seemed to be a person underneath the pile of fabric. Only the back of his head, a white scarf, and a pair of brown leather shoes were visible. The man seemed tall, much taller than most Chinese or Japanese. A full head of curly, toffee-brown hair defined him as a Westerner. He was definitely *not* Japanese!

Jasmine cautiously moved a little closer. The man wrapped within the parachute did not move. She held her breath. With her right hand still gripping the knife, she used her left to lift an edge of the fabric. Slowly, she removed the cover from the figure. As soon as she spotted a patch sewn onto the back of the flight jacket, she dropped her arm that held the knife. Taking a few deep breaths, she turned around, waved her arm, and signaled for Daisy to come.

Moments later, the reluctant young cousin joined her. "Who is he?" she whispered, eyebrows furrowed.

"Look…" Jasmine sounded excited, pointing to the writing on his back. In Chinese, it read: "This foreigner has come to China to help in the war effort. Soldiers and civilians, one and all, should protect him." The flag of the Republic of China—red with a navy blue patch bearing a white sun with twelve triangular rays—was painted on top of the cloth.

This Blood Chit was issued by the Nationalists to the American Volunteer Group, addressed to any citizens who might come across American pilots in difficult circumstances.

"He's a *Fei Hu*! A Flying Tiger!" exclaimed Daisy.

"Exactly." Jasmine squatted down. "Hello," she called out, touching the man's arm. "Can you hear me?" She spoke in English, her voice soft and full of concern. Receiving no answer, she gently turned the man over. The pair gasped in unison.

The pilot's eyes were closed. The left side of his forehead had a deep laceration along the hairline. Dried blood had matted his brown hair and had dried upon his cheek and neck. Dark spots spattered his white scarf. A few droplets of blood blemished the image of a winged tiger leaping out of a Victory "V" on his chest. His left arm and leg seemed to be injured.

Daisy covered her mouth with her hands. Nibbling the knuckles, she asked, "Is he dead?"

Dropping to her knees, Jasmine placed her right index finger under his nose. "I think I can feel him breathing. He's still alive!"

"What should we do?"

Jasmine doubted that they could carry him back to the village. It was a long walk over rugged terrain.

"What should we do?" Daisy asked again.

"We must get help, but we can't just leave him like this."

"How do we get help if we—"

"You go to the village. Find Doctor Wang."

"I can't go all by myself. I don't know the way."

"It's not hard. We've been here many times."

"But I've never paid attention. I just followed you."

Jasmine touched the young man's face. His cheeks were warm with fever. She looked up at Daisy. "Then you stay with him. I'll go back to the village."

"I can't stay here with him."

"Look, there are only two choices." The elder cousin was adamant. "You can go back to the village to get help, or you can stay here with him. I'm sorry we have to split up. But we can't leave him injured and alone in the wilderness. It's too dangerous."

Seeing that Daisy was about to argue, Jasmine lifted her palm. "It will get dark soon. Choose!"

Reluctantly the seventeen-year-old chose to go back to the village. "Are you sure you'll be okay out here alone with him?"

Jasmine wasn't sure. But what choice did she have? The man lying in front of her was an American pilot who had come halfway around the world to fight for her homeland. She just couldn't leave him behind without protection. "I'll be okay. Go, before it's too late!"

Daisy turned to go.

"Remember to turn right after you cross the third creek. Don't go straight."

Daisy nodded as she waved and ran. Like Jasmine, she was in typical student outfit—blue cotton shirts, slate-gray skirts, and black cloth shoes. A pink scarf flapped behind her slender neck.

"Wait!" Jasmine called after her younger cousin.

"Yes?"

"Send someone to tell Uncle and Birch. They have to know what has happened here."

Chapter 23

▬ ▬ ▬ ▬ ▬ ▬ ▬ ▬ ▬

After Daisy was out of sight, the reality of her situation chilled Jasmine: she was alone with a wounded man who might die at any moment. She had no idea how she could help, but she couldn't simply watch him take his last breath while doing nothing.

As a girl who had grown up in cities, Jasmine didn't know much about traditional medicine or herbs. Luckily, though, she'd lived in this mountainous area for a year now, and as one willing to learn, she'd picked up some basic treatments from Doctor Wang, a sixty-year-old herbalist.

The sun slanted toward the western sky, and the rays crowned the snow-tipped peak with a hazy orange halo. Jasmine guessed that she had a couple of hours of daylight left, so she went into action. Fortunately, forget-me-not, the herb she most needed, grew all around her. It was about two feet high and produced ample sprays of small flowers during summer. With dazzling blue petals and a sunny yellow center, it was one of the prettiest of the little wildflowers.

Jasmine had seen Doctor Wang smash forget-me-nots to treat a little boy's cuts on his knee and elbow. What could she use to mash the flowers? She quickly gathered a handful of the wildflowers and returned to the pilot's side.

Taking the square red scarf off her neck, she wrapped some blue flowers in it and beat them with a rock the size of her hand. Once they were mashed, she placed the puree carefully over the cut on his forehead and tied a knot to make sure the herbs stayed in place.

Since her experiences in Nanking, Jasmine hated blood. It made her sick, but that didn't stop her now.

The injuries to his leg and arm also needed attention. She unbuckled him from the parachute. That was easy compared with taking off his clothes. He was dead weight, and she didn't want to cause more damage. So she took out the knife from her pocket and tore open the sleeve of his jacket.

What else can I use? She considered using the parachute. *But what if it's still important to him?* She didn't want to destroy something vital to his mission or his survival. Her eyes dropped to the long white scarf around his neck. Even with bloodstains, it was a fine silk scarf. She took it. *I'll buy him a new one,* she promised silently before tearing it into several strips. Again she wrapped forget-me-nots inside the strip, smashed the flowers, and placed the herbs on his wounds.

The injury on his arm was bad, but his leg was worse. She let out a horrified gasp after slicing through his pant leg. Between his left knee and ankle was a dark hole caked with dried blood. The flesh around it was pink, yellow, and speckled with leathery brown and black burnt spots. Jasmine recoiled at the thought that she might hurt him. Her hands shook, and she took a few deep breaths to stabilize them. Catching her lower lip between her teeth, she gently placed the herbal strip around his wound.

It was lucky he was unconscious. Jasmine doubted she could do anything for him if he were wide awake. Treating him as she watched the pain in his eyes would be impossible.

Is his leg too damaged? Her frown deepened. If they were in a big city, they could seek immediate medical help from a Western hospital. *What would the doctor do? Amputate his leg?* She felt deep sadness for this Flying Tiger. Without a leg, how could he walk? How could he fly?

Hopefully, Doctor Wang has Yunnan Paiyao. The medicine, known as White Medicine from Yunnan, was powerful. The hemostatic powder had gained prominence as a miracle drug after it had been used on an army commander. He'd recovered from a severe injury with no amputation, which a French doctor had originally recommended. But

Yunnan Paiyao wasn't cheap, and even if the herbalist had it, there might not be enough.

Her mind wandered as she worked. Once finished, she let out a breath, as if she'd held it for hours.

The sun had already slipped behind the mountains. Late afternoon shadows slanted across the land. She covered the pilot with his parachute. She still needed to find another herb. Sweet wormwood wasn't so abundant in this area, even though she knew what it looked like. Doctor Wang had used it to treat Daisy when she'd come down with a cold several weeks ago.

Jasmine wished that time would slow down so she could find the herb before dark. Running along a creek at the edge of the woods, she checked the undergrowth and shrubs. Frantically she searched for the life-saving medicine.

She let out a cry of relief when she spotted the tall shrub with fern-like leaves and primrose-yellow flowers. Reaching up, she smelled the plant, and her face broke into a dimpled smile. It was sweet wormwood. She was familiar with its distinctive aroma. She tore off the top part of the plant and dashed back to where the flyer lay, but as she reached him, her smile disappeared. This medicine was usually served to a patient as soup, but she had no means to cook. She'd been so focused on finding the herb that she'd forgotten about this practical issue.

Jasmine didn't know anything about this pilot, but she knew about the Flying Tigers, a group of American volunteers who were courageous enough to risk their own lives to help China. Cousin Birch had told them many stories. She felt bad that she wasn't able to help the American more. He'd been injured while fighting for her country!

Chapter 24

━ ━ ━ ━ ━ ━ ━ ━

Only the tree line in the distance was discernible in the waning light. Jasmine sat at the pilot's side and stared at him with sad eyes. His condition was growing worse. His forehead was damp with sweat, and he was speaking almost incomprehensibly. The only words she understood were "Jack" and "sorry." *Who is Jack? Why does he keep saying sorry?* When she touched his face, the wounded man grabbed her hand. "Jack!" he called out. His big brown eyes gazed at her face as if he was trying to figure out who she was, but before she could react, he closed them again.

Jasmine felt a sudden flush of heat. Traditionally a female couldn't be touched in any way by a male before marriage. Although she was in college and thought of herself as a modern woman, she had never held hands with any man outside of her family. Not even Peter Peterson, the American teacher who had proposed to her.

Automatically, she tried to withdraw her hand, but the unconscious pilot held on to her with a death grip. She couldn't pull away from his grasp.

"I don't know who Jack is, but he must be very important to you. Is he your brother? Wake up! Jack is waiting for you. Your mother and father are waiting for you back in America. Do you have a sister? If you do, I'm sure that she is worried about you."

The pilot did not respond. After a while, he let go of her hand. His body trembled then spasmed.

Panic gripped her. "Help is on the way. Don't give up. You're a Flying

Tiger, a brave man. You can't give up. Fight!" She shook his hand to encourage him, but felt only his tremors.

She touched his face. He was burning hot. Jasmine prayed that Daisy would show up soon.

Silence enveloped them as dusk turned to evening. She was utterly alone with a gravely injured man. In the moonlight, he seemed young and innocent.

Who are you? Why did you leave your beautiful homeland to come here? Jasmine had seen pictures of America. Peter Peterson was a talented artist, and the splendor and serenity of his landscapes had taken her breath away. She couldn't believe that such places were real, but Mr. Peterson had assured her that all his paintings were inspired by natural settings.

Most Westerners don't know enough about China to care. Why are you so willing to risk your life to fight for us? Are you like Father John and Auntie Valentine, who think that saving lives is a service of the highest kind? Or are you just fearless?

She knew that there were few men like this man. Birch had told them all about the Flying Tigers. There were fewer than one hundred, and she'd never anticipated meeting one of these brave flyers.

I don't even know his name or how he really looks. Jasmine wished she had water to clean the blood off his face. *Water!* Now she remembered the water carrier. In the midst of anxiety and worry, she'd forgotten about it.

She dashed to where they'd left their sketchpads. The light from the full moon was bright enough for her to find her way. The bamboo water container was about two and-a-half feet long with several sections, a string tied to the ends of the bamboo for easy carrying. Shitou, Doctor Wang's grandson, had made it for them.

Dropping to her knees, with both hands holding the water carrier, Jasmine tried to drip water into his mouth. But the elongated carrier wasn't easy to use. "Please, open your mouth!"

He didn't respond. The water barely touched his lips.

"Please!" She raised her voice. Concern and frustration tightened the muscles around her shoulder blades.

For a time, Jasmine gazed at the wounded Flying Tiger. A cluster of clouds scudded past the swollen moon, casting a melancholy pall across his features. She felt a pang of sympathy for him, for his family and friends back home. They might never see him again. He would disappear within this faraway foreign land. They would lose him forever, just like she'd lost her parents and her aunt.

The thought of losing a loved one made her throat swell. She imagined the man as Birch. They were about the same age. Both were brave pilots, and they fought the same enemy.

What if he *were* Birch? What would she do to save her beloved cousin? Birch had saved her from drowning, and she would do anything to save him. *Anyone who fights the Japanese is my hero, my friend, my family.*

And she had to repay the kindness of Father John and Professor Valentine. The Americans had saved her life. *Try everything,* she told herself.

With a determined look, she lifted the carrier to her own lips and took a gulp of water. Bending down, she pressed her lips to his. With one hand still holding the bamboo carrier upright, she clutched his chin with the other. Drop by drop, she let the water dribble into his mouth. She wasn't in a hurry, yet her heart thumped, as if she were running a marathon.

It worked. The wounded man swallowed. Repeatedly she fed him, a mouthful at the time, half afraid that he would wake up and she would be embarrassed, and half wishing she actually had such power.

This small victory encouraged her. Picking up the sweet wormwood, she took a big bite. The herb had a bitter flavor, not something she would normally enjoy eating. After chewing for a minute, she leaned down and pressed her mouth on his. *I'm so sorry...I don't have a better way.* Little by little, she fed him the sweet wormwood, alternating with gulps of water.

Crickets bickered, and a bird sang a lonely song. A breeze stirred the nearby woods. The temperature plunged. Hugging her arms around herself, she ran her hands over her shoulders.

The cold was too much for the injured man. His lips trembled, his teeth chattered. Jasmine tucked the parachute tightly around his body. Sticking her arms under the fabric, she rubbed his hands, trying to generate warmth.

She was alarmed by high fever followed by shivering. *Does he have malaria?* The fatal disease was well-known in Southeast Asia. The symptoms were easy to identify. She hadn't suspected he had the illness until now, only because she'd thought his fever was due to his injuries. *Dear God!* A cry caught in her throat.

The pilot moaned. His head swayed from side to side. At one point, he turned to his right. His hands went to his left knee, seemingly trying to repress the pain in his injured leg. The sight was heartbreaking. *After all this, I'm going to lose him.* Her shoulders dropped as if her thoughts were pulling her downward.

Heroic stories about the Flying Tigers had already touched Jasmine. Now, witnessing the pilot's sacrifice moved her to tears. She was lost in admiration. The physical contact between them, no matter how unintentional, heightened her emotion, for it was the first time she'd been so close to a man.

If he's going to die, I won't let him die alone. If this is indeed his last moment on earth, then at least he'll know that someone cares about him and is with him at the end. With that thought, Jasmine slipped under the parachute and lay behind his back. She threaded her right arm under his neck and wrapped her left arm around his upper body. Carefully, she peeled his hands from his knee and clutched them in hers.

In the soundless darkness, she folded their interlocked arms and hands in front of his chest and pulled his body close to hers. As her cheek touched the back of his head, the tang of blood and sweat greeted her. "I'm here with you. Just stay with me. Don't give up. Don't leave me," she whispered over and over in his ear.

Oh, dear God! Dear Guanyin, the Goddess of Mercy, Jasmine prayed in silence while blinking back the tears that burned her eyes, *I beg you to show your mercy. Don't let him die! He's too young. He shouldn't be left in a foreign land. He deserves to go home, to be with his family and loved ones.*

Throughout the sleepless night she pleaded.

Chapter 25

Jasmine awoke to the chirping of birds. The first light of dawn rimmed the surrounding woods, and the sky was leaden with a thick layer of gray clouds, so low that the mountains were hidden. Withdrawing her numbed arms from the man at her side, she eased out from beneath the cover, then checked the wounded man in the dim light.

He was in a deep sleep, or perhaps still unconscious. "Can you hear me?" she called out softly. His eyes remained closed, but his eyelid moved slightly. Jasmine touched his face. It was still hot, but not dangerously feverish. Whatever she'd done, it seemed to have stabilized his symptoms.

A small victorious smile graced her lips as she brushed away pieces of grass that had become entangled in her untended hair. *I know you'll be okay. You're a tough man. A brave man!* Still, she knew she needed to take him to Doctor Wang as soon as possible.

Where was Daisy? Jasmine scanned the perimeter of the meadow. There was still no sign of anyone. As she waited, she decided to feed the pilot more sweet wormwood. It seemed to have helped him. She ran to the creek; it took her no time to find it. Drops of dew shimmered on the fern-like leaves.

She dashed back and fell to her knees beside him. Taking a big bite, she chewed the bitter-tasting leaves. Her face burned as she bent down to face him.

It had been dark when she had last fed him, but now, in broad daylight, she could see him clearly. Her hands were shaky as she clutched his chin to open his mouth. Her heart drummed so hard that she thought she was going to wake him. Calming her nerves, she carried out what she needed to do to save this Flying Tiger.

She hadn't drunk a drop since the previous day because she know she had to conserve the water for him; there wasn't much left. The water from the creek wasn't drinkable without boiling—she'd been warned by the villagers.

Daisy, where are you? Come quickly!

Dark clouds that hovered above them warned of a coming storm. She just wished it would hold off a little longer. She tucked the parachute around his body as the rain began to fall.

Bending down, she leaned over his upper body to shield him from as much rain as possible. Her hands were wrapped around his head; her chest was only inches above his face. Her cheeks grew hot even in the cold shower. But she did not back away; she remained stubbornly in the same protective position. Her solitary goal: keep this Flying Tiger alive!

Chapter 26

Daisy showed up a couple of hours after daybreak. "I'm so sorry," she apologized, short of breath. "I got lost." Despite Jasmine's warning, she'd missed the turn. It had been getting dark, and she was in such a hurry. Luckily, the moonlight was bright. By the time she'd stumbled into the village, she was too tired to get help, and she knew she could never make it back in the dark. So she waited until dawn to gather two young villagers, Shitou and Mutou, to come with her. "How is he?" she asked.

Jasmine shook her head. "Not good, I'm afraid."

"Is he really a Flying Tiger?" asked Shitou, his voice filled with curiosity and admiration. He took off his conical straw hat to fan himself.

"Yes," Daisy answered with a slight lift of her chin.

"May I see the Blood Chit?"

"Not now," said Jasmine. "Plenty of time later—"

"Ghost!" cried the other villager. Fear glazed his eyes as he spotted the man's blood-stained face. The simpleton with buck teeth, greasy hair, and ill-fitting clothes backed away two steps and hid behind Daisy. "No," Daisy assured him. "He is a great man, an American pilot. He helps us fight the Japs."

"The Japs? Who are they?"

"Stop!" Jasmine held up a hand to put an end to the dialog. "We must go now." Her tone was so imperative that all heads turned toward her.

She alone understood that time was crucial in this life-or-death race.

The young villagers had brought a bamboo-pole sedan chair. Built by fastening two poles to a reclining bamboo chair, this carrier was common in the mountainous regions of Southwest China for transporting anyone too weak to walk.

"Don't touch his wounds," Jasmine called as they lifted the pilot's body. "Be careful!" she instructed as they placed him on the chair.

"He's so tall," said Shitou, lifting an eyebrow. He'd never before seen a Western man.

Designed and constructed for Chinese, the carrier was too small for the American. His feet rested upon the footstep, but his knees bent awkwardly.

"Mutou, take the front," Jasmine ordered. Most of their path was downhill, and putting the taller boy in the front prevented the unconscious man from sliding down.

Shitou positioned himself at the rear. With a shout of "One, two, three," the young men lifted the bamboo poles onto their shoulders and hoisted the carrier into the air.

"I hope he won't fall out," Daisy said.

Jasmine agreed. She'd taken this type of sedan chair, and going downhill was hair-raising. "Why don't you stand on the other side?" she asked Daisy as she grabbed the pilot's arm. The two girls walked close to the chair, making sure the wounded man was safe. "Go slowly, everyone," Jasmine said as they descended over the rocky pathway.

The clouds had parted and sunlight burst over the peak of the mountain. Tree branches extended over the trail, offering dappled shade and breaking the sunlight into dozens of golden beams. The scent of honeysuckle and other wildflowers hung in the air. Before long Mutou whined, "I'm tired." The American was heavier than anyone they had ever carried.

"You're such a sissy," scolded Shitou. Beads of sweat fell from beneath the brim of his hat, trickling down his temple. "Don't be a baby," he added, panting. His footsteps sounded hefty.

"Mutou, this is important!" Jasmine encouraged.

"Too heavy," Mutou protested. Scrunching up his nose and wiggling it from side to side, he set the carrier down.

Shitou had no choice but to follow. Taking off his hat, he mopped his face and head with the rag around his neck. Then he unbuttoned his shirt and used it as a fan. His bare chest was as bronze as his tanned face.

"Mutou," coaxed Daisy. "Would you like some candy?"

"Yes." A crooked smile spread over the young man's face.

"How many do you want?" Daisy teased him.

"Two."

"Why two?"

"One for me, and one for Shitou…"

"If you carry him all the way to the village, I'll give you six; three for you, and three for Shitou."

Candies were like treasures to the village youngsters. Only at Chinese New Year did they get a couple pieces if it was a good year. Having enough food for everyone in the family was a hard task for most people. A snack wasn't even a concept. Jasmine and Daisy had brought lots of candies when they came to the village and asked their family to send more, yet the supply was still limited.

Mutou lifted the sedan chair without further complaint, and Jasmine gave an appreciative nod to her younger cousin.

Chapter 27

— — — — — — —

"Doctor Wang, you must save him," Jasmine blurted as they stepped inside the herbalist's house. "He's a Flying Tiger. He—"

Lifting his right hand, the gray-haired man interrupted her, "I know." He was in his early sixties, with steadfast eyes, a tanned face, and a no-nonsense manner. His gray tunic and cotton trousers were patched in several places, but clean.

"Grandpa wanted to go with us," said Shitou, wiping his face and neck.

"He twisted his ankle a few days ago," Daisy explained. "Remember?" She panted, a telltale pink stain on her cheeks.

"Mutou," the herbalist sighed, "wasn't my first choice."

Jasmine nodded. She knew there weren't any strong men left in the village.

"Put him on the bed," Doctor Wang instructed. He sat on the edge of a wooden-framed bed and took the patient's arm. His three middle fingers rested on the young man's wrist. One of his eyebrows shot up for a moment as he felt the pulse.

The room was quiet. No one dared to make noise. All eyes were on the herbalist's face. Boxes and jars with labels filled two shelves lining both sides of the room. Several bamboo baskets full of drying plants lay on the floor. A distinct smell of herbs hung in the air.

"Malaria," said the herbalist. "He has malaria."

A collective gasp broke out.

Jasmine put a hand over her mouth. Doctor Wang's diagnosis had confirmed her fear.

"You'll be able to cure him, right?" Daisy asked with a shaky voice. "You cured me."

The old man felt the pilot's pulse again. "Maybe," he said. He looked up at Jasmine. "What did you give him?"

"Sweet wormwood," she stammered.

He nodded his approval. Then he turned back to her, a curious glint in his eyes. "How?"

Jasmine opened her mouth but didn't know what to say. A rush of heat colored her cheeks. Luckily, the doctor didn't ask again. He was in a hurry. "Shitou," he called to his grandson. Listing several herbs, he told the teenager to prepare the medicine. Sweet wormwood was at the top of the list.

Shitou opened various boxes and jars. After filling the ceramic pot with the ingredients, he left the room to cook the mixture. At sixteen, he was well trained. Children in poor families grew up fast; they had no choice.

The herbalist lifted his patient's head and unwrapped the silky red scarf. When he spotted a clot of dark blue substance, he shifted his gaze to Jasmine again. "Forget-me-not?"

She nodded as she twisted her hair around her finger.

Doctor Wang cleansed the wound, sprinkled some white powder on it, and wrapped it with gauze.

"Did you just use Yunnan Paiyao?" Jasmine asked. She'd prayed that the herbalist had this miracle medicine.

"Similar ingredients. Magic White Powder—I make it. What do you think of the name?" In spite of his slight build, Doctor Wang had the look of a competent man who had experienced life and survived many trials. Hard living had carved deep lines into his leathery complexion.

"Very good," said Daisy.

But is it magical? He could certainly use some magic right now, thought Jasmine.

The herbalist turned his attention to the patient's leg.

"Can you save his leg?" Jasmine moistened her lips.

"I think so." He looked up, meeting her troubled gaze. He added, "It takes time, Jasmine. I'm a pretty good herbalist. But—"

"The best," interrupted Daisy.

Doctor Wang gave an appreciative nod. "This powder is first-rate. The best you can find anywhere. But his leg is badly damaged. It will take time. Hopefully, he'll be able to use it one day. But not anytime soon, I'm afraid."

The old man treated the wounds one after another. "You know," he said, grinning at Jasmine, "with sweet wormwood and forget-me-not, you might have saved his life. Good job, girl." His smile accentuated the wrinkles around his eyes and mouth.

Jasmine let out a breath of relief. Her fingers finally let go of her long hair.

Chapter 28

Bright sunlight and soft music woke Danny Hardy from sleep. His memories were uncertain, incomplete, and the strange environment compounded his confusion. He remembered his plane had been shot down and he'd been wounded. The last thing he recalled clearly was sliding open the canopy and scrambling out of the falling aircraft into a chilly wind over what had appeared to be wilderness. But he couldn't even remember how he'd managed to pull the ripcord of the parachute.

As his consciousness returned, and his memories grew clearer, he seemed to recall a young woman with silky skin, delicate features, and long shiny hair. She had talked to him, touched him, and hugged him. She'd done everything she could to keep him alive.

She even kissed me!

But surely, such memories must be the product of his imagination. Or perhaps a dream… No Chinese woman would give him a kiss, or even touch a man's hand…

In the early 1940s, few Westerners knew much about China or any Asian country. Danny was an exception. Born into a missionary family, he'd lived in China for several years when he was a little boy. Such an upbringing had made him curious about this Oriental country. He'd long harbored a desire to revisit this part of the world. Living in San Francisco, he'd visited Chinatown many times and learned to speak Mandarin from his mother.

Born in 1914, the Year of the Tiger, Danny had the characteristics of a Tiger—bravery and competitiveness. He loved challenges and had never worried about risk. Which was why he'd come to China—to help protect the place where his family had lived. Nanking, where the horrible massacre had occurred, had been his home and held a special place in his heart.

"I'm in," he'd stated without hesitation when a commander secretly recruited pilots to join the American Volunteer Group under President Roosevelt's executive order. It was the summer of 1941, and America wasn't yet at war with Japan, so the volunteer pilots had traveled to China as civilians and then enlisted in the Chinese Air Force.

By then, Japan had captured vast areas of China, controlling and blockading the entire coast. Vital military supplies couldn't be brought into China from friendly countries, including the United States. The only remaining supply line was the Burma Road, a treacherous unpaved path stretching hundreds of miles from northern Burma to Kunming in China. Keeping this lifeline open was the American Volunteer Group's primary mission.

"Where is Burma?" Danny had asked. He didn't even know where they were going exactly, but he'd signed up anyway.

"That sounds exciting," said Jack Longman with an enthusiastic grin. "If you're in, I'm in."

Danny's fascination with China had rubbed off on Jack. They'd been best friends since elementary school, and Jack was eager to see the exotic and ancient land with his own eyes. The only problem was that he'd had to postpone his wedding because married men weren't eligible.

"Susan is going to kill me!" Danny exclaimed. Jack was engaged to Susan Hardy, Danny's younger sister.

Guilt snapped him out of the past and into the present. *If it weren't for me, they'd already be married. Now they'll never have the wedding they wanted...*

But Jack was as much a daredevil as Danny and had joined the Flying Tigers on his own. Danny hadn't purposely put his best friend at risk. Still, such facts didn't soften the pain of losing his childhood friend, his wingman, and his would-be brother-in-law. Tears seeped out of his closed eyes.

"Don't worry," a sweet voice said nearby. Soft fingers wiped away the tears. "You're doing fine. Doctor Wang says you'll be okay. Your fever finally broke. No need to worry, you'll be well in no time." Her hand patted his shoulder as she spoke.

His eyelids flickered. Her voice sounded familiar. Was this the goddess in his delirious dream?

Slowly, Danny pried open his eyes and blinked against the sunlight. He was in a simple mud-brick room, lying on a wooden bed with white mosquito netting draped along three sides. A painting of mountains and rivers hung on one wall; below it stood a timeworn ebony table and two chairs. Sunlight came through a window on the other side of the room.

A young woman sat by the side of his bed. One look at her, and he knew she was the girl in his dream.

"You're awake," she whispered, "finally!" She shot to her feet. "He's awake!" she called out, turning toward the door. Her long hair swung with the movement of her head.

A crowd of well-wishers poured into the room chanting a chorus of greetings. Suddenly it was packed with smiling old men, women, and children, some folks even stood by the open window and craned their necks to catch a glimpse of the airman. Most wore ragged cotton shirts and slacks; more than a few seemed undernourished. Danny could tell that they were poor peasants, except for the young woman who wore a lilac silk blouse and a matching long skirt with a red scarf tied around her neck, and another girl dressed in apricot georgette.

Arching his neck against the pillow, Danny struggled to sit up. Dizziness thrust him back down.

"Would you like some water?" asked the young woman.

Before he could answer, the girl in apricot georgette picked up a cup from the table. Squatting beside his bed, she spoon-fed him.

Danny nodded in appreciation and managed to say in a raspy voice, "Ni...hao." Clearing his throat, he repeated the greeting.

A collective exclamation came from the crowd. It happened every time he spoke Mandarin. These people were amazed that a foreigner could speak their language. Although his vocabulary wasn't as large as he wished, his pronunciation was impressive. Thanks to his early years in China, he had no trouble handling the "four tones" going up and down as most Westerners dreaded. "Ni hao," he said again, an infectious smile on his face.

"Ni hao! Good. How are you?" the crowd chorused.

Just then, someone near the door shouted, "Doctor Wang is coming!"

Chapter 29

The throng parted. A man with gray hair and a wrinkled face walked into the room. He moved with determined strides, and when he reached the pilot, he dipped his head slightly and lowered himself onto a chair beside the bed.

Doctor Wang took Danny's hand and felt his pulse. He checked the young man's eyes. Then he opened his mouth and stuck out his tongue, as he signaled his patient to do the same. Danny followed the instructions.

The room was quiet as everyone focused on what the herbalist was doing, anxious to hear his assessment. A pleased smile came to Doctor Wang's face after the exam. He patted the American on the arm and uttered a string of words in a thick local accent.

Danny had no idea what the herbalist was saying. He could get by in Mandarin, but he didn't understand all the dialects—there were too many to count—but from the contented look on the herbalist's face, Danny guessed that whatever he'd said was good news, and all he could do was to return the same grin.

"Doctor Wang says you're doing great," the young woman translated for him. A brilliant smile lit up her face.

Danny was astonished that she could speak such good English. Before his plane went down, he'd noticed that he was flying over mountainous terrain. Most people in rural areas were illiterate, especially women. Few Chinese females were educated. Even elementary school was a luxury for a girl. Then he remembered—the goddess of his dream had spoken in English that night.

"Your malaria is under control," the girl continued, "but you still must take the herbal medicines three times a day and have acupuncture."

Malaria? The fatal disease had killed countless people worldwide, including a member of the ground crew he knew. No wonder he'd felt deadly tired those days before the last mission. It wasn't a cold after all. Malaria is hard to cure, even with modern medicine, which was obviously lacking in rural areas. Danny was surprised that he was getting better. "How long have I slept?"

"More than a week; you were in terrible shape," replied the young woman.

His jaw dropped. "Thank you," he said to the herbalist, and then to her, "for saving my life!"

She lowered her head to hide a blush.

Turning around, Doctor Wang looked for his medicine bag.

"May I?" the red-cheeked young woman asked. Her gaze dropped to the American for a moment before she averted her stare.

"Yes," said the herbalist, standing up. "You're a fast learner. Go ahead. I'll watch you."

She put the box on the nearby chair, opened it, and took out a fine needle three inches long. Carefully, she removed the blue-and-white cotton quilt from him, revealing half of his body. He was wearing only his underwear.

Exposed in front of a roomful of people, Danny stiffened. Quickly, he pulled the coverlet back, even though he knew privacy was a concept that hardly existed in China.

"It won't hurt," she assured him. Her voice was soft. The sweet smile had never left her face. "I'll be gentle."

The young woman took his hand. She measured three left fingers above his wrist crease and positioned the long needle over a meridian point. Looking up, she waited for the herbalist's confirmation before she pricked the needle between two tendons. She twisted and twirled the thin needle between her delicate fingertips. One after another, she placed two dozen needles on his head, limbs, and body.

The one on his stomach tickled. He twitched slightly.

"Did it hurt?" Immediately, her head popped up, and she looked him in the eye. "Are you okay?"

"Never better," he joked. It wasn't a lie. Surrounded by kind people and treated by the girl in his dream, Danny felt safe.

Even when he was a boy, he'd had special feelings for girls from Asian countries. Although he couldn't remember much, his upbringing and the good memories buried in his subconscious made him feel close to the people with whom he'd grown up. His first crush in middle school was for an Asian girl. She was so shy that she never talked to him much. In college, he briefly dated a Chinese woman. Back in the mid-1930s, interracial marriage or courtship wasn't a norm, and her family had forced her to break up with him. A year later she married an Asian man.

When he decided to join the American Volunteer Group, Jack had joked that Danny could date as many Chinese girls as he wanted. "Heck, you can even marry several, if you want." Having more than one wife was seen as desirable, though only rich people could afford to marry more than one woman.

The problem was—Danny had been so busy fighting the Japanese that he'd not had time to get to know anyone. The reason he'd volunteered to take this last mission, even when he was worn to a frazzle, was due to a lack of pilots. The American Volunteer Group was small, only one hundred pilots. Within half-a-year, a handful had left the group, more than a dozen had died, and many were injured. Even though vastly outnumbered by the enemy, the Flying Tigers had turned the tables on Japan in China's skies.

Danny had pushed himself beyond exhaustion, and he badly needed rest. His accident seemed to be an opportunity to relax and recuperate. "By the way, my name is Danny Hardy," he said. "What's yours?"

"Bai Moli."

"You're White Jasmine?"

"Call me Jasmine."

"What a beautiful name! It's fitting. No wonder you smell so sweet." Danny flashed a smile. He wasn't joking. Jasmine flower exuded an intoxicating fragrance. "Jasmine stands for purity and gracefulness, you know?"

Jasmine nibbled her lip, flattered by his compliment. Open praise, especially from a young man to a young woman, was rare.

"Jasmine flower is also the embodiment of everlasting love. Have you heard that, too?" said the girl in apricot georgette. With shoulder-length hair and a pink scarf around her neck, she looked very much like a younger version of Jasmine.

"No, I hadn't. Sounds even better. And your name?"

"Bai Chuju. It means White Daisy."

"How charming! Fresh as a Daisy. What else does your name mean?"

"Innocent, wholesome, cheerful…all that good stuff."

"Just like you, right?"

"Of course," replied Daisy, her voice sweet and full of pride. "You know, my brother is like you. He's also a pilot. He was trained in the U.S."

"Really? What is his name?"

"Bai Hua. He—"

"Let me guess. He's tall and strong, just like the Birch tree."

"Exactly!" Her eyes lit up with pure joy. "But…but he's not as tall as you. No one in China is as tall as you. Anyway, we've already told him you're here. And he said to get well. Relax, he's already reported to your commander." Her English wasn't as good as the young woman's, but she sure liked to talk, if given a chance.

Danny tipped his head in appreciation. He knew his friends in the squadron and his commander, General Chennault, would worry about him.

"Let me introduce you to the villagers while you…" Daisy indicated the needles on his body. "This is Shitou. It means Rock." She pointed to the teenager with a toothy grin. He had just brought a bowl of dark soupy medicine into the room. "He's Doctor Wang's second grandson. His father joined the Army, like most of the healthy men. Linzi, his brother, is the one who went down the mountain to send the message to my father and brother."

Now Danny understood why only old men, young boys, and women were there. "Where is your brother?"

"He's in Chungking, hundreds of miles away," Daisy said. "Now," she pointed to a little boy standing near the bed, "this is Xiao Pang—Little

Fatty—Doctor Wang's youngest grandson."

Wearing only a red apron over his chest, the toddler with chubby cheeks was barely three. With a tiny sprout of hair shooting up on top of his skull, he looked like a cartoon character. His shoe's toecap was made of scarlet red cloth and embroidered to look like a tiger's head.

Danny couldn't help but wink at the child. "Cute shoes."

"Tiger-head shoes are used for babies and toddlers in the country-side," explained Daisy. "According to legend, the tiger became real when the child was in trouble. He helped protect him and his family. I'll tell you the story when you get better."

"Okay." Once again, Danny learned how important the tiger was in China.

"This is Mutou," Daisy lowered her voice as she introduced a young man with a smudged face and filthy clothes. Most villagers had plain but clean clothes. This teenager was an exception.

"His name is Wood, right?"

"Correct. It also means Wooden." Unwilling to let everyone hear, Daisy switched back to English. "He's eighteen, but he's like a two or three year old. Retarded, you know. Born prematurely, I heard. But he's strong. He and Shitou carried you down the mountainside."

"Carried me?"

"Yes. What else could we do? You were out cold. Mutou almost dropped you. He wanted to quit. I had to bribe him with candy." Her lips arched to an impish grin.

Danny felt even more grateful.

One by one, Daisy introduced the other villagers to him.

"What's the name of this place?"

"Tao Hua Cun—Village of Peach Blossoms."

"That's beautiful!" Danny made a mental note to remember it. He wouldn't tell anyone, not until the war was over. Right before his last assignment, he'd heard about a tragedy. One of the American pilots was rescued by a group of Chinese civilians after he bailed out. When the injured airman was interviewed back home in the U.S., he named the village in order to thank the people. The Japanese intelligence picked up the information and sent troops to the village to retaliate. Everyone there—men, women, and children—was slaughtered.

A half hour later, Jasmine removed the needles and covered Danny with the cotton quilt.

"Let him rest," ordered the herbalist. "He's not well yet. I'll be back later to treat…" He gestured to Danny's head, arm, and leg, then to the bowl of medicine. He chased everyone out except the two girls.

Jasmine picked up the bowl of herbs while Daisy helped Danny sit up in bed. Without a word, the younger cousin slipped her body behind his back to support him.

"Are you sisters?" rasped Danny. Moving made him dizzy and short of breath.

"No, we're cousins," Jasmine replied and lifted the bowl up to his lips.

"No wonder you look so much alike," he said before drinking the medicine. It was bitter and unpleasant, but he didn't question what was in it. Only afterward he made a face, sticking out his tongue, "I'll be damned. *Liang yao ku kou*. I understand the phrase now."

"Good medicines do taste bitter," agreed Daisy. "Personally, I prefer Western pills."

Jasmine offered a cup of water for him to rinse his mouth.

"Forgive me if I'm being nosy." Danny wiped his lips and pressed his fingers together beneath his chin. His gaze bounced between the two women with open curiosity. "You girls don't look or act like typical country gals."

"You're right," Daisy answered as she helped him lie down again. "We're from Chungking, you know, the wartime capital. Jasmine was in college, and I was in high-school before the bombing forced us to quit."

"How did you end up in Tao Hua Cun?"

"My father sent us here to hide us from the war. He's a colonel in the Chinese Air Force," explained Daisy with pride in her voice. "He sent my brother to the front, but he doesn't want us to have anything to do with the war."

"Your father is right. Young ladies like you have nothing to do with this war."

"He calls this place *Shi Wai Tao Yuan*."

"Shangri-La?"

"Yes, it's a haven of peace and happiness shielded from the hostile outside," Jasmine said, tightening the blanket around him.

"How did he find it?" Danny's interest was piqued. He couldn't wait to see the village with his own eyes.

"Years ago Doctor Wang saved him when he was lost in the nearby mountains. Since then this remote village has been part of his life, and ours. My brother is crazy about this place. Mom loved it, too. The flowers…she loved…" All of a sudden, Daisy's smile faded, leaving only sadness in her almond-shaped eyes.

Jasmine reached out and caressed her back.

"What's wrong?" asked Danny.

"Nothing." Blinking rapidly, Daisy dredged up a smile, but it didn't reach her eyes. "You must be starving. Shitou made rice porridge. I'll get it." She hurried out of the room.

"Is she okay?" asked Danny, concern written on his face.

"Daisy is tougher than she looks."

"What happened?"

"A year ago her mother, my aunt, was killed during a Japanese bombing."

Danny cursed under his breath. The pain of losing Jack rushed back.

Chapter 30

Danny let loose a low whistle as he watched Jasmine and Daisy enter his room. The girls wore white silk cheongsams, the body-hugging, ankle-length dresses wrapping their slender figures. A flaming peony was painted on the left side of Jasmine's cheongsam, while fuchsia roses dotted Daisy's dress. Jasmine was more mature and always had a graceful composure. This stylish outfit further accentuated her elegance. Daisy was younger and playful. Yet her beauty was no less than her cousin's.

Though both girls took his breath away, his gaze remained on Jasmine. His eyebrows creased. Somehow the red wavy lines dangling from the peony troubled him, filled him with gloom. They looked like blood!

"What's wrong?" Daisy checked Jasmine's dress, trying to see what troubled Danny.

He shook his head and pulled himself out of the daze. "You girls surprise me..." Fidgeting in his bed, he fought to keep his eyes off the peony. "What's the occasion?"

"To celebrate—" said Jasmine, her face as flushed as the flower on her dress.

"Celebrate your freedom," interjected Daisy.

"What?" Danny scratched his head.

"Would you like to take a walk outside?" the younger cousin asked. A mischievous sparkle came into her eyes.

Jasmine thinned her mouth, the corners of her lips twitching with the need to smile.

"Finally!" Danny heaved a sigh of relief. It had been several weeks since he woke up. He still had a bandage wrapped around his head, but he felt better by the day.

Doctor Wang hadn't allowed him to go out of the room. "Not yet. You're too weak. You need to rest."

Danny protested, "I've already made up the sleep for the past six months and stocked enough for next year."

But the herbalist was adamant. It was the Chinese way.

"I'm house arrested by Doctor Wang," Danny joked.

Now, finally, he was able to breathe the fresh air, to feel the warm sunlight, to see the beauty of the village.

Wrapping his arms around the girls' shoulders, he struggled to a standing position. One on each side, they supported him as he maneuvered with one leg. They had both been so shy the first time they helped him, and Danny smiled at the memory. Fighting to stand on his own, he'd swayed and stumbled, and both cousins had rushed to catch him. He could see their faces burning as they snatched his arms.

The sight of the trio was heartwarming, yet a little comic. As Chinese, both girls were quite tall—Jasmine was five-feet six, and Daisy a little shorter. But they were dwarfed by Danny, who was six-feet three. He leaned down as they stood on the balls of their feet and inched forward.

Warm sunlight greeted him as he stepped out the door. He squinted and lifted his head. A smattering of white clouds floated across the sky, and a soft breeze caressed his face. Closing his eyes, he took a long breath, drawing the fresh air into his lungs.

They were standing at the highest part of the community. A few yards away, several rows of mud-brick houses dotted the hillside. Smoke wafted from the chimneys. Lush green mountains surrounded the village on three sides. In front of them, the hill slanted down to a fog-blanketed valley.

Danny loved the storybook like scenery. But he was most impressed by the massive steps carved into the steep slopes. The terraced fields seemed like emerald woven cables laid out over the land. In the rice paddies, water shimmered in the gaps between the crops. "How did they do this?"

"By hand," Daisy replied.

"It is stunning."

"Wait until autumn," Jasmine said. "They look like golden ribbons." She paused, and then murmured, "Maybe you'll still be here in a month or so..."

Danny didn't know what to say. Of course he would love to stay in this beautiful village with these two incredible young women. Yet, on the other hand, he wished he could return to the front soon. His friends in the squadron would be happy to have him back, and he missed them and also craved the excitement. But for now, while he recovered, he would enjoy every minute of it.

The village wasn't modern; the people here had lived a primitive life for thousands of years. They used oil lamps and drew water from wells. They grew crops and raised livestock. Women spun thread and wove cloth, trading their handy work at the market in exchange for other essential supplies. Some residents also hunted, but that was before most of the healthy men had gone to fight the war. Doctor Wang and his family collected herbs for a living.

Danny had a strange sensation that he'd somehow been transported back in time.

"Would you like to see Doctor Wang's house?" asked Daisy.

"I'd love to."

"Let's go," Daisy chirped, stifling a giggle.

A smile graced Jasmine's lips, creating two dimples on her silky cheeks.

"What's so funny?" asked Danny. He turned his gaze back and forth between the two girls.

"Nothing," the younger cousin answered with an impish grin.

Chapter 31

— — — — — — —

Danny knew the answer once they had stopped in front of Doctor Wang's house. The pair had tricked him. It wasn't a casual visit. They'd planned to take him there. Six tables filled with food stood in the courtyard, and mouth-watering aromas permeated the air. Dozens of people, probably everyone in the village, greeted him with grins upon their faces. His lips parted in wordless surprise. Before he could say anything, he heard Daisy shout to the crowd, "One, two, three!"

"*Sheng ri kuai le!*" A roar erupted. "Happy birthday!"

Danny blinked in disbelief. He'd forgotten that it was his birthday. Jasmine had asked him once, and Daisy had brought up the question a second time. He'd never given it a second thought, but now everyone in the village was wishing him happy birthday *in English!* Most people here, he'd learned, were illiterate even in their native language. How hard was it then for the girls to teach them the salutation?

"*Xie xie!* Thank you very much!" Balancing on one leg, Danny folded his left palm over his right fist and raised them before his chest. His proper manner was well received. People returned the same gesture, and their smiles broadened.

"Come here, Son," Doctor Wang called out. He wore a formal outfit, a navy blue one-piece garment extending to his heels.

Everyone, even without a formal dress, had clean and relatively new clothes.

The two girls helped Danny walk to the herbalist.

"Sit here." Doctor Wang pointed to a seat for the guest of honor.

Danny sat between the herbalist and the two cousins. A couple of gap-toothed old men were also seated at the table. He was surprised to notice that no women sat at any table, except for Jasmine and Daisy; the other women remained standing nearby with young children.

The herbalist stood up and raised his bowl full of rice wine. Everyone at the tables followed. Daisy cupped Danny's elbow and helped him to his feet.

"We're here to celebrate this brave young man's twenty-eighth birthday," Doctor Wang said in a booming voice. He turned to the American. "We wish you a happy, healthy, and long life!" Raising his bowl, he clinked it with Danny's and turned to the crowd. "*Gan!*"

"Bottoms-up!" the crowd repeated.

Tilting his head, Danny finished the drink in one long swallow. The rice wine was sweet, but the villagers' gesture was sweeter. "Thank you!" he said, showing his empty bowl.

The crowd cheered.

Shitou placed a bowl of noodles in front of Danny. Steam rose from the dish.

"Taste it," said Doctor Wang.

"What about…?" No one else had a dish.

"It's Longevity Noodle, only for the birthday boy," explained Daisy.

Danny knew better than to argue. Using a pair of chopsticks, he scooped up the noodles, put them in his mouth, and started to chew.

"No!" everyone cried out, forgetting their manners.

"No, no, no!" Jasmine hurried to say. "Don't bite. Don't break them. Longevity Noodle symbolizes long life."

"You have to slurp!" Daisy drew in a big gulp of air with a sucking noise, "until no more can be stuffed inside your mouth. Try it!"

Danny did as he was told while everyone stared at him. He stuffed so many noodles inside his mouth that he felt short of breath. The crowd cheered. Daisy beamed while Jasmine released her breath and relaxed in her seat.

Then the men at his table piled his bowl with bits of everything.

"That's enough!" Danny waved his hands over the container.

No one listened to him. They kept adding more. When they were done, the not-so-small bowl held a mound of food. He looked at the cousins for help, but they only grinned at him.

"You better eat it all," Daisy teased. "There is no dessert." She wasn't pulling his leg. Dessert wasn't a concept in this remote countryside.

Danny knew he had to finish; it was a sign of respect. But it was not difficult. The food was delicious. The Roasted Duck was cooked with pine needles to impart a unique flavor, and the Yunnan Steamed Pot Chicken was stewed to falling-apart perfection. Decorated with colorful flowers, the Pineapple Rice was the perfect complement to the spicy food. Even the wild mushrooms and dark green ferns were tasty.

Meat dishes are served only on holidays, Danny thought. Evidently they were treating his birthday as a holiday. He ate everything, and when he finished, he wiped his mouth and said, "One more grain of rice will kill me." Covering the bowl with one hand, he lifted the other to his throat and made a slashing gesture.

The villagers laughed.

When the meal was over, the two cousins gathered all the girls and lined them up under a big tree with strings of white flowers. Waving her arm, Daisy led the group in singing:

What a lovely jasmine
What a beautiful flower
Sweet, charming, full of blossoms
White and fragrant, everybody loves
Let me pick one
Give it to my loved one
Oh, jasmine, my sweet jasmine.

Most village girls couldn't carry a tune, and some were so shy that they hid behind others. Only the two cousins' honey-smooth voices moved the song along. Once they were done, the village girls fled to their parents and buried their red faces on their mothers' chests. The audience cheered and clapped.

Beaming from ear to ear, Danny applauded the loudest. The famous folk song was as sweet as the fragrance he'd detected from the white flowering tree. He focused more attention on the young woman who had the same name as the song, and he had to use all his willpower to tear his eyes away from her.

Daisy's job wasn't done. She signaled Shitou to stand up.

At the next table, the boy held a flute in his hand. He'd been playing every day, and Danny often woke to his delightful music. Still, he fidgeted in his seat, reluctant to perform in front of the entire village.

"You promised!" Daisy scolded him, then coaxed, "Danny will be so happy, if you play it for his birthday."

It worked like a charm. Shitou stood up. Soon he filled the air with lilting music.

"My brother gave him the flute when he was five," whispered Daisy, leaning close to Danny. Pride was written all over her face. "Shitou carries it everywhere. I've seen him play on top of a water buffalo."

Danny remembered one of Jasmine's paintings portraying such a peaceful scene. Putting two fingers in his mouth, he whistled loudly. His smile was as bright as the gorgeous sunshine.

Shitou's eyes lit up like fireworks when he heard the pilot cheering. He smiled back, and as a result, he missed a couple of notes.

Then it was Doctor Wang's turn. Standing with feet apart and shoulders braced, he opened his mouth. His voice was full of energy. His eyes were bright with unwavering fortitude.

"Peking Opera," Daisy explained. "In theaters, performers wear elaborate and colorful costumes."

"What does it mean?" Danny whispered back.

"The play is based on an historical event. This particular piece happens right before the hero's execution."

Danny nodded. He didn't understand the words. But from the way the herbalist was singing, he guessed it must be something along the line of bravery.

People shouted "Hao" from time to time during the performance.

"It's a long-standing tradition," Daisy clarified, "to shout out praises if the actor is doing a good job."

"*Hao!*" Danny cheered at the top of his lungs and applauded until his hands hurt.

The performances continued. The pageantry was in full swing when Shitou stood up and said, "Tell us a story, Danny." There was nodding all around.

"How about the attack at Salween Gorge?" Daisy suggested.

"I've told you many times."

"Tell us again."

"Yes," the masses chorused. "One more time; one more time!"

Danny understood. At this moment, when China was severely beaten, any success was a boost to their morale. Salween Gorge Battle was a key victory for the Allies. It was his favorite story. So he gave the hem of his button-up shirt a tug and straightened, ready to stand.

"Sit down, Son." Doctor Wang pulled on his arm. "No need to stand."

Danny nodded his appreciation and started to tell the story.

Chapter 32

"Salween Gorge is impressive," Danny began, eyes glowing. "Has anybody ever been there?"

Everyone shook their heads.

"Well, you have to know what the place looks like before you can fully understand how the attack worked. Salween Gorge is near Paoshan in western Yunnan. There is only one path across the river—a suspension bridge at the bottom of the gorge. When I say the bottom, I mean it!" He spread his long arms, one up and one down, to indicate the distance. "There is a mile drop from the top of the plateau to the river!"

"That is," Daisy clarified, "more than three *Li—Chinese mile*." The crowd murmured, amazed at what they'd heard.

"It is thirty-five miles down a treacherous path to the bridge."

"More than one hundred *Li*," added Daisy.

"Right… There are dozens of switchbacks." His right hand twisted and turned a few times. "On the other side, the road winds in the same way up to a plateau. And the Japanese 56th Division was getting ready to cross the river. Kunming is only two hundred miles east of Paoshan. In between, only a limited number of Nationalist troops—"

"The 66th Division," interrupted Shitou.

"…remained to defend Kunming." Danny acknowledged the boy for remembering the details. "If Kunming, the capital of Yunnan, were captured, it would be devastating to China and to the Allies."

Everyone leaned forward.

"To slow the enemy's advance, the Nationalist Army destroyed the suspension bridge. It was a painful decision. There were still Chinese soldiers on the other side of the river." Danny pulled a hard breath into his lungs. The ones who were left behind had had no chance of survival. But for the greater good, it was a necessary sacrifice.

"So that stopped the Japs?" one of his listeners asked impatiently.

"No, it only halted them for a while. The instant the Japs reached the river they started to build a pontoon bridge. Hundreds of vehicles, armored tanks, and thousands of soldiers packed the thirty-five-mile road. They waited there to cross the river, eager to destroy the Chinese troops. Fighting for weeks, only a small part of the Nationalist's 66th Division was left, and they were exhausted. The Japs were sure that they would win the battle. But first they had to cross the river..."

"No chance," said Shitou, full of confidence. "The Flying Tigers would not let them succeed."

"Shitou is right. We couldn't allow that to happen." Danny grinned playfully at the crowd. "In mid-morning, eight Flying Tigers took off from Kunming, including my friend Jack and me. Four planes were assigned as top cover. The other four P40s were loaded with fragmentation and demolition bombs under each of the wings. Believe it or not, the bomb racks were homemade. Our planes are fighters, not bombers."

Danny inhaled deeply. "By the way, Jack was a great pilot. He was one of the toughest." His voice caught on a lump lodged at the back of his throat. Longing appeared on his face. He hadn't told anyone in the village about Jack. During the past few weeks, whenever he thought about his dear friend, he'd felt a void in his heart. By not bringing him up, Danny hoped he could shut out the pain. But it hadn't worked.

"Tell us what happened next, Dan Ni." Shitou stood behind the American and nudged him with an elbow.

The boy's enthusiastic request brought Danny back to reality. He inhaled again and gave Shitou a crooked grin. Straightening his shoulders, he held his head high. "The day wasn't the best for flying. In fact, it was terrible and dangerous. Towering thunderheads lay in our path. The rain came down in buckets; it pounded our planes. Luckily, the clouds broke when we reached the gorge. I guess Lao Tian Ye was on our side, or God was willing to help us."

Everyone latched onto his words.

"I've never seen so many Japs in one place. Thousands of troops and hundreds of tanks and trucks lined the path. All were waiting for their engineers to finish building the bridge. Immediately, we formed a single line and dived down. Together we released our explosives." Excitement flooded Danny's suntanned face, as if he were back in the battle.

"What happened then?" Shitou knew the event by heart, but he still couldn't restrain himself.

"What happened was better than any of us could have imagined. I pulled into a sharp turn and saw"—Danny's mouth stretched into his inimitable smile—"the tank I had aimed at blow up. Pieces slammed into the cliff. Huge slabs of rock peeled off from the cliff and crashed onto the road below. I could hear the noise as they landed. *Whump!*" He raised his voice as he imitated the sound. "*Bam! Bam!* In waves, we blasted the enemy all along that road."

Cheers erupted from his listeners, and Danny felt the same flush of exhilaration he'd experienced at the time of the attack. His eyes sparkled. "Clouds of dust filled the air at the gorge as my friends and I kept dropping bombs. Can you imagine it? Trucks and tanks spun out of control, fell down the cliff, and exploded on the road hundreds of feet below. Rocks of different sizes rolled off the hillside and crushed the helpless Japs to death."

"Or buried them as they screamed!" Shitou added.

Danny scanned the crowd. Everyone was absorbed in his story and thrilled with the result. Perching her chin on interlaced fingers, Daisy turned her face to him in a way that made him think of sunflowers turning toward the sun.

With a dimpled smile and open admiration, Jasmine blossomed like the peony on her dress. His gaze lingered on her. He knew he shouldn't do this, but he couldn't help himself. Jasmine wasn't just another gorgeous girl; she was the one who had saved his life. And he was crazy about her!

Forcing his attention back to the story, he continued, "The better part is that our attack caused a massive landslide. It destroyed the road and cut off the enemy's only escape route. Now the Japs had nowhere to run. No place to hide. The twisting path became a curse upon them. We passed back and forth along the road, killing anyone that moved. It was a fine sight."

Feeling like a coiled spring, Danny was ready to go back into action to score another victory like that one. "The explosions went on and on. Along with punctured gas tanks and secondary explosions, the road looked like an inferno."

He lifted his right hand and asked, "Where could the Japs go with a rocky wall on one side and a steep drop on the other? Where?"

"Go to hell!" someone in the crowd yelled. And everyone cheered.

"Hell is exactly where they went. And you know what? Salween River is also called Nu Jiang—Angry River…"

Laughter filled the courtyard.

"At one point, Jack called out over the radio, 'O Danny Boy, are you ready for some action at the bridge?' And I glanced at him on my left and gave him a thumbs-up. I knew what he wanted to do. 'Count me in,' I said. Side by side, we zoomed toward the bottom of the gorge. The Japanese engineers swarmed over the shoreline like little ants. With each of our six guns, Jack and I fired and made sure that they would never build or repair another bridge."

"*Hao!* Excellent!"

"Wait! That's not all," Shitou yelled, as if he were one of the pilots, his eyes bright with enthusiasm.

"Shitou is right. During the next few days, we returned to the gorge flight after flight and attacked the poor Japs. Within a week, no functional Japanese unit remained within a hundred miles of the gorge. We taught the bastards a lesson."

"I doubt the Japs will ever dare to go back to the gorge," said Jasmine.

Daisy agreed, "It would be suicidal. They wouldn't be that stupid."

"Wonderful!" A collective roar went up from the crowd. Everyone, old or young, men or women, clasped their hands or waved their arms.

Danny remembered seeing the same exuberant expression on faces of the Nationalist troops on the other side of the gorge. Watching the

Flying Tigers' attack unfold, the unkempt, drained 66th Division had been unexpectedly surprised by the winning battle. Along the river's edge, the Chinese soldiers had cheered, embraced one another, and jumped up and down for joy.

"Excuse me, Son, are you saying that no one fired at you?" asked Doctor Wang after the applause had subsided.

Chapter 33

— — — — — — —

"I'm glad you asked, Doctor Wang," replied Danny. "Yes, they did engage us when we first appeared. We had to be quick. The Japs shot at us with everything they had as soon as we came into range. Speed was our only advantage. Gunfire was flashing all around me. In fact, I was hit—thirteen holes to be exact!" A collective gasp went up, and he hurried on. "Don't worry; it wasn't serious. Nothing we couldn't fix later."

The villagers let out sighs of relief.

"Where did you learn to fight like this?" asked the herbalist.

"My friend Jack and I were both pilots in the U.S. Navy. Believe it or not, we'd never had any combat experiences before we came to China. None of the Flying Tigers had tangled with an enemy in the air. I wasn't even trained to fly a P-40."

The audience shook their heads.

"In fact, one of my friends left his gun switched off the first time we were in the air." Danny chuckled, remembering his colleague's crestfallen expression. "Things like this happened a few times before we learned our lessons."

"Unbelievable!" exclaimed Doctor Wang.

"That's why the Japs thought so little of us at first. They already had four years of fighting experience. They had a more maneuverable aircraft. The odds were against us. But we gave those arrogant bastards a surprise!" Danny beamed. With sheer determination and courage, the Flying Tigers had turned the tables on Japan in China's skies.

"Were you ever afraid?" someone in the crowd asked.

"You bet!" Danny felt like he was giving an important press conference. "But we didn't have time to acknowledge our emotions."

Everyone grinned at him.

"One time Jack and I were alone in the air for about fifteen minutes. We had to face two dozen enemy fighters. The Japs took us by surprise. Most of our pilots were away from the base that day. Some had just come back and landed. And the rest of our planes were in the middle of maintenance or repair. Actually, Jack and I were enjoying our days off. I was reading a book. He was writing a letter to his fiancée, my sister."

"Jack married your sister?" Shitou exclaimed.

"He was going to, but married men were not allowed to join the American Volunteer Group. So they postponed their wedding. He… was…killed during our last mission." Bitterness crept into his voice. "We were going to be brothers-in-law." He lowered his head to hide the hurt in his eyes.

Daisy touched his arm.

"I'm so sorry," murmured Jasmine.

Others offered their sympathy.

Danny lifted his head, acknowledging their words. He cleared his throat before continuing. "Anyway, when we heard the report that the Japs were coming, we dropped whatever we were doing and raced for our airplanes. Luckily, two planes were ready to go. We jumped into the cockpits and took off."

The herbalist was tongue-tied: "Are you saying that the two of you were going to fight twenty-four enemy fighters?"

"For about fifteen minutes, yes."

"Why? Why did you take the risk?"

"We had to. It would have been a disaster if the Japanese had gotten through to our base. The planes on the ground were defenseless. They would have destroyed every single one of them. We had to hold them long enough so that the other Flying Tigers had time to refuel and take off."

The listeners shook their heads as Danny continued: "Jack was an excellent pilot. I couldn't have picked a better partner." He wondered if he would ever have another great wingman like Jack.

Daisy touched his sleeve.

Danny tipped his head and said, "Soon two dozen Japanese fighter planes showed up. They were ready to tear up our base. Side by side, Jack and I roared down on them, opening our guns. We broke their rigid formation and sent them scattering in all directions."

"What happened then, Dan Ni?" Shitou took a nervous breath.

"I snapped off bursts of fire as I dived. One Jap plane was hit and spun out of control. But I didn't have time to check on it. There was another in my line of fire, so I jumped at the chance. A stream of bullets hit its tail and fuselage. It turned into a fireball and plunged toward the ground."

"Wa!"

"After that, I climbed to a higher altitude, ready for another dive. Jack did the same. He zoomed down, opened fire, pulled away, climbed, and dived back down. Again and again, the two of us repeated the maneuver, catching several Japanese fighters by surprise. We held up the line and blocked their advance—"

"So, instead of destroying your base, they had to deal with the two of you?" Jasmine asked.

"Yes. Fifteen minutes later, more Flying Tigers joined the fight. These pilots didn't have time to leave their cockpits before they were airborne again. I'm sure they urged the ground crew to hurry."

Shitou wiped his forehead in relief.

"By then, the Japs had lost their advantage. It wasn't their day. They'd already lost five planes. During the next twenty minutes, they lost three more. Believe me, the Japanese are not bad flyers; they have good training. They're not cowards, as some people think. But after eight planes had been destroyed, they'd had enough, and they fled."

"Thank goodness!" The crowd let out a sigh of relief.

"During the fight, both Jack and I were hit multiple times."

The audience tensed again.

"My plane wasn't too bad. There were a dozen holes in it, but nothing critical. Only my ammunition ran out. Jack had taken a bad hit. The

Japs had punched several big holes in his plane. I shouted over the radio for him to bail out." The phrase rang such a familiar bell. *How many times I'd yelled at him like that? And how many times he'd barked at me in the same way?*

"He jumped out of his plane, right?" asked Shitou, leaning closer.

"He didn't."

"But you said he was hit badly."

"His cockpit was riddled with shots. His engine sputtered and coughed. Smoke shot back along his fuselage. He—"

"So why didn't he bail out?" Daisy implored.

"Because he was trying to save his plane."

"Giving his life?"

"Yep. I could hardly breathe when I heard his engine quit."

"What did he do?" Shitou's eyes widened.

"He stayed with his P-40 and did a damn good job putting it in a river. Our ground crews fished it out of the water later. Believe it or not, they were able to repair it. Jack—"

"How was he?"

"He was all right. He came out of it in one piece—only minor injuries."

"Thank God!" both Jasmine and Daisy cried.

Everyone nodded their agreement.

"So, back to your question. Was I scared? You bet I was scared! But there was no time for feelings. We were on a mission. To keep fighting is all that matters."

"You're so brave," the two cousins said in unison.

"Jack always said that bravery didn't mean a lack of fear." Danny lifted his chin, his voice rising. "It was knowing that something else was more important than the fear. What I like to say is: Courage is doing something when you're scared half to death."

Doctor Wang spoke up: "It is the highest honor to meet you. I'm sure that there isn't one of us who doesn't want to thank you."

The crowd murmured its agreement.

With a gleam in his eye, Doctor Wang slapped Danny's back. "*Hao yang de*. Excellent!" The herbalist raised his bowl again. He waited until everyone followed suit before offering another toast. "To Jack! We'll never forget his sacrifice." He clinked his bowl with Danny's. "And to you, *wo men de Fei Hu!*"

Tears welled in the American's eyes.

The tiger was considered the owner of great strength and vitality in Chinese culture. Fei Hu—a Tiger with wings—symbolized unparalleled power. Danny was touched by being called *Wo men de Fei Hu—our Flying Tiger*.

Chapter 34

- - - - - - - -

After the party ended, Jasmine accompanied Danny back to his room. "Best birthday party ever," he told her. The next time he opened the guns or dropped bombs, he knew that he'd have his Chinese friends in mind.

"Hold on. Not done yet." Jasmine lifted her right index finger then spun around and ran out of the room. Before Danny could blink, she returned with a homemade purple-and-black patchwork bag. She handed it to him, apologizing in her soft voice, "Sorry, I can't find any gift wrapping."

"No, no, no," he said. "No need to give me a gift." He opened the bag. Inside, there was a white silk scarf. He didn't know what to say.

By now he knew that Jasmine had used both his scarf and hers to bandage him that night. She had apologized for shredding his scarf. But she hadn't related any details. No matter how much he pressed her, she only smiled, her fingers twisting a strand of her long hair.

"I know it's not as good as yours," she said. "I asked Linzi to buy one. This is the best he could find in Anning."

"This is beautiful." While it was true, the quality of the new scarf wasn't as good as the old one, the kindness of her gesture overwhelmed him. "I don't know what to say," he repeated. He was rarely tongue-tied. "You are the one who saved me; I should give you a gift—"

"It's not my birthday." A shy smile created two dimples. She pointed to the bag. "There is another…" Her voice was almost inaudible.

Danny put his hand into the bag and fished out a red sachet. "This is so pretty." A white jasmine flower was hand stitched on one side, and a cute little tiger was embroidered on the other. A mischievous sparkle came into his eyes. "Isn't he a bit chubby?" He pointed to the tiger. Its tiny wings seemed almost comic. "I doubt this fat little tiger can fly very high."

"It's my...first time. I..." She lowered her head.

"You mean you made this?"

She nodded. The redness on her cheeks deepened, but she lifted her head as her dark eyes blazed with pride. "Smell it."

Danny put the sachet under his nose and inhaled deeply. A pleasant fragrance he'd already detected became stronger. "So sweet. What did you put in here?"

"As many flowers as I could find. I added a couple of herbs good for repelling insects. I checked with Doctor Wang. Hopefully, mosquitos won't bother you anymore. You can't afford to get malaria again."

Once again Danny was speechless. "Another bout of malaria would kill me. I'll keep this with me at all times. Thank you, Jasmine!"

Such simple words didn't come close to his feelings. Bending closer, Danny picked up her right hand and lightly planted a chaste kiss on it. From the night he'd caught a first glimpse of her, it was love at first sight—something a tough man like Danny had never expected. He fought the urge to pull her into his arms, because he knew that a full embrace might be too much for her comfort.

Even in the faint light, stars danced in Jasmine's eyes. She bit her lip. But she didn't pull her hand away as she'd done the first time he'd taken it that night. Her heart fluttered as if it had sprouted wings and flown into her throat. She longed to stare into his eyes, but she was afraid he would see the blush on her cheeks. Neither broke the silence, each mindful of everything that went unsaid.

Her hand was still in his when Daisy burst into the room. Immediately, Jasmine stepped in front of him, trying to hide the red sachet.

But Daisy paid no attention to what they were doing. Blood had drained from her face, and fear shone in her eyes.

"What is it, Daisy? What's wrong?"

"The Japs are coming!"

Chapter 35

▬ ▬ ▬ ▬ ▬ ▬ ▬ ▬

"Oh, my God!" gasped Jasmine. "The Japanese troops are looking for you, Danny." She grabbed his right hand and flung his arm over her shoulder, ready to take him away. But where could they go? Where could they hide him?

"Wait!" Danny gestured with a wave of his other arm. "How many are there? Where are they now?" If they were close, he couldn't allow the young women to stay with him. That would be too dangerous. He would order them to run. But where could they hide? The village was so small, only a dozen houses. It would be easy for the enemy to find them. Perhaps he should tell them to run up the mountainside and into the forest. The Japanese wouldn't know that area.

Daisy was breathless. "They captured Anning yesterday. Linzi just came back from the town."

"Are they on their way to the village?" Danny was surprised that the Japanese had seized the nearby town so quickly. They'd been hundreds of miles away when he'd checked just a few days ago. Through Daisy's father, General Chennault had told him to stay put and take care of his injuries and his illness. If the enemy troops were closing in, then the General wouldn't have taken the chance—for his safety and everyone else's. Japanese were notorious for punishing whoever assisted American pilots. The tragic news of an entire village being slaughtered simply because they'd saved a Flying Tiger flashed through his mind and sent chills down his spine.

"I don't know," replied Daisy. "I left when I heard the Japs were in town. I'll go back to—"

"No need." Doctor Wang entered the room, his thin face hard. "They're not here, not yet. But we have to go. We can't take any chances."

"That's right," Danny agreed. "We can't afford to… But where are we going with so many people? Where can we find a safe place?"

"Not the whole village. Just you and the girls—"

"What?" chorused all three.

"There's nowhere for us to go. This is our home."

"But—"

"Don't worry about us. We're just farmers, villagers. They can't kill everyone in the country."

"No, it's too risky." Danny shook his head. His stomach was tied in a knot. "What if they find out an American pilot is here?"

"I told everyone not to mention you to any outsiders. No Japs will know you're here. Besides, this village is tiny and remote. There isn't an official road, only a footpath known by the locals. It's hard to find. I doubt the Japs will even come up here. Sending you away is just a precaution. No need to worry about us."

"But—"

"Danny!" interrupted Jasmine. "Listen to Doctor Wang. Where can an entire village hide? This is their home."

"Where are we going?" Daisy asked. Worry knitted her brow.

"A small cave. A secret hideout. No one except my family knows the place." Doctor Wang shifted his gaze to the cousins. "We'll meet here again shortly. Take clothes, food, and medicines. I don't know how long you'll have to stay there—at least a few days."

The herbalist rushed toward the door then turned back to face the trio. "I've already sent Linzi back down the mountain. It may take him a little while now that Anning is occupied by the Japanese. But relax; he'll find a way to inform Colonel Bai and Birch. I'm sure they'll send someone to pick you up soon."

At least that was what the herbalist hoped. Colonel Bai had trusted him to provide safety for the young women. Now he wasn't certain he could carry out such a task.

———————

Danny's eyes widened when Doctor Wang and Shitou returned with the bamboo-pole sedan chair.

"Let's go." The herbalist signaled the wounded pilot to get in.

"No, I can't let you…" Danny waved his arms, shaking his head. "I can handle it." He bounced on one leg. Turning to Shitou, he said, "Find a couple of sticks for me, will you?"

"No, you can't." Doctor Wang grabbed the American's arm. "Look, it's going to get dark in a few hours. If you insist on hopping like this, we won't get there until midnight or later."

"But—" Looking at the teenager and the older man, Danny was embarrassed. An unfamiliar sense of helplessness washed over him. He was a man, a tough fighter. Even in his wildest dreams, he couldn't imagine being carried. He'd felt awful when he had learned that two teenagers had walked hours to transport him to the village. At least, unconscious, he hadn't seen it happen. *Damn!* He cursed his broken leg.

"Don't worry about me. I've done this before," Shitou said with a smile. "You're heavy, but I'm strong." He winked at Danny while puffing up his chest.

"And I'm stronger than the boy," said Doctor Wang, jutting out his chin.

It was a simple statement of fact. The herbalist wasn't bragging. He'd been living in this area all his life, collecting herbs in the mountains to make a living. It wasn't easy. Sometimes he was gone for days with his son or grandsons. Returning home, they all carried heavy loads. Short and wiry, the sixty-year-old could still handle significant weight.

"We can pitch in," Jasmine said as she moved one step closer to the sedan chair. She'd changed into a plain cotton shirt and slacks. Two bags hung over her shoulder and crossed her chest. She held more bags in her hands.

"No." Doctor Wang dismissed her with a shake of his head. "You girls need to carry all the supplies."

"Why don't we ask Mutou?" Daisy suggested. "He did a good job last time. I don't have any candy left, but I promise I'll give him some later." She put her bags on the floor and turned quickly. "I'll go find him."

"Wait!" Doctor Wang called after her. "Don't ask him. Mutou can't tell right from wrong. Not his fault. But we can't afford to take chances. The fewer who know where we're going, the better." He waved an impatient hand. "Now, come along. We can't waste time."

Chapter 36

- - - - - - - -

"Stop," called Doctor Wang, after walking several hours up the main path of the mountain. He and Shitou set down the sedan chair.

The afternoon was comfortable with warm sunshine and a light breeze. Shitou wore nothing but gray cotton trousers and a conical straw hat. The toffee-brown rag around his neck stuck on his bronzed chest. He was bathed in sweat. A smile hovered at the corners of his mouth as he mopped his face with the cloth.

"Sorry, Son," the herbalist said, sucking in his breath. "We can't use the chair anymore." He pointed to the woods. Only a discreet footpath cut through the forest.

Danny nodded in appreciation as he stepped down from the chair.

"What about the chair?" asked Jasmine.

"We'll come back soon to take it to the village," answered Doctor Wang.

Danny headed toward the trail with quick hops. The rich smell of the earth greeted him. The path was narrow. He grabbed the tree trunks on either side to steady himself and sidestepped rocks and roots on the ground. The sun had already gone down behind the mountains, and without direct sunlight, the forest was dark.

Doctor Wang walked in front of the group, calling out warnings from time to time.

Danny panted.

After walking a couple of hundred yards they reached a small opening in the woods.

Danny rubbed his face and squinted to drive the sweat from his eyes. A steep cliff lay in front of them.

"The cave is up there," said the herbalist. He sounded more concerned than excited.

The bluff was about one hundred feet high and very steep. A natural rock staircase led straight up. The steps were irregular: some short, others over two to three feet high.

"You'll need to get down on all fours to climb up," said Jasmine in a shaky voice. "But how can Danny—?"

"There's no way for him to climb up," agreed Daisy.

Shitou leaned his head back, his eyes glued to the upper staircase.

"I'll carry him," said Doctor Wang, a tinge of steel in his voice. Before Danny could comment, he stepped in front of him and bent his body forward. His small frame was dwarfed by the American's six-feet three inches.

Danny was mortified by the old man's suggestion. Being transported on the sedan chair was awkward, but being carried by a sixty-year-old man up a steep cliff was unthinkable. He retreated a few steps and limped around the herbalist toward the cliff. Jasmine and Shitou each grabbed an elbow to steady him and pull him back, but he shrugged them off.

Standing straight, Danny raised his right arm. His left arm, like his left leg, was still too injured to be useful. His fingers groped the cracks on the rocky step in search of a good grip. Taking a deep breath and using the strength of both his right leg and arm, he jumped and landed on the first footstep.

The second step was much harder. The foothold was higher and narrower. It was impossible to jump and land precisely on the small surface.

"Be careful!" called Daisy.

"Stop it, Danny! Come down, please," Jasmine begged.

But Danny wouldn't give up. Again he reached up with his uninjured arm. The rock above him was smooth, and he couldn't find a good handhold. Clutching whatever he felt was best, he jumped. This time he wasn't successful. As everyone gasped, he slipped down.

Luckily, the herbalist and Shitou were prepared. They stood beneath him with outstretched arms and caught him when he fell. Blood seeped through his white sleeve where he'd scraped his right elbow.

"Are you okay?" Daisy asked.

"Danny, listen to Doctor Wang. Please!" Jasmine pleaded, gripping his hand.

The herbalist put his hand on the American's shoulder. "Son, don't feel bad. You're one of the two bravest young men I've ever met." He turned to Daisy. "Birch is the other one."

The young girl beamed with pride for her brother.

Doctor Wang's eyes were calm, and his expression was that of a man who had seen the worst of life and still had faith. "You're severely wounded. You almost died fighting the Japs. You've done things none of us could ever do..."

Jasmine, Daisy, and Shitou nodded quickly.

The herbalist continued, "Now, it's time for us to take care of you. It's our job to look after you. I don't know how much we can do, but we'll try our best." He squeezed Danny's shoulder. "You're a Flying Tiger with injured wings. Take good care of those wings. Once they're healed, you can soar into the sky. Fight for all of us. We know you will. We believe in you!" His wrinkled face shone with steadfast strength. "Let us take care of you now. Don't let the Japs or the sickness defeat you when you're down."

A lump lodged in the back of Danny's throat. The only thing he could do was make a promise: *I'm going to get well. I will fly again and fight for all of them. I promise! I swear!* He pressed his nails into his palm and set his jaw in grim determination.

Chapter 37

— — — — — — — —

"Jack!" cried Danny, waking from a bad dream. It was the morning after they'd reached the small cave. His eyes were closed, but his expression was pure panic. His hands waved in the air, seemingly trying to grab something or someone. A sheen of perspiration clung to his forehead.

The news of the Japanese coming had brought his frustration and fright to the surface.

He had no weapon. No aircraft. Even if he had his P-40, he was in no shape to fight. How could he protect anyone? He was afraid to lose these people to whom he'd grown close, just as he'd lost Jack. He was a Flying Tiger, but he had injured wings. How could he fly without healthy wings?

"Danny, wake up!" Jasmine sat cross-legged on the rocky ground. Her fingers rubbed his cheek, trying to pull him out of whatever disturbed him. "It's just a nightmare."

Disoriented, Danny blinked a few times, struggling to open his eyes. Once he caught a glimpse of Jasmine, he relaxed.

Jasmine gazed at him with concern.

Danny rubbed his eyes with the heels of his hands. A faint smile flitted across his face. Wearing a forest green silk blouse and a matching long skirt, Jasmine was a vision of beauty.

"Before you get up," she lightly touched his cheek again, "let me use the needles."

This ancient method of treatment was based on the idea that illnesses were caused by a disruption of energy that flowed naturally through the body. Using the needles at identifiable points helped to restore the disrupted flow and bring back health. For thousands of years, this technique had been used to treat many diseases.

Jasmine felt lightheaded when her hands grazed his bare skin. Her heart thumped so hard that she thought it would burst. Time and again, she wondered if he could hear her heartbeats, and she scolded herself for being so foolish, so obvious.

Danny didn't mind the pressure from the needles, and her sweet "jasmine" scent made him feel dizzy. Her soft touch sent fresh energy throughout his body. That was why he was a little disappointed when he heard the girls' conversation.

"I thought you had the bag." Daisy sounded tearful. She whipped her head around. All kinds of food, personal belongings, and pots and pans surrounded them. But there was no sign of the medicine bag.

"No, I told you—" Jasmine stopped. No use to blame anyone at this point. The upsetting truth was that in haste, they'd left the bag behind in his room. Now they had no needles or herbs for his malaria, or the Magic White Powder or the gauzes for his wounds.

"What are we going to do?" asked Daisy anxiously.

"Relax," Danny assured them. "I'm fine. No need to worry."

But he wasn't fine. Everyone knew it. Malaria was hard to cure even with advanced medicine. It clung tenaciously, sometimes forever. He still had a low fever. His wounds still needed treatment. He was lucky that Doctor Wang had given him the homemade Magic White Powder that had saved his leg. Nonetheless, he wasn't healed.

"The old way," said Jasmine. "We'll use forget-me-nots and sweet wormwoods. At least we can cook now—" She didn't finish. The thought of her feeding him mouth to mouth made her blush.

"My turn to pick the herbs," said Daisy, oblivious to the sparks between the other two. Taking a switchblade out of her pants pocket, she made ready to leave.

Something about the knife seemed familiar to Danny. "May I see your knife?" he said to Daisy as he held out his hand.

Daisy handed the switchblade to him. "It was a gift. My brother gave it to me. He gave one to Jasmine, too. But she didn't take it. She hates—"

"Hates knives?"

"After what happened to her parents, she hates anything sharp," Daisy answered before Jasmine could say anything.

"But…but the knife, the needles—"

"She'll do anything for you," said Daisy, looking remarkably innocent. "Did you know she practiced the needles on herself before treating you? She was afraid of hurting you, so she hurt herself as she learned the techniques."

Danny lifted his head.

Daisy continued, "You told us courage is doing something when you're scared half to death. Jasmine was courageous when she rescued you. I wish…"

Jasmine's cheeks flamed.

"This is the knife that she used to cut off your clothes."

Danny was wearing his own clothes: a pair of beige trousers and a white button-up shirt with the sleeves rolled up above his forearms. His brown flight jacket was folded and served as a pillow, the long white scarf by its side. Doctor Wang's daughter-in-law had done a good job mending his torn clothes. Patches of similar cloth now stitched the tears and shreds.

"My brother likes knife-throwing," Daisy blabbered. "He can hit any target. Maybe twenty or thirty yards—he's great!" She lifted her chin slightly.

Daisy always felt proud whenever she mentioned her big brother, and it dawned on Danny that his sister probably had similar feelings when she talked about him. "I'm pretty good at knife-throwing, too." He twisted the knife in his hand. "Your brother and I seem to have a lot in common. I'd love to meet him one day. He sounds like a great brother and a fun friend."

"I'm sure he'd like to meet you. He's the best brother one could ever have!"

"Daisy is right. Birch saved my life," Jasmine said. "I call him Ge—Big Brother, just like Daisy. We grew up together."

"Jasmine is lucky. She had five more years with my brother than I did." Daisy laughed.

"You're not jealous, are you?" Danny teased the younger cousin.

"Jealous? Of course not; I know he loves us both."

Danny nodded. One corner of his lips pulled up into a playful grin. "So, if we were to have a contest," he said, "knife-throwing, I mean, who do you think would win? Your brother or me?"

Daisy parted her lips to speak, but said nothing. After a moment of serious consideration, she answered, "Both of you will win!"

Chapter 38

The cave was the size of the room that Danny had occupied in the village. The steep, natural staircase led to the outcropping above the tree tops. Underneath it, a green coverlet spread across the hill, sloping down the mountainside. A hazy blue lake lay in the distance. Over the valley, another massive mountain range loomed on the horizon.

To the right of the cave, a narrow ledge extended around the corner of the rock face, winding and twisting up the mountain. After a couple of miles, the herbalist had told them, the trail would converge with the main path, leading to a gorge, Dead Man's Pass. From there, one could navigate down the mountain. The only other way out of the area was to go through the village.

How in the world did he find this place? Danny wondered.

Years ago, the herbalist had injured his leg during an outing with his son. It was late, so they couldn't go back to the village that night. As they made their way through the woods, they stumbled upon this shelter. Since then, they'd used it whenever they had to stay a few days in the area. Over the years, they'd made their "gathering hut" very homey—a fire pit, stored wood, and a layer of dry straw on the ground for a more comfortable sleep. Not far along on the ledge, water from a spring trickled from the rock.

The sun was rising, its upper edge peeking between the clouds and the distant horizon, splashing the hills in a rich golden-yellow hue. Sitting upon this natural balcony, Danny was awestruck by the spectacular vista. "Jack would have loved this," he exclaimed. The words just popped out of his mouth. He wished his friend were there. They'd always enjoyed being outdoors together. A nostalgic look came over his face.

Danny missed Jack tremendously. The fact that he couldn't save his best friend had made him relive the critical moment again and again. He'd spent sleepless nights and long days in recuperation, trying to figure out what he could have done to save him.

"You know…" Jasmine spoke softly as she caught his soulful eyes. She was wearing a garland of forget-me-nots. Danny had asked Daisy to pick extra flowers and made two wreaths, one for each girl, to cheer them up. "…Jack was luck. He had a great friend like you. He'd be happy knowing that you think about him. You still love him. What more can a person ask? I'd be thrilled if…someone remembered me like that."

Danny held up his hand. "You'll always be remembered," he assured her. Turning to face Daisy, he said, "You too, sweet girl."

"Tell me what Jack looked like, Danny." Jasmine picked up a piece of charcoal from the fire pit and stood up. "So that I can preserve this friend for you, for us, for whoever happens to be here in the future." In the past two days, she'd already drawn several large images on the smooth rock wall.

In one picture, Danny sat inside an airplane, Tiger Teeth painted on the nose of his aircraft. The canopy was open. He was wearing a flight jacket, a long scarf coiled around his neck and flapping behind him in the wind.

In another portrait, a life-sized Danny was standing on the ground next to his plane. His left arm rested on the wing. Shoulders back, head held high, he revealed every bit of his strength and confidence. A devilishly charming smile spread across his face.

The next panel showed a fight scene in the air. The planes were too small to detect a pilot. The tiger teeth painted aircraft zoomed down, sending tracers tearing through the sky. In the line of fire, a plane with a Japanese Rising Sun spiraled down, leaving a characteristic puff of smoke.

At the bottom right corner, two young women sat on the ground, their knees bent, legs tucked under them. Each held a garland on her head and leaned back staring at the sky. Their faces lit up with pure joy. In the background, tall mountains rose into peaks resembling "the Hump."

Flying Tigers had flown many times over "the Hump" to transport military supplies from India to China. Danny had told many heroic stories of flying this treacherous stretch of the Himalayan Range. The stories had left such a strong impression that Jasmine had had to incorporate "the Hump" into her drawing.

Danny loved her life-sized rock art and praised Jasmine many times. Her pictures captured the essence of the moment. He felt sorry that such a talented young woman couldn't finish college. *Maybe she can go back to school when this damned war is over*, he thought.

"Jack and I look very much alike," he explained. "Some thought we were brothers. Well, we were brothers. When we were young, we swore to be brothers after I read a classic Chinese novel."

"*Romance of the Three Kingdoms?*" asked Daisy.

"That's right! Since then, I wanted to have a couple of sworn brothers. No one who had read the story could ever forget what the three men had said as they took their oath." He paused, using the two fingers on each of his hands as quotation marks before continuing, "Though not born on the same day of the same month in the same year—"

The two girls joined him, "We merely hope to die on the same day of the same month in the same year!"

Everyone in China knew the unforgettable pledge taken by the three close friends. For centuries, their vow had been quoted as the ultimate fraternal loyalty.

"Jack was the perfect candidate. Well, the only candidate. We were best friends since elementary school."

"But what did he look like?" asked Jasmine. "You say he looked like you." She lifted her arm, holding the charcoal close to the wall. "I can't draw another you and say that it is Jack."

"Okay, he was about the same height as me, but heavier. He had straight, dark brown hair, not curly like mine. Always a crew cut. He had a stubble over his chin and cheeks. There was a faint scar on his right forehead, about an inch long. He fell when we went rock climbing during our first summer in college. He lost a lot of blood. It scared the hell out of me. But girls loved his rugged good looks, even the scar. Susan was crazy about him. Who could blame her?"

Jasmine continued to draw as she listened to the description. She turned around when she finished and caught Danny's stunned look. "Let me know what I can change. It's hard without seeing him in person. I—"

"No, no, no!" said Danny. He slammed his right fist into his left palm. "Damn! That's Jack!"

On the wall, Jack stood next to Danny. His left arm encircled Danny's shoulders, his right hand resting his own waist. The stubble on his chin and cheeks couldn't hide a wide smile on his ruggedly handsome face. Now the two brothers would be together on that rock wall forever, along with the two young women who admired them.

"Where did you learn to draw like this?" asked Danny.

Just like in the picture, Jasmine sat with her knees bent, legs tucked underneath her. "I've always liked art, even when I was little. My father taught…" Her voice trailed off and she swallowed hard a few times.

Aware of her family tragedy, Danny put a hand on her arm and patted her lightly.

Jasmine cleared her throat and pressed on: "I'm lucky to inherit my father's talent. My teacher in college—"

"He's also American," said Daisy. The topic brought a gamine smile to her lips. "Poor Mr. Peter Peterson! He loved Jasmine. He really wanted to marry her, I remember."

Danny's eyebrows shot up. He leaned forward.

"I…I couldn't…" Shaking her head, Jasmine hurried to explain. "I didn't love him." Just then a breeze stirred the treetops. Her hand flew to secure the garland in her hair. The air smelled of wildflowers, delicate and subtle.

"She loves heroes. Someone like you." Daisy winked at Danny. She tilted her head and tapped her cheek with two fingers. "It's been over four years. I wonder how Mr. Peterson is doing now. At least he's safe in the U.S."

Chapter 39

—————

With sweet wormwood three times a day, Danny's malaria appeared to be under control. He still had a low fever, but his symptoms had stabilized.

His injuries, though, especially the ones on his leg, seemed to take a turn for the worse. Forget-me-not was good for stopping the bleeding, but useless for relieving pain.

Danny hid his discomfort during the day. He even insisted on exercising. But the impact of bouncing up and down sent shivers of pain up his wounded leg. He had to use all his strength to keep going. Whenever he put the slightest weight on the left leg, he winced, but only for a second. He knew the young women were watching. He didn't want them to worry.

It was a different story at night. In his sleep, the excruciating pain was too much to endure. His hands clutched the knee of his injured leg, trying to suppress the throbbing sensation. His face contorted in agony. From time to time he moaned.

Jasmine watched Danny helplessly in the flickering firelight. She wanted to get up, to rush to his side, to ease his pain. But she had nothing to help him. She wanted to lie down next to him and wrap her arms around him like their first night together, to let him know she was there for him. Yet with Daisy sleeping nearby, she didn't dare. Danny tugged at her heartstrings so hard that she stared at him for hours with teary eyes.

On the fourth evening a storm broke. The wind-driven rain fell horizontally, turning the night chilly. Because of the cold and the humidity, Danny seemed to be in greater pain. He touched his wound instead of his knee in his sleep. Jasmine had no choice but to intervene. She rose. With legs tucked underneath her, she crouched beside him, peeled his hands off his leg, and clasped them in hers.

For hours she sat, holding his large hands in hers, rubbing his knuckles with her soft fingertips. In the fire pit, logs sizzled and flames flickered. Smoke curled up, stinging her eyes. The night was long. Dark clouds loomed, blotting out the stars and the moon. In the distance, lightning crackled and thunder boomed. An air of melancholy hung heavily over her.

When the storm tapered off after midnight, everything became eerily quiet. Only an owl made rhythmic *whoo-whoo-whoo* noises in a tree somewhere down the cliff.

Then Danny moaned.

Jasmine skimmed her palm over his cheek and down his chin. With a feather-light touch, she caressed his face. "Shhh," she murmured in a soothing sound. It seemed to work—Danny stopped groaning and fell back asleep.

But Jasmine could stand no more. A pang of sympathy for the man she loved threatened to overcome her. "I'm going back to the village," she announced over breakfast. Her voice was calm, unwavering. She'd made up her mind.

"Why?" asked Danny. He held a steaming mug of herbs with both hands, trying to ignore the knife-like pain in his leg. "We don't need anything, at least not for a few days."

Daisy agreed, "Doctor Wang promised he'd bring more food. He should be here soon."

"We need the medicine for Danny's leg now," said Jasmine. Her eyes had dark circles from lack of sleep. But she sat ramrod straight, her chin tilted high. "Even when he comes, he won't bring the medicine bag. It's in Danny's room. Doctor Wang won't check there. He probably thinks we have it."

"Don't worry. I'm fine." Danny raised the mug of sweet wormwood soup. "See, we've got the herb!"

"No. We need the real medicine, especially the Magic White Powder." Jasmine held up a hand to quiet Danny's protest. "You want to save your leg, don't you?"

Of course she was right. A few days without it might be okay, but in the long run, he needed the medicine.

"And we have to find out where we're going next," Jasmine added. "Hopefully, Uncle and Birch received our message. We can't stay here forever."

Sullenly, he rolled the earthenware mug between his palms. After a moment, he drained the potion in a few swallows and complied. "Let's go then." The storm had dissipated, but the sky was still overcast. A fragile pink dawn crawled over the eastern hills. He looked outside. "It's a nice day to walk."

Jasmine knew that Danny hated being useless, yet she had no choice. "I'm going. Alone."

"It's too dangerous. The Japs—"

"This is a remote village. The Japs won't come here."

"No! It's not a good idea to go down the mountain alone. I can—"

"Danny!" Jasmine interrupted, stretching her arm, and then pulling back from his cheek. "You can't even get down this cliff." She hated to say it, but she had to be blunt.

"I'll go with you," offered Daisy.

"No, you have to stay. Danny needs—"

"We can take the longer route." Danny pointed his chin toward the ledge that led to the main path.

Jasmine shook her head again. "You know that's not practical, Danny. Besides, if worse comes to worst, you can't run as fast as I can. It'll be dangerous…for me."

The situation was clear. Helping a wounded man through enemy-occupied territory would be suicidal. Danny knew it too. His shoulders sagged. He plunged his fingers into his hair and gritted his teeth.

After a long silence, he stood up. Balancing on his good leg, he pulled her up from the ground and lifted her palm to his cheek. His gaze swept her face like a physical touch. The power of his stare held her in place. After a few moments, she whispered, breathless, "I'll be back…soon."

Instead of letting her go, Danny folded her into his arms and held her tightly. His tall frame swallowed her small figure. Jasmine was astonished. Her instinct was to withdraw, but he was so strong, warm, and comforting. How could she resist such magic? Chewing her lip, she slid her arms around his body and surrendered to his embrace. She stood to the top of his collarbone, so she straightened to her tiptoes and nestled her cheek against his chest.

Danny said nothing, but his silence was louder than words. Jasmine could hear the pounding of his heart and felt his overflowing emotion. They held each other for a long time.

Finally, Jasmine broke away. She knew if she didn't, they would hold each other for a lifetime. She pulled her shoulders back and gained a measure of composure. She had things to do. She had to be strong.

"When the war is over, if…if I'm still alive, I'll—" murmured Danny. His Adam's apple bounced to accommodate a dry swallow. His hands still encircled her slender waist. Jasmine raised her arm, put a finger to his lips, and nodded. Danny tucked a wayward strand of her hair behind her ear and tightened the red scarf on her neck. With a heavy sigh, he said, "Be careful!"

Before she stepped down the rock staircase, she turned and waved goodbye. It was then she realized that for the past few minutes, she'd forgotten her cousin. A grin blossomed on Daisy's lips. Her eyes flickered, translucent with pure delight. Jasmine flashed a sheepish smile at her cousin before disappearing down the cliff.

Chapter 40

From the moment Jasmine vanished from his sight, Danny missed her. A hawk drifted in the sky above him. With several beats of its mighty wings, it swooped and plunged. A shrill cry broke out as it disappeared into the valley below. Danny sighed, envious. The bird could follow Jasmine. He couldn't. *Where the hell are my wings when I need them?*

He'd wanted to tell her how he felt. The words were on the tip of his tongue, but he'd resisted the urge. He was afraid to hurt her. Love was a luxury for a soldier. He might be killed at any moment, especially now that the enemy was close and he had no means to fight back. If they found him, they'd kill him. When Jack was killed, Danny imagined Susan's pain. He didn't want to put Jasmine through such grief.

Now, he doubted his decision.

Sooner or later everyone dies. That shouldn't stop us from expressing our feelings. What was I thinking? A gust of wind tossed the leaves around him that had fallen during the storm. He tightened the white scarf around his neck. The rain had turned the day cold.

What if Jack had never told Susan that he loved her? Danny was sure his sister would have preferred to know, and not knowing would have been far worse. *At least she was loved. Isn't that what we all want?*

Sliding his hand into his pants pocket, he felt the soft sachet she'd given him. A slow grin turned his mouth up as he imagined the moment he took her in his arms again and whispered his love to her. Immersed in thought, he didn't notice the other girl staring at him with her big eyes full of adoration.

———————

Daisy was flying. She was the pilot, and her brother sat beside her. Danny and Jasmine had taken seats in the back. The sun was shining and the sky was crystal blue. She was having so much fun, zooming through the puffy clouds, an iridescent phoenix soaring alongside. Suddenly Birch yelled, "Watch out!"

She looked up. An airplane with the bloody Rising Sun on its wings loomed in front of them. She gunned the engine.

"Turn left. Now!"

She ignored her brother's order. With death in her eyes, she chased the Japanese before she realized another enemy plane was firing at them from behind. She swerved to the left, but it was too late. With a deafening bang, her plane shook violently.

"I told you to turn!" Birch exploded, his face suffused with anger.

Daisy was shocked that her brother had raised his voice. He was always so nice to her, especially after their mother's death. She'd never seen him so upset.

His livid expression scared her, but she shot back a venomous look. "I want to kill the Japs. Tell him, Jasmine. Did I do anything wrong, Danny?" She whipped her head around, and her mouth opened in a wordless scream. Part of the fuselage was gone. Danny and Jasmine were nowhere to be found.

No!

Daisy awoke with a start. She sucked in one deep breath after another to supplant the panic attack. The dream was too real. She jammed her palms against her eyes, trying to break from the grip of her nightmare.

The sun was barely above the horizon, and the sky was a gorgeous blend of lavender, pink, and orange. The morning was cool. In the first light of the dawn, Danny sat on a rock near the edge of the cave. He wore a blue shirt with the sleeves rolled back to his elbows. His flight jacket draped the top of her blanket. Daisy pulled his clothes closer and inhaled deeply, savoring his scent. *Thank God Danny is safe.*

Like Jasmine, Daisy had never felt like this before. The handsome, courageous Flying Tiger had swept her off her feet and caught her up in a whirlwind. The seventeen-year-old was in love.

Danny was kind to her, but Daisy could tell that he loved Jasmine. This didn't make her feel bad. She'd seen the sparks, and she was happy for them. She loved them both. All she wanted was a chance to be with him, to see his attractive face, to hear his thrilling stories. As long as they included her in their lives, she was content.

Daisy sat up, yawned, and made circles with her head to work out the stiffness. She set a pot of water over the campfire for cooking the herb. *Sweet wormwood is helpful, but we need the needles and the real medicine. Oh, Jasmine, where are you? Come back quickly.*

She walked toward him. "Good morning," she said in a sweet voice.

"Good morning, Daisy." Danny flashed a quick smile before turning his gaze back to the distant hills. He stared at the valley, a pensive look on his face. Beads of perspiration covered his forehead and glinted in the light.

"You've already exercised?" Daisy lifted her arm and dabbed his sweat with her sleeve. "Take it easy, Danny. Don't push too hard. No need to hurt yourself."

"Thank you," he said, fixing his eyes on her. His brow knitted. The anxiety on his face was undeniable.

"Relax." Daisy tried to sound nonchalant. "Doctor Wang probably doesn't want Jasmine to walk back and forth in one day. It takes several hours one way, you know. They'll come today. You'll see."

Danny dropped his head. Absentmindedly, he rolled the carmine red sachet between his hands.

"Did you…?" Daisy was going to ask if he'd had a good sleep, but she changed her mind. *Even if he didn't, he won't tell me.* She'd noticed that Danny tried to hide his discomfort from her. "Did Jasmine give it to you?"

He nodded.

"May I?"

Danny handed the scented bag to her.

Daisy took it and examined it. "I didn't know she could…" she murmured. "It's lovely." Putting it closer to her nose, she inhaled.

"Isn't it beautiful?" Danny sounded proud, as if he had made it himself.

"It takes a lot of time—"

"And lots of effort, I know."

"But if I had made it"—Daisy analyzed the images again—"I'd let the Tiger work out a while before I put him on." With a playful smile she winked—that was something she'd picked up from the American. She loved the way he winked at her.

Danny responded with a broad grin. "A fit Tiger would be better, I agree."

"Would you…" she said, her expression turning serious, "accept mine if…if I give you one?" She lowered her head briefly before lifting her eyes. Her cheeks flushed. But she didn't avert her stare.

Danny was startled. "Of course I would."

"You will?"

"I wouldn't refuse a gift like that."

"You…you don't know?"

"Know what?" Danny scratched his head.

The redness on her porcelain cheeks deepened. Daisy rolled the sachet in her hands, "It is a special gift."

"Special?"

"You know," she caught her lip between her teeth before speaking again. "A woman to a man when she—"

Now he understood. His heart flipped over. While he had doubts about expressing his feelings, Jasmine had already shown hers. Her affection for him wasn't surprising. Yet her openness caught him off guard.

"It's more than a symbol of affection," explained Daisy. "It represents her blessing. She wishes her loved one to be safe and to come home soon."

Danny's shoulders fell. "I didn't tell her." He put his head in his hands and rubbed his thumb across his furrowed brow.

"It's okay, Danny." Daisy touched his arm, reassuring him. "She knows. Even I can tell." At that moment, she seemed more mature than her age. "When she comes back, tell her. Tell her how much you care about her. She'll be thrilled." A soft smile graced her lips. Her eyes twinkled. No jealousy. No possessiveness. Only pure affection for the two people she loved. She wanted the two of them to be happy. All three being happy together would be even better, of course.

Chapter 41

—— —— —— —— —— ——

Two days passed. No sign of Jasmine. What happened to her? Danny and Daisy had discussed it countless times but couldn't find an answer. Doctor Wang had said the village was hard to find. There was no well-defined road, only a narrow footpath known only by the locals. No outsider knew an American pilot was in the area, so most likely she hadn't run into Japanese. But why hadn't she returned? Had she fallen? Did she twist her ankle? Even if something had delayed her, Doctor Wang should have been there by now. Or Shitou should have been there. Or Linzi, if he'd already finished making the phone call in Anning to Colonel Bai or Birch.

"I should go to the village," Daisy said.

They were standing near the edge of the cave, looking out at the valley. A thick mist hovered above the tops of the trees.

"Yes, let's go," Danny answered.

"No, I should go."

"I can't let you go alone."

"Danny, don't argue with me." She stood toe-to-toe with him. Almost a foot shorter, she had to tilt her head back to look at him. Her slender body seemed so frail before the broad-shouldered man, but she didn't budge. "Don't make me repeat what Jasmine said. You know she was right."

Danny shook his head, his eyes hollow from lack of sleep. Whether he liked it or not, he knew that Daisy was right. He wasn't healthy enough to climb down the cliff. And his presence would only add danger. Nevertheless, he didn't have the heart to let the teenager leave without protection. He looked up at the gray sky that lay like a thick blanket over the mountains. "Something isn't right. She should be back by now."

"We have to find out what happened. And soon we'll run out of food. But going with me won't help."

Danny cursed his incapacitated leg for the hundredth time. His head hung between his hunched shoulders. An overwhelming sense of helplessness engulfed him, and the sky mirrored his mood.

"Relax," said Daisy. Her lips arched with a trace of a smile. "I'm just going to check it out. I'll be right back."

She picked up a magenta-and-black patchwork bag and slung it over her shoulder. Spinning back, she pointed to the container near the fire pit. "Don't forget to drink, three times a day. There's enough for two days." She'd prepared the herb earlier in the morning.

"Wait," Danny shouted and bounced a few steps closer to her. Gravel crunched beneath his boots. "Be careful!" He grabbed her arm and fixed an unblinking stare on her. "Look for signs. If you see anything out of the ordinary, come back! We'll find another way." He squeezed her arm, trying to inject some sense into her. "Don't do anything foolish. You understand? Your safety is most important."

A beam as bright as summer sunshine blossomed on her lips. "Don't worry." As she started to leave, she turned. Quickly, she took something out of the patchwork bag. Thrusting it into his right hand, she took his left hand to cover it. She raised her head and met his gaze. Her almond-shaped eyes filled with affection. A moment later she rushed off. "You said you'd accept it," she called out before disappearing down the cliff.

Danny opened his hands. His mouth made a perfect O. She'd given him a red sachet. This one wasn't as elaborate as Jasmine's, and it seemed to have been done in a hurry. A white daisy was displayed on one side and an airplane on the other. Had the seventeen-year-old girl slept at all last night? Or had she already made the sachet before they'd come here?

Chapter 42

Daisy was more than determined, but her anxiety grew as she drew closer to the village. A cool mountain breeze rustled through the green leaves. Branches creaked and sighed, and she shivered and clutched her bag closer to her chest. She wanted to turn back and run to safety with Danny. But she didn't turn. She needed to know what had happened to Jasmine. And she had to get the needles, the medicines, and more food. Moving forward was her only option.

Daisy loved the stories Danny had told them. The Flying Tigers' bravery inspired her. Now it was her turn. She had to be strong. She ignored her nerves and walked quickly. The wind blew grit in her face, so she closed her eyes for a moment. Then, crossing her arms and hugging her elbows, she pressed onward.

It was noon when she reached the village. Immediately, she knew something was wrong. No children playing; no sounds of laughter or music from Shitou's flute; no one working in the terraced rice paddies. The silence fell heavy on her.

Then she smelled it. A strong putrid odor pervaded the normally fresh air. She wrinkled her nose. The sickening stench was foreign to her. *Is this the smell of death*, she wondered?

Again Daisy thought about turning back. But if she did, they would never know what had happened. *Danny said courage is doing something when you're scared half to death.* Fighting back the urge to flee, she tiptoed toward Doctor Wang's house.

When she stepped into the herbalist's front yard, she stopped abruptly. Her hands flew to her mouth to stifle a scream. Her eyes opened wide. She wanted to run. But she couldn't move her legs; fear locked her in place. She was so afraid to look, yet her gaze was glued to the pile of bodies that lay before her.

This was the first time Daisy had witnessed Japanese atrocities up close. She'd been sheltered by her parents in Chungking. When her mother died, the mortician had done such a good job that she looked as if she were in a deep sleep.

But this village now wore the look of unending misery. Dozens of bodies were scattered in the spacious yard. The people had been shot or stabbed to death. Dark blood was splattered everywhere; some of it had flowed into wiggly lines before drying. The absolute terror on their faces was frozen in time: some of their eyes stared sightlessly into space; others had their mouths agape as if in the middle of a scream. Flies had picked up the scent and were buzzing madly. Maggots were feasting on the dead. The entire place reeked of rotten flesh and congealed blood. Daisy almost fell backward, reeling from shock. In spite of the offensive odor, she drew in one deep breath after another.

She caught sight of familiar faces. Doctor Wang, the kind and tough herbalist, sprawled face-up, a single stab wound to his left chest. Partly on top of him, Shitou, the boy with a ready smile, lay face down, his back riddled with wounds, his flute still pinned around his waist. Little Fatty, the three-year-old boy, lay nearby, his head smashed. His Tiger-head shoes were still on his feet, but they had failed to protect him or his family.

Is this real? For a moment, Daisy wondered if she was dreaming. She dug her fingers into her eye sockets, trying to pull herself out of the nightmare. Only a few days earlier they had celebrated Danny's birthday in this lovely yard. Everyone had been in high spirits. Music, singing, storytelling, cheers, and laughter still lingered in the air, and she could still recall the sweet fragrance from the strings of white flowers on the big tree, and the delicious aroma of all the food. Now the people were gone, and the tranquility of the village was forever shattered.

Is it possible? Remembering that day brought hot tears to her eyes.

The warm memories threatened to overtake her, making her shake even harder. Daisy felt paralyzed. The sight of surreal terror gripped her heart. She staggered sideways, tripping on Mutou's body. Several candies were scattered around him; a couple of pieces were still in his hand. His belly was ripped open; his intestines spilled out.

She shrieked at the top of her lungs as she frantically scrambled back onto her feet. A few moments later, her face white as chalk, she threw up. The little breakfast she'd eaten splattered on the ground. Even after she emptied her stomach, she continued to retch.

"Daisy!"

She jumped. The call terrified her. Whirling around, she saw a young man in a blue cotton shirt and gray trousers running toward her. Mud and drops of dark blood stained his patched clothes. "Ge!" She tumbled toward him, collapsing in her big brother's protective arms.

"I'm here; you're safe." Birch hugged her tightly.

A cry broke from her frail frame. Daisy could hardly breathe. Birch stroked her back and rocked her in a gentle embrace.

"What…happened?" she asked after her cries subsided a little. Tears stained her ghostly white cheeks.

"The Japs came—"

"But why? Why kill everyone?" She couldn't understand such senseless brutality.

"They were looking for the American pilot." Birch smoothed his sister's hair and hurriedly asked, "Is he okay? Is he safe?"

She gave a series of little nods. Tucked under her big brother's strong arms, she hid her face on his chest.

"Take me to him, Daisy. We have to leave here as soon as we can."

Reluctantly, the terrified teenager left her brother's shelter. Like an obedient child, she followed him as he half-led, half-dragged her.

Suddenly she stopped. "Where is Jasmine?" Still sniffling, she turned to scan the bodies and narrowed her eyes. She was petrified to find her cousin among the dead, but where else could she look for her?

Birch hesitated before taking Daisy by the elbow and pulling her back. "She is…gone," he said in a tormented whisper. His expression turned grave.

"Gone? Where did she go?" Daisy stared at him, incomprehension in her eyes. She couldn't accept the true meaning of that sorrowful word.

"I'll tell you later. Now we have to go!"

"Wait," Daisy pulled her brother toward the house where she'd lived. "We have to pick up the medicines—"

"No, we don't have time to use—"

"When we rest. Please! It won't take long. Danny is in pain!" Her voice was strong, pleading, and full of affection.

Birch's eyes searched hers. Something told him that his sister was no longer a little girl, that she was growing up to be a fine young lady. With a nod, he followed.

Danny's room was in total disarray. The mosquito netting was torn from the bed. The pillow, sheet, and blanket were scattered on the floor. The muted green-and-blue paintings were ripped in the middle. One of the wooden chairs had lost a leg. Pieces of broken china were strewn everywhere. The medicine bag lay sideways under the table.

Daisy bent down and picked it up. "Do you know how to use…?" she asked as she raised an acupuncture needle.

Birch shook his head.

Never mind. Caring for Danny was now imperative. She had to take over for Jasmine. The thought of her older cousin brought tears to her eyes again and threatened to overcome her, but there wasn't time to be weak. She replaced the needle inside the bag. The Magic White Powder was all-important. Gauze would be useful too. She collected enough herbs for three days and put everything inside her patchwork bag.

Now they could leave for the mountain hide-out.

Chapter 43

━ ━ ━ ━ ━ ━ ━

One look at Daisy and the young man with her made Danny's heart skip a beat. A bad feeling came over him.

In his twenties, the Chinese man was handsome and athletic. He was dressed in farmer's clothes. But his sharp eyes, stern expression, and erect posture conveyed the message that he was a man in uniform, not a plain farmhand. His bulging pants pocket and the waistband were other suspicious giveaways. The newcomer was startled for a few seconds when he glanced at the murals on the cave wall.

"Danny," Daisy greeted him in a rare small voice. "This is Birch Bai, my brother." She spoke plainly, without her usual sweet smile. Her eyes seemed red and puffy.

The two men shook hands and tipped their heads in curt bows. There was no hint of warmth. Birch did not smile. His face gave away nothing.

Knowing Daisy, Danny might have expected her to bounce up and down when she introduced them. She'd shown such excitement whenever she'd mentioned her brother, and from all he'd heard, Birch was a brave pilot. Presumably, they had much in common.

"Where is Jasmine?" Danny asked.

Daisy opened her mouth, but no sound came out. She looked at her brother for help. Her innocent eyes glistened with tears.

"We have to go," said Birch, ignoring Danny's question. His strong legs were braced slightly apart. "We don't have much time. The Japs could be here any minute." Now that they knew an American pilot was in the area, they would search high and low for him. They wouldn't give up easily. A Flying Tiger was invaluable to them. Birch knew that. He'd already seen some of them while trying to find his sister, his cousin, and the airman. If it weren't for his knowledge of the area, he might not have eluded them.

"Where's Jasmine? I'm not going anywhere without her!"

"We must leave now," Birch said, speaking sharply.

"Are you crazy? I can't—"

"I'm sorry, Danny." Birch softened his voice. "There is nothing we can do for Jasmine now." Taking a deep breath, he continued, "I'll tell you everything once we're safe."

Danny threw back his head and released a roar of frustration. "Like hell I'll leave without—"

"Listen to him, Danny," pleaded Daisy, gripping his right arm. "My brother never promised anything he didn't do. He always keeps his word. Trust me. Trust him. Really, there is nothing we can do..." A single tear seeped out of the corner of her eye. Her pale lips quivered.

"Please," said Birch, "let's go before someone else gets hurt."

Danny finally understood. He saw it in their eyes. *Jasmine is gone!* And he had to move quickly before someone else got hurt. No time to grieve now. Through trembling lips, he managed to say, "You will tell me the first chance..."

Birch gave a firm nod. "Now, let's get out of here."

"Which way are we going?" asked Daisy.

"Through Dead Man's Pass."

"No! You know I'm afraid of heights. I can't do it."

"We have to," Birch insisted. The other way wasn't passable for a Westerner, especially an injured American. Even for the Chinese soldiers, it was dangerous. Three soldiers sent to assist him had died along the way. If it hadn't been for one of them who stopped a bullet, he wouldn't be alive.

Daisy opened her mouth to protest, but then swallowed what was on the tip of her tongue. She rubbed her hands up and down her arms as if she were suddenly chilled. Birch tucked an errant strand of her hair behind her ear and skimmed a knuckle down her jaw. "Don't worry, I'll help you. I'll carry you piggyback and you can close your eyes. Everything will be all right." His gaze turned tender. Trying to put her at ease, he offered a smile. "We'll be safe once we get down the other side of the mountain."

Chapter 44

— — — — — — — —

Danny was an excellent hiker and rock climber. Jack had joked that they could race up a hill on one leg with their eyes closed. Danny didn't know how hard it would be to close his eyes, but he already knew that it was challenging to rely on one leg. He still couldn't put any weight on the injured leg, so how was he supposed to hop several thousand feet up a mountain? Sweat formed across his forehead, cascading down his temple. His brown hair looked like it had been washed. His clothes were soaked. If not for his top-notch shape, mental toughness, and determination, he wouldn't go far.

Wherever the path was wide enough, both the brother and the sister supported his arms. Occasionally, Daisy raised her small hand and wiped the sweat dripping into his eyes with her soft fingers. She felt sad for Danny. He had to work hard, but more importantly he had to fight his sadness over Jasmine's death. *I'll love you, Danny, as much as Jasmine. I promise!* she shouted repeatedly in her mind. She was more determined than ever to safeguard this Flying Tiger. Whenever the path narrowed, she dropped away and walked behind them.

Then the ledge became very narrow, only a couple of feet wide as it followed the contour of the cliff edge. With a sheer rock wall on one side and a drop of several hundred feet on the other, Birch moved ahead of Danny to give a helping hand. He grasped the American's right hand to stabilize him. At the same time, he had to make sure their arms and legs didn't bump the rock. He kept his eyes glued to the path.

"Wait!" shouted Danny after they'd gone a few yards. He tightened his grip and tugged on Birch's hand, preventing him from backing up further. A hole in the path loomed a step away. Birch was so focused on helping Danny that he hadn't noticed it as he dragged his feet backward. It would be a disaster if he tripped. He lifted his head to give an appreciative smile.

Danny nodded.

They inched forward. Once past the ledge, Birch sat Danny down on a rock and went to his sister.

Daisy had turned pale. "I can't do this," she stammered. Her voice tinged with fear and frustration. "I'm going back," she announced, retreating a few steps. Her knees quivered, and she wound the hem of her lilac shirt around her finger. "I'll go down from the cave…and use the main path. I'll meet you at the bridge."

"No!" Birch yelled. "We can't split up. It's too dangerous."

Daisy recoiled at the thought of crossing this narrow shelf hundreds of feet above ground.

"Don't look down," ordered Birch, extending his hand to his sister. A couple of loose rocks tumbled down as he moved.

Daisy couldn't take her eyes off the long descent. A gust of wind suddenly threw her off balance. His hand shot out to catch her.

"Look at me, Daisy," Birch urged. "Hold on to my hand. I won't let you fall. You know you'll be safe with me, don't you? Take one step at a time." He hated to make his beloved sister suffer in any way, but the path was too narrow for him to carry her on his back. "Whatever you do, don't look down. Look at me!"

Daisy nodded but was still reluctant to venture a step. Her legs began to buckle, as she stole a glance over the edge. The canopy of green trees seemed so far down.

"Try sideways," said Danny. "That way you don't have to look down." Sitting on the rock, he fidgeted, all pins and needles, as anxious as the man on the ledge.

"Right," agreed Birch. "Turn your body. Face the rock wall. C'mon!"

Twisting the cloth bag behind her back, Daisy did as she was told.

She pushed her chest up against the craggy surface and moved one tentative step to the left. Then she froze. "I can't do this!" she cried. Terror pinned her to the spot. She panted, "Ge, don't make me do this. Please!"

Birch's heart tightened. They were stuck on a narrow ledge hundreds of feet above ground, and he didn't know what to do.

Should we turn back? But if we do, then how can Danny get down the staircase? And even if he can, he'll be exhausted. We still have a long way to go. How can I add more burden to him? We don't have much time. It's getting late. God forbid, if anything happens to either of them...

He rubbed his forehead, and his fingers came away wet. He was between a rock and a hard place—on one side was the sister he adored; on the other was a pilot he admired. How could he choose between them?

"Daisy," Danny called out, his eyebrows furrowed with worry, "you told me your brother never promises anything he doesn't do. You told me that he always keeps his word. Remember? You told me to trust him. So, you must trust him! He won't let you down. He'll never let you fall. I have faith in him. So should you."

Daisy trusted her brother beyond any doubt; it was herself that she doubted. Her fear of falling off the cliff, and taking her brother with her, paralyzed her. *What would Jasmine do?* Instinctively, she knew that Jasmine wouldn't get stuck here. She would keep going no matter what. Taking a deep breath and willing her body to relax, Daisy took a tiny step.

"I won't let go of you," Birch promised.

The narrow section was only ten yards, but it seemed longer than the Great Wall. Her heart beat frantically, and her breath came in short gasps.

Courage is doing something when you're scared half to death. Over and over she recited what Danny had told them. The cadence of the words acted like a drumbeat in her head. *I'm scared, but I can do this.* She inched her way along the ledge. Each step was as difficult as the Long March.

"You made it!" Birch exclaimed once the ordeal was over. Relief flooded through him.

"Next time, I expect you to walk backwards and lend me a helping hand," joked Danny, winking at her and eliciting a smile. He offered her his hand when she reached him and felt the sweat in her palm.

Chapter 45

— — — — — — — —

They continued for another hour. Birch held on to Danny, and Daisy brought up the rear. Just before they reached the main path, both men stopped abruptly, their soldier's intuition suddenly keen. Daisy almost bumped into them. Before she could say anything, Birch spun around and put his index finger on his lip to hush her.

They slowed their steps and edged forward in silence. Soon they could hear the low hum of conversation. At the crossroad, several dozen yards ahead of them, two Japanese soldiers sat on a fallen log, eating and talking.

Birch drew his pistol. But Danny stopped him. "Too noisy," he cautioned.

Birch nodded. Switching his gun to his left hand, he took a knife out of his pants pocket. Pantomiming a stabbing gesture, Danny asked Daisy for her dagger. As he took the knife, he signaled for her to hide behind a large tree.

On their bellies, the two men crawled toward the Japanese soldiers. When they were twenty yards away, Birch gave Danny a hand signal, and a silent agreement passed between them.

Together they threw their knives at the Japanese. Their aim was impeccable. Both soldiers dropped forward without a cry. They were dead before they knew what hit them.

Daisy let out a cry of relief. The thought that she might have encountered the enemy alone made her cringe. Luckily, her big brother had good sense.

When the trio reached the bodies, she winced and tried to avoid looking at the bodies, but a single curious glance revealed the knives protruding from the backs of the enemy's necks.

The men pulled out their weapons. Danny wiped off the blood on the dead man's clothes. *This one's is for you, Jack! Just wish you could see it.* They had always cheered for the other's success, and then worked hard to match it. They had been as competitive as they were loyal. Would he ever find another friend like Jack?

Danny folded the blade before handing it back to Daisy. "You were right. Your brother and I won together, just like you predicted."

They pressed onward, and in a couple of hours reached a creek with crystal clear water splashing from boulder to boulder then cascading down the steep mountainside. The thunderous sound of rushing water drowned out any other noise. The moist air turned the area to a lush green. Tall trees thrust up to the sky, their branches covering the trail and creating dappled shade, with sunlight breaking into dozens of golden beams. Shrubs and patches of emerald moss carpeted the forest floor; clusters of red and blue wildflowers dotted the grass along the creek. If they hadn't been pressed for time, they might have stayed longer.

Again—it happened. This time it was a surprise to both parties.

Two Japanese soldiers appeared around a bend in their path. For a second, everyone stood still. Then all hell broke loose—screams, shouts, gunshots. Without a weapon, Danny whirled around. Ignoring his multiple injuries, he tackled Daisy and threw her to the ground. Jumping on top of her, he tried to shield her. Bullets sailed over their heads, and one grazed Danny's left shoulder. Blood spurted out. He sucked in a harsh breath as the fiery sting ripped down his arm and splintered toward his head.

At the same time, Birch drew his pistol, opened fire, and dove for cover. His shooting was as good as his knife-throwing, and with several bursts, he raked the enemy. Two bullets caught one Japanese soldier right between his eyes. A couple of slugs hit the head of the other, who dropped to one knee, his face masked in blood.

In a matter of seconds, it was quiet, except for the ever-flowing water. And Daisy's scream.

Everything had happened so quickly. She'd been two steps behind the men and didn't understand why Danny had shoved her down. Out of the corner of her eye, she caught a glimpse of the Japanese firing at them, and out of fear for the two men she loved, she screamed.

"It's over, Daisy." Birch shook her. Then he pulled Danny to a sitting position, his heart still jackhammering in his chest.

Daisy cried out when she caught sight of the blood spurting from Danny's shoulder and from her brother's forehead. Fear glazed her black eyes and twisted her delicate features.

Birch had sustained a shallow hit when a bullet grazed his scalp. The injury looked messy, but luckily it was superficial.

A collar of terror tightened around Daisy's neck even as her hand darted to the cloth bag she was carrying to search for the medicine. Her fingers were so shaky and numb, she couldn't feel anything.

"Stop, Daisy," said Birch. Blood trickled down his cheek, chin, and chest.

"My God…your head…his shoulder…medicine…" Her gaze swept from her brother's temple to Danny's shoulder.

"We don't have time," exclaimed Birch. He knew that the gunfire would soon draw more Japanese. He hauled Daisy to a standing position, cupped a hand on her elbow to stabilize her, and reached out to Danny with the other. "We'll be fine. We'll be fine."

Just then, Daisy found the bottle of medicine. She twisted off the top and shook the Magic White Powder first onto Danny's wound, and then onto her brother's laceration.

They were on their way again when Danny turned to Birch. "Your little sister can certainly scream, but I hope next time she screams"—he rubbed his ear and made a puckish face—"I'm a little further away from her." He could always find a joke to lighten the mood; that was the only way to stay sane in an insane world.

However, his untimely joke would haunt him the rest of his life.

Chapter 46

One look at Dead Man's Pass, and Danny understood why Daisy didn't want to take this route.

The gorge was one of the deepest canyons in the world. Between sheer rocky cliffs, the two sides were connected by a narrow bridge made of rough wooden planks intertwined with ropes. It was no more than twenty yards, but it wasn't for anyone with a faint heart. One missed step would send one down the deep gulch.

The bridge was too narrow for two men to walk side by side, and it was not possible for one to hop from one plank to another. Wasting no time, Birch bent down in front of Danny, and before the American could argue, Birch picked him up on his back. The two hundred-pound weight made him stumble. Sucking in a breath, he stabilized himself. With both his hands he readjusted and secured the man's position on his back. Without turning, he shouted to Daisy, "Wait here. I'll be right back."

At five feet ten, Birch was tall for a Chinese. He'd grown up tall and strong, just like his parents wished for him when they named him after the white-barked birch tree. Danny was six feet three, a heavy load. The primitive bridge was challenging for anyone to cross, but it seemed like an insurmountable task to carry another person on one's back.

Birch bent forward, adrenaline coursing through him as he trudged one step at a time. His heart hammered wildly, and his pulse quickened. The decayed boards and rotten ropes threatened to break at any moment. No matter how brave he was, he couldn't help but wonder if the old bridge could hold their combined weight.

"Grab the rope," yelled Birch. Two lines at waist level flanked the bridge. The one on the left side was limp, almost useless. Danny clutched the rope on the right.

The planks creaked and the bridge swayed under their weight. The springy movement brought a ripple of goose bumps onto Birch's skin. Cold mountain updrafts sent chills up his spine. Below he spotted a hawk. With several deliberate beats of its powerful wings, the bird drifted, swooped, and dove suddenly when its prey came into view. With a shrill cry, it disappeared into the fog above the river at the bottom of the gorge.

The endless abyss took Birch's breath away. But he remained focused and proceeded slowly. At one point, a piece of plank broke. He didn't see it happen, but he heard it—the snapping sound and then Danny's gasp. His heart sank. *How big is the gap? Will it be trouble when I come back for Daisy?*

Sweat poured into his eyes, but he didn't have the time or a free hand to wipe them clean. Sheer determination propelled him forward.

Halfway across, they heard yelling from a short distance away. It was in Japanese, "*Yamero!* Stop!"

Birch picked up the pace.

Daisy had watched nervously as Birch navigated the bridge. To prevent herself from crying out loud, she bit her knuckles.

So focused was she on her loved ones that she didn't hear the Japanese closing in from behind. They laughed and shouted at her, signaling her not to move. But Daisy broke into a frantic run and sprang onto the bridge.

It was too late. A couple of steps later, with a loud blast and her scream, the old bridge broke in the middle. The soldiers probably meant to frighten her, to slow her down, but the hand grenade had damaged the already-rotten structure, and it snapped, cutting off the only escape route she had. Now she was separated from the two men she loved.

Birch was a step away from the end when the explosion hit. Both he and Danny seized whatever was within their reach and their bodies slammed into the mountainside. Wood shattered. Debris sprayed and plunged into the rocky chasm.

Birch snatched a nearby tree branch. A large piece of skin on his left elbow tore away, and blood oozed through his blue shirt. His forehead, grazed from the bullet, started bleeding again. Pain stole his breath. Ignoring the wounds, he hauled himself up and over the rim.

Danny held onto the rope with his one good arm. His left arm and shoulder were too injured to be useful. His right leg found a foothold on the rocky wall. A second later the rock broke loose under his weight, and he slipped. Rough rope ripped the skin of his palm. A thousand pinpricks stabbed him. He almost let go of the lifeline.

"Hold on!" yelled Birch. Hanging by one hand to the tree branch, he reached down with the other and seized Danny's right bicep. "Hold on!" he repeated. Using every bit of his strength, he dragged his companion to safety.

The two men lay breathless on their stomachs. It took a few seconds to get their breath back. When they peeked over to the other side of the gorge, their hearts stopped. "Oh, shit," mumbled Danny. Birch just stared at his sister's small frame hanging from the cliff.

Daisy had stepped onto the bridge as it snapped. Her instinct for self-preservation had driven her to grab a piece of the plank as she fell. She was left dangling against the sheer cliffside thousands of feet above ground.

Even more frightening was the sight of four figures in muddy yellow uniforms ogling her from the rim. Her body stiffened. She couldn't move. She couldn't breathe. Terror stifled the scream that filled her throat.

Before she could blink, two soldiers gripped her by the arm. She screamed, her legs kicking the air. The right sleeve of her lilac shirt tore apart, and for a moment she hung suspended. Then the soldier's rough hands hauled her up and over the edge of the gorge.

Birch whipped out his pistol and fired.

Danny picked up a rock and threw it at the enemy.

One Japanese crumpled from a shot to his chest. Another slapped his hand over his head, blood spurting between his fingers. The rock hadn't killed him, but it had hurt him. Enraged, he lifted his weapon and sprayed a hail of gunfire.

Both Danny and Birch ducked. Bullets slashed all around them, hair-raisingly close. Then, abruptly, the shooting stopped. They caught a glimpse of an officer slapping the soldier who had fired. Apparently, they had seen the American and wanted to capture him alive.

Birch aimed at the officer, but in a split second he'd pulled Daisy in front of him, using her as a human shield. Birch tilted his pistol up, and the bullet sailed over their heads.

They were so close, yet so far away. An unbridged gap lay between the girl and the two men.

Danny could see a look of horror on Daisy's pale face. A hand snaked out from behind onto her chest. She screamed. Kicking and yelling, she struggled to get away, but there was nowhere for her to go. She leaned forward, trying to jump over the cliff, but hands clasped her arms and legs from behind, holding her in place. She shrieked while rough hands tore at her clothes.

Birch took aim again. No one was in sight, except Daisy. She stood with arms pinned behind her back. The front of her shirt had been ripped open. The Japanese were in hiding. One cowered behind her. Two crouched on either side of her, clutching her legs; their bodies protected by large boulders in front of them.

Daisy bit the arms and hands around her. She jabbed her elbows backward.

Most Chinese women were taught at a very young age to be submissive. But Daisy was an exception. Growing up in a military family, she was encouraged to be an independent and confident woman, and now she fought her captors ferociously. Yet she had no means to free herself.

"Ge, open fire! Kill me!" she yelled, panic-stricken.

Birch squeezed his eyes shut. A vein bulged in his neck. Daisy's wails and pleas made his blood run cold. He lifted his pistol, his hand steady, yet he felt nothing but turmoil in his head. Taking a ragged breath, he squinted his eyes as if in this way he wouldn't see his sister die. Then he pulled the trigger.

"No!" roared Danny. He bumped Birch and the bullet missed Daisy. It hit one side of the cliff and sent a few small rocks tumbling down the gully.

The hands from behind Daisy had already ripped off her clothes.

It was clear that the Japanese were going to rape her right in front of the helpless men. Profane laughter mixed with her hysterical cries.

Danny turned his gaze along the gorge, trying to find a way back. As far as his eyes could see, there was no way to cross. Even with healthy legs and supreme rock-climbing skill, it would take a day or two to get down and up again. An unreachable gap opened between them and swallowed up any hope of reaching the young woman.

While Danny inspected the gorge, Birch watched helplessly as his sister struggled. Daisy's suffering completely unhinged him. He again raised his arm and aimed. A muscle quivered in his jaw as he pulled the trigger before Danny could bump him again.

No bullets were left in his gun.

"Please, Danny!" Daisy begged. She looked at Danny like a drowning woman in search of a lifeline. Her eyes grew larger as hands started to fondle her bare breasts. Her pale skin lay in stark contrast to the pink scarf around her neck. Enemy's blood, bright red, trickled down her mouth. "Please!"

Her pleading cut into Danny's heart. Grinding his teeth, he lowered his head. He couldn't stand to watch her suffer. The rock was still in his hand. Instead of throwing it, he squeezed it as hard as he could. Blood from his ripped palm stained the rock. He was a Tiger trapped over an impassable gulf.

Meanwhile Birch moved a few inches away from Danny. His eyes were moist. Torn by sorrow, he bit his lower lip until he tasted the salty flavor of his blood. He didn't hesitate for long, though. In response to the urgency of her cry, he had to act. And act fast!

He tossed the empty gun to the ground and pulled two hand grenades from his waistband. Clasping the handles in his right hand, he used his left index finger to secure the safety pin's pull ring. In one heart-stopping motion, he removed the pin. With one hand blocking his companion, he threw the grenades at his sister.

"No!" A wail lodged in Danny's throat. He gazed at the hand grenades in the mid-air as they flew toward Daisy. Time seemed to slow as he watched the terror on her face dissolve into peace.

Daisy Bai, a girl as fresh as a daisy, would forever be seventeen.

Chapter 47

▬ ▬ ▬ ▬ ▬ ▬ ▬

Pieces of her pink scarf floated on the wind, twisting and turning, refusing to fall, but finally making a last circle and then spiraling, one by one, into the abyss.

"No! God, no!" Danny's bloodcurdling wail echoed through the canyon. He beat the earth repeatedly with the rock that he still held in his hand. Then, with all the agony, frustration, and strength that he had, he hurled the rock across the chasm to the spot where the enemy had gathered. Then he turned and punched Birch in the chest, knocking him to the ground.

"What have you done?" In a fit of anger and grief, he lifted his arm, ready to seriously hurt the man who had blown his own sister to pieces. But before his fist landed on Birch's face, he stopped.

Before him lay a fallen man, a body turned to stone, a bloodstained face frozen in a mask of agony. Danny's heart broke, and his hand changed direction, landing instead on the rocky ground beside Birch's head. Instantly, his knuckles were covered with blood. The impact with the hard surface sent shivers of pain up his arm. Yet he didn't care. He needed physical pain to take away the sorrow he didn't know how to endure. Raising his arm, he prepared to hit again.

"Stop!" Birch grabbed the American's elbow, trying to stop him.

It was too late. Danny's fist hit the stony ground again. Then, for a third time, Danny raised his arm. "Why?" he shouted, his eyes glowing with fury. "Why did you do it?"

"I had no choice. No choice…"

"We could have gone back. We might have found another way. God knows, as long as she was alive, there was a chance. There was…hope."

Birch shook his head. His throat became so constricted that he could hardly speak. He closed his eyes, keeping Danny from seeing the depth of his despair. A thousand memories dragged him to the edge of madness.

He still remembered the day Daisy was born. She was cute, adorable, and always sweet. The first time she smiled at him, the ten-year-old boy had melted. When she gripped his finger with her soft hand, he had vowed to protect her with his life. When she called him "Ge" for the first time, he was as proud as he could be. During the past seventeen years, a day hadn't gone by without him thinking of her. She was his beloved sister.

Such vivid memories nearly paralyzed him. He felt the world closing in on him, squeezing his neck, and suffocating him. Daisy had loved him. She had always looked up to her Big Tiger Brother. She trusted him to protect her, to shield her from harm. *What have I done?* Never in a million years could he imagine that this was how their relationship would end.

Daisy! Silently he screamed her name. His hands clenched into fists so tight that all the blood was wrung out of them. *I'm sorry. I'm so sorry!* Tears collected at the corners of his closed eyes.

Danny could feel Birch's sadness. And his heart wrenched again. Yet he had no idea how to handle his own pain and sorrow. Picking up a couple of sticks, he stood up and stumbled away, fleeing from the sad scene.

Birch opened his eyes and snatched the empty pistol. Seizing Danny's arm, he tried to keep him from falling.

Danny brushed aside Birch's hand. "Leave me alone!" he barked. Eyes bulging, he looked ready to kill. "You hear me? Keep your hands off me!" He stormed off, leaving his companion open-mouthed.

"Wait, Danny. Turn left," Birch called after him. "We have to go this way."

Chapter 48

- - - - - - - - -

Danny had a nightmare. It had started rather well. Jack was in the dream. Jasmine and Daisy were there, too. They were all sitting on a magenta-and-white blanket in a meadow carpeted with forget-me-nots. Yellow butterflies, their wings marked with black lines and dots, floated all around them. The air smelled of honey. He was thankful that no bees were there. Jack was allergic to bee stings. It was an idyllic afternoon. The sun was shining. A turquoise lake lay at the bottom of the hillside, and a snow-capped peak jutted straight into the blue sky. A soft mountain breeze touched his cheek. *Is this Yunnan Province in China or California in America,* Danny wondered?

They talked while drinking Chinese rice wine. Danny talked most. The cousins regarded him with admiring smiles. He was perplexed that his best friend didn't talk much. Jack was never tongue-tied in front of women. Girls were crazy about his rugged good looks. Maybe, Danny reckoned, his friend was just missing Susan. They were planning to get married. *But when will that be?* He remembered how happy his sister and Jack had been when they'd become engaged. The wedding would be soon. Right?

As he strained to remember, a huge red dragon swooped down and sprayed fire from its mouth. In a split second, the meadow became an inferno. Both Jack and Daisy turned into fireballs. "No!" Danny cried out.

Where is Jasmine? He couldn't do anything for Jack or Daisy, but he

192

might be able to protect Jasmine. If he could only find her!

Frantically he searched the area. No sign of the beautiful woman who had been so close to him only a moment ago. She had simply vanished in a sea of red hot fire.

Danny jerked awake. He fluttered his eyelids, trying to pull himself out of the frightful dream. When he caught sight of Birch by the campfire with a stick in his hand, he knew why he'd dreamed of fire.

The night was quiet. The air smelled of smoke. Wood crackled. Orange flames danced and flickered with cobalt tips.

Birch had seldom displayed great emotions during daytime, but in the middle of the night, while he thought his companion was asleep, his face contorted into a haunting expression of agony. Sitting cross-legged by the fire, his shoulders sagged. Firelight reflected the liquid on his cheeks and illuminated the tears in his dark, soulful eyes, and Danny had the strange thought that the eyes he was seeing were Daisy's eyes. Or Jasmine's…

He felt sympathy for Birch. He knew the pain of losing a loved one. He'd known Daisy for only six weeks, and yet the pain of her death was unbearable. Birch had lived with her for seventeen years. How could he bear such a loss?

Danny had an urge to rush to the fellow pilot's side, to tell him that he understood his pain, and to assure him that he wasn't alone. Yet he did none of those things. He wasn't ready. How could he counsel someone when he himself desperately needed emotional support?

Closing his eyes, he turned away from the campfire. Shadows claimed his features at once. He hid in the darkness. His lips clamped together, his jaw quivered. Curling his right hand into a fist, he pressed the knuckles onto his mouth to stifle a cry. Rivers of tears he'd tried so hard to suppress during daylight now flowed in the dark.

That night, both men nursed their own wounds in isolation.

Danny hadn't spoken to Birch since Daisy was killed. He relied on two sticks to move, stumbling and tripping. When he staggered, Birch tried to catch him, but each time Danny brushed him aside.

Danny was angry with Birch, but he was more furious with himself. He was supposed to protect the people in China; that was the reason he'd come here. Instead, wherever he went, people died. Jack was gone. So was Daisy. She and Birch had not used the word "death," but Danny knew from their faces that Jasmine, too, had been killed. He wished he knew exactly what had happened. There hadn't been time for Daisy to tell him, and he doubted that she would have given him any details. He wanted to ask Birch what had happened, yet how could he? Birch had his own tortuous grief to confront. Facing his pseudo bravery, Danny wasn't even sure he could handle hearing the truth. Danny Hardy was a Tiger trapped in a cage.

Chapter 49

— — — — — — — —

For three days they walked in silence. On the last afternoon they reached a river with murky water rushing headlong over rocks and logs in the middle. There wasn't a bridge in sight. "This is Shallow River. It will take us only a couple of hours from this point," Birch called out.

Danny approached the riverbank. After struggling for three days in pain with a wounded leg, he was exhausted, and he was glad there were only two hours left in the journey. More importantly, his company with this Chinese pilot would end soon. He couldn't wait to get away from him, from the negative energy between them. Perhaps he wouldn't feel so much pain if he didn't have to look at the cousin of the woman he'd loved, the brother of the girl he'd cared for.

Birch stepped in front of Danny, blocking his way. "Your injuries—" He didn't get to finish. The American walked around him and continued to limp toward the river.

"Wait!" Standing with feet planted slightly apart, Birch opened his arms. "Let me carry you."

"No!"

"But the water—"

Danny dismissed him with a wave of his walking stick. He started hobbling again then murmured, without turning, "Over my dead body."

"The water isn't deep, but it's cold and dirty. It could be bad for your malaria, and your wounds might become infected again. You—"

"I don't care!"

"I care. Daisy and Jasmine would care." Birch's face darkened. "They would be sad…if they could see you—"

"Tell me what happened to Jasmine." Danny glared at Birch. This was his last chance. Soon they would part ways.

"Only if you let me carry you…" Birch glared back, not backing off. His chin went up.

"You—"

"Please." Birch softened his voice. "You know your leg isn't just yours anymore."

Danny knew it well. Even his life didn't belong only to him. People had given up their lives to save his. What could he do? He couldn't intentionally damage his health when others valued his life and well-being so highly. The tough fighter pilot had no choice but to comply. Taking a frustrated breath, he tipped his head in an almost imperceptible nod and flung the sticks away.

Birch let out a pent-up breath and snatched one of the sticks. For the second time since they had met, he carried the American on his back. Wrapping his left hand around Danny's left thigh, he made sure that the injuries were well above the unclean water. He leaned his body forward, putting weight on the stick in his right hand.

Sunlight shimmered on the surface of the river. The mountain water was cold, but even so, beads of perspiration soon appeared on his face. The salty sweat stabbed like pinpricks on his cuts.

The current was deceptively swift. Rocks of different sizes and shapes lay at the bottom of Shallow River. Luckily, the water was mostly knee high. Birch waded one step at a time, careful not to catch his feet in the cracks and crevices. Some of the rocks were slippery with moss, and several times he slipped, but not once did he fall. He was determined not to let Danny's wounds be submerged. With unwavering determination and the strength of a soldier, Birch plodded across the river.

"Thank you," Danny muttered after they reached the other side.

Birch was out of breath. "You're welcome." His face was the color of a ripe tomato. He was drenched from head to toe by the cold river water and by his own sweat.

Danny pointed to a tree trunk not far from the shore. "Should we?"

They rested for a few minutes, enjoying the warm sun on their backs.

Birch began to speak: "As I promised, Jasmine…" His voice trailed off. His throat constricted to a point where he could hardly force the words out of his mouth. Taking a ragged breath, he pulled out a red scarf from his pocket. He'd found it in the village. The carmine red scarf had been hanging on a tree branch, flapping in the wind. He knew that it had belonged to Jasmine. He had given it to her when he'd escorted them to the village, a place he and his father had assumed would be safe.

"May I…may I keep it?" Danny asked, staring at the scarf.

Birch really wanted it, but he handed it to Danny without hesitation. On their way back to the cave, Daisy had told him what had happened over the past few weeks. He could tell that both his sister and cousin had fallen in love with this gallant Flying Tiger.

Danny grabbed the scarf with both of his hands and pressed it to his chest. A single tear seeped from the corner of his eye and made its way down his cheek.

Seeing Danny's emotion, Birch felt relieved. He knew Jasmine would be pleased if she were watching. As for himself, he didn't need anything to remind him of his sister-like cousin. They had shared twenty-three years together, and she would always be in his heart. He just wished he could erase the last few hours of her life. The images were too painful to relive, yet they were stubbornly hard to forget.

Swallowing the dryness in his mouth, Birch began the most difficult story he'd ever told. "Jasmine's fate was sealed the moment she went back to the village…"

Part Three

Forget You Not

Chapter 50

—————————

"What are you doing here?" Doctor Wang called when he spotted Jasmine stepping into his front yard.

"We forgot the medicine bag. Danny is in pain. I've got to—"

"Oh, no! Is he okay? Other than the pain?"

"He's okay, I think. We've used sweet wormwood three times a day. It works well for his malaria. But forget-me-not is useless for pain."

"I know. I'm sorry. My fault. I should have looked through his room—"

"No, it was our fault." Jasmine waved her arms.

"Well, I'll go up to the cave with you after lunch. You'll need more food soon."

"Have you heard anything from my uncle or my cousin?" She moistened her lips with a nervous lick.

"No, not yet. I was waiting for Linzi. That's why I wanted to wait a few more days before bringing supplies. I was hoping we might learn something by then."

"He's not back yet?"

"Not yet. Don't worry, Jasmine." Doctor Wang narrowed his eyes as he stared at her. "Linzi is reliable. He'll find a way to inform them. It takes time, now that the Japs are in Anning."

She nodded, hoping the herbalist was right. "Should we..." she ventured, "should we send Shitou to the town as well? It's been several days."

"Point taken," agreed Doctor Wang. "Let's have a quick lunch. I'll send Shitou down the mountain afterwards. Then I'll go up with you. All is in order. Do you feel better now?"

"Yes," said Jasmine, dipping her head. Storm clouds crawled above, stealing sunlight. Shadows fell across her face.

"Do you think the Japs will come here?" Jasmine asked at the dining table with the herbalist's family. She held a bowl of rice, but she didn't hurry to eat.

"I don't think so. As I said, this is a tiny village. No need for them to come here. No outsider knows about Danny. I've reminded everyone repeatedly to keep it a secret." He picked up a piece of her favorite wild mushroom and put it in her bowl. "Stop worrying so much, girl. Eat!"

Next to Jasmine, Shitou glanced at his grandpa, fidgeted in his seat, and lowered his head. Jasmine noticed the boy's awkwardness. *Has he told his friends in town?* Knowing Shitou, this wouldn't be a surprise. The teenager was so proud of his part in the rescue of the Flying Tiger that he couldn't stop talking about it to anyone in the village who would listen. *But had he been able to control himself when he went to the town?* She hoped that the boy had listened to his grandfather and kept his mouth shut. The result of a loose tongue could be disastrous.

Jasmine knew how efficient the Japanese spies were. The destruction of Jiaochangkou Tunnel was the work of their secret agents. They had informed and directed their bombers to destroy the entrances of the shelter. Several thousand people had been locked inside and died, including her aunt.

"What if…" Still deep in thought, she chewed the mushroom without tasting it. "What if—"

Shouts and screams erupted from outside. Jasmine looked up, her eyes widening. Doctor Wang shot to his feet. Before anyone could do anything, two Japanese soldiers kicked down the door and stormed inside. All the fear, pain, and hatred that she'd experienced in Nanking rushed back, robbing her of her ability to think, to react. She sat paralyzed on her seat.

A soldier grabbed her upper arm. He jerked her to her feet with violent speed and shoved her so hard that she staggered and fell to the ground.

Shitou jumped up. He extended his hand to help Jasmine stand.

"*Ike*. Go! Get out," the soldiers barked. With bayonets fixed on rifles, they herded the family outside.

Soon all the villagers were crowded in the herbalist's front yard.

"What the hell?" Doctor Wang mumbled under his breath. "Why? How did they find…" His voice trailed off as he stared at his grandson.

Shitou would not meet his grandfather's eyes.

"You…" The old man glared at the boy.

Jasmine stood behind them. Her suspicion had turned out to be true. The worst nightmare had become reality. She was once again face to face with the Japanese. *How much do they know? Do they understand my involvement?*

Even without knowing her role in assisting the American, they might single her out. She wore a shapeless cotton tunic and loose-fitting trousers like a farm girl. Yet her beauty stood out, working dangerously against her. Without the protection of Father John and Professor Valentine, she was in serious danger. Jasmine lowered her head, trying to make herself inconspicuous.

———————

"My name is Sadao," a Japanese officer spoke through an interpreter. Unlike a military man in charge, his voice was soft. He was in his late twenties, of medium height and good build, with a pleasant face and close-cropped hair. "I'm sorry to inconvenience everyone," he apologized, adjusting the star-studded cap on his head. "But we need your help. An American pilot bailed out in this area. We heard he was injured. We'd like to find him. We want to talk to him. We'll take care of him, if he's badly hurt."

Sadao scanned the frightened crowd. The Japanese intelligence agency had picked up a rumor of a downed American pilot in the area but they had no idea in which village to search. Several small communities were scattered throughout this mountainous region and accessible only by foot. The interpreter was a Japanese businessman, who lived in the town of Anning. He knew the unofficial paths.

"Now, will anyone tell me where he is?" continued Sadao. He was genial as if he were talking to friends. His gentleness lay in stark contrast to his men who were surrounding the villagers with rifles. A machine gun was trained on the crowd. A huge German shepherd glared at the captives.

Behind the herbalist and Shitou, Jasmine couldn't see the Japanese clearly, but his nonthreatening voice and politeness startled her. She was bewildered. She'd seen firsthand how cruel Japanese soldiers had been in Nanking. Was he different? Nevertheless, she remained perfectly still with her head low, unwilling to draw attention.

"Don't worry," the officer went on, "we won't hurt him. He's a warrior. We're all warriors. It's just business. No need to be afraid. Not for him. Not for yourselves." He signaled the moon-faced interpreter.

Dressed in a black V-neck tunic over loose-fitting trousers, the interpreter opened a cloth bag he was carrying.

"Now, just to show we've come in peace and mean no harm to anyone"—the officer stuck his hand into the bag and brought out a handful of candies—"these are for the kids."

The residents relaxed. Some of the children still buried their faces in their parents' protective arms, but a few looked at the candies with shining eyes and wet mouths.

"Here…" Sadao stepped closer to the crowd. Bending down, he handed candies to the children. Some brave youngsters came up from the back to get the treats. In a few seconds, the mood had changed. Kids peeled the wrappers and licked the candies, sweet smiles spreading over their innocent faces.

"May…I?" Mutou ogled the bag of colorful candies.

"Of course," said Sadao. Before handing them to Mutou, he asked, "Do you know the American pilot?" The handful of sweets dangled in front of the retarded young man. "Do you?" the man in charge pressed, keeping the candies as bait.

Ignoring Doctor Wang's cautionary voice in the background, the simpleminded teenager bobbed his head.

"Where is he?" The hand with the treat inched closer to the boy.

Mutou ran his tongue over his buckteeth and lips again. He pointed his finger at a house on higher ground.

With a wave of his arm, Sadao sent several soldiers to search. He snickered at the childlike young man as he dropped a few candies in Mutou's hands.

Minutes later, the soldiers came back with the parachute.

Doctor Wang's jaw dropped. After he'd transferred the pilot and the young women to the cave, he'd instructed Shitou to burn the chute. How could it still be here? He turned to his grandson and caught the boy's contrite look.

Shitou was in awe of the Flying Tiger. He admired Danny too much to destroy the things he'd used, so he'd hidden the parachute under a pile of firewood, thinking it would be safe. How could he know that his innocent action might bring disaster?

"Where is he?" the man in charge asked again.

Mutou gave an indifferent shrug and wiped the drool from his mouth with the back of his hand.

"Who takes care of him?" More candies dangled before Mutou's face.

"Mutou, stop talking!" barked Doctor Wang.

The young man hesitated a few seconds. He licked his thin lips, shiny with saliva, while his ravenous eyes stayed glued to the lure in front of him.

"Relax," said Sadao with an easy smile. "We just want to find him. To give him some candies, you know. Now, tell me who takes care of him?" The treats got closer to the young man's face.

Mutou turned, pointing his fingers behind the herbalist and his grandson.

The officer threw the candies toward Mutou and took a few large strides. Shoving the old man and the boy aside, he pulled Jasmine out from hiding. With one hand clasping her arm, he lifted her downturned face with the other. A startled expression flashed in his eyes. Even in plain peasant clothes, her beauty stunned him. For a moment, he just stared at her, forgetting where he was and what he was supposed to do.

Chapter 51

Jasmine had listened nervously to the conversation. *Mutou can't tell right from wrong. He's going to give me away.* She stood hugging her arms around herself.

Dragged from hiding, her skin rippled with goose bumps and her heart skipped a beat when Sadao lifted her chin. She summoned all her strength to force a calm expression that belied the trembling inside her.

"What is your name?"

"Jasmine."

The officer grinned. "You are not a farm girl, are you? A student?"

"I was…" She shot him a bitter look. She wanted to say she couldn't be a student anymore because of him and his fellow soldiers. That she was now motherless and fatherless because of him and his fellow soldiers. But she thought better of it and decided not to provoke him.

"What did you study?"

"Art. Oil painting."

"Painting? That's great. I took an art class in college. Landscape painting is my favorite." He swept his hand left to right, encompassing the lush mountains around them. Except for the gloomy sky, the scenery was breathtaking. "Isn't this a perfect place? Perhaps you could show me your paintings later. I'd love to see them."

Jasmine remained quiet. She had an odd feeling. If it weren't for all the guns surrounding them, she might have thought that they were friends carrying on an interesting conversation.

After a moment of weighty silence, he stopped beating around the bush. "For now, will you please tell me the whereabouts of the American pilot…?"

Jasmine shook her head.

"Come on. It's okay. Tell me. We won't hurt him."

Like you didn't hurt Lu Ping and the hundreds of thousands of disarmed soldiers in Nanking. The image of Lu Ping's blood-covered body lying on the church floor flashed through her mind, but she said nothing.

"You know where he is…I can tell. Be a good girl."

His voice was still calm, yet with an undertone of cold brutality. His demand gave her the shivers, still Jasmine didn't say anything.

In a rising voice, Sadao repeated his question several times. His nose flared. His gentleness disappeared, replaced by a malicious expression. His hands tightened on her arms, and he shook her violently. "Where is he?"

"Let go of me!" cried Jasmine, struggling to pull away from his tenacious grasp.

"Tell me. Now!" he shouted. "This is the last time I'm going to ask nicely. If you don't tell me, you'll be very sorry." His narrow eyes burned with a cruel glare. "You'll tell me, sooner or later, one way or another. I assure you."

The Japanese interpreter added his own warning. "He's not kidding. He'll hurt you. Just say the words. Don't wait. He has a reputation of being…very persuasive."

"She's just a girl," Doctor Wang said as he took a step forward. He'd been trying to intercede, but he'd been pushed back by a soldier with a bayonet pointed at him. "She doesn't know anything. Let her go!"

A rifle butt hit the herbalist in his gut.

Shitou yelled, and he, too, was held back by a gun.

Jasmine began to shake. All the horrifying stories she'd heard in Nanking leaped into her mind. She wanted to run. She wished she could hide. But she was going nowhere, her arms in the grip of iron claws.

Sadao gazed at the terrified young woman one more time, trying to decide if he would carry out his threat. It didn't take long. With a wave of his arm, he summoned two soldiers. They planted themselves on each side of her. Upon seeing their superior's nod, they began to strip her.

A gasp erupted from the crowd. Shouts, cries, and screams filled the air. People surged forward, trying to interfere.

Bang!

Sadao took out his pistol and fired once into the air. "If anyone passes this line"—he drew an imaginary line in front of the crowd with his gun—"he'll be killed. No questions asked. Understand?"

———————

Jasmine kicked, punched, and cried as the chaos broke out. But she had no chance of escaping from the two strong men. Soon all her clothes were gone. Caught by a draft, her red scarf flew up and tangled on a nearby branch.

The two soldiers dragged her to the tree that was strung with white flowers. They bound her hands behind her back and used extra ropes around her ankles. Sadao walked toward her with measured steps. "It's not too late." He brushed her long dark hair off her chest, exposing her bare body. "Tell me where the American is and I'll let you go," he said as if he meant it.

"Let her go! She doesn't know anything," bellowed Doctor Wang, iron in his voice. "I'm the one who takes care of the pilot. I'm the one you're looking for."

The officer ignored the herbalist. Interrogating a naked woman was much more enjoyable. He might question the old man later, but he doubted it would be necessary. "How long do you think she can last?" he asked the interpreter without taking his eyes off her. The corner of his mouth tilted upward in a sadistic half-smile.

Jasmine waged a futile struggle against her bonds.

"You're a beautiful girl. I don't want to hurt you if I don't have to. But you're not giving me a choice," he said, taking out his Samurai sword.

She paled. Her eyes were filled with terror when he pointed his blade at her chest.

"You like painting, right?" he said. "If you don't start talking, I will paint a picture on your chest."

The tip of the sword pressed on top of her left breast. Jasmine closed her eyes, too afraid to look. Her hands clutched together tightly in her bonds.

Sadao paused for effect. He knew the power of threat. He wasn't in a hurry. Blood oozed out of the cut, dripping down her smooth chest. "Tell me!" he barked, with daggers in his eyes and the sword in his hand.

No sound came from her except the chattering of her teeth.

His nostrils flared. "All right, you asked for it!" He took a step back, and with a swift motion, he swept the Samurai sword down around her breast, slashing her flesh.

Jasmine screamed. A shudder racked her body, and tears gushed out of her closed eyes.

The crowd gasped. The villagers groaned and shouted in anger. Women lowered their heads, unable to look. Parents clutched their children and held them close, hoping to shield them from the sights and sounds. Doctor Wang and Shitou pushed and shoved the soldiers, but they couldn't break through.

"Where is he?" the Japanese officer repeated, his voice shrill with frustration.

A sudden gust of wind fluttered her dark hair around her ashen cheeks. She let out a horrified gasp as the tip of the sword poked at her breast again. *No! No, God, please!* Blood pulsed in the injured flesh, sending fiery sensations throughout her body. She didn't think she could stand another cut.

But the blade went down again, ripping her flesh.

Jasmine shrieked as the sword went up and down her naked body. Her face contorted in agony.

Sadao was serious when he'd said he was going to paint a picture on her chest. Soon a bloody image appeared with wiggly lines carved on her upper body. The cuts were controlled and skillful: deep enough to draw blood and create piercing sensation, but not deep enough to kill her. He asked the same question each time before sending down the blade.

Jasmine wailed at the top of her lungs, as if her cries would stop the pain. What was the alternative? The only way to stop her suffering was to tell them where Danny was hiding. But she couldn't let these monsters torture him, or kill him.

Don't give him up! Never tell them where Danny is! Never! Never! Never!

Again and again, as the sword pierced her flesh, she swore to herself that she would not back away from this impossible promise.

Chapter 52

The tip of the blade went up to Jasmine's left cheek. Her eyes flew open, undeniable fear glazing her eyes. "No, please…don't…" For the first time she begged him, her speech slurred by pain and terror. Her dark hair was plastered upon her face with sweat and tears, accentuating her pallor.

The moon-faced interpreter took pity on her. He fired a rapid exchange with the man in charge. Then he turned to Jasmine. "For heaven's sake, tell him where the pilot is," he urged. "They are soldiers. It's war. It's their job to fight. Not yours." He was in civilian clothes, dressed like a Chinese. "You're a young woman. Why are you doing this? No need to go through this for anyone. Don't be a hero. It's not worth it."

Jasmine just looked at the man with the sword pointed at her cheek. Through numb lips, she pleaded in Japanese, "Dear God, no more. Please!"

"I'm glad you can speak our supreme language, but there is no need to beg me," Sadao stated with a shrug. His thin lips curled in a venomous sneer. "You have the power. You're the one holding the key. Just say the word."

This was the hardest part. She wasn't entirely powerless; she could end the torture by telling them where the American was hiding.

But she couldn't let Danny go through the hell that she was going through. It was his blood or her blood; she chose her own blood. It was her suffering or his suffering; she chose her own suffering. Not for a moment would she consider the alternative. It was her life or his life; she chose to give her life so he might live.

"You've really tried my patience," Sadao barked. "How on earth can a girl like you be so stubborn? Tell me where he's hiding. Now!"

Jasmine closed her eyes, knowing her plea had fallen on deaf ears.

The blade went down, ripping her flesh. This time, instead of slashing her once and questioning her in between the cuts, he did it several times in a row, leaving three long crimson lines on her left cheek.

Darkness whirled at the edge of her vision. Jasmine fainted.

Sadao slapped her right cheek, demanding her back to consciousness.

"Stop!" Doctor Wang roared in anguish. He'd had enough. He'd been beaten by the soldier for trying to push through the line. This time, he punched the Japanese in the face. As the man with a bloody nose staggered backward, the herbalist shoved beyond him. It was suicide, yet he had no choice. He couldn't stand to watch the young woman under his care tortured anymore. He'd rather die while trying to save her.

With bare arms, Doctor Wang flung himself at Sadao.

The man in charge twirled around. Without batting an eye, he lifted his sword and thrust it into the herbalist's chest. Before anyone could blink or cry, he yanked the blade out.

Blood surged from Doctor Wang's chest, staining his oyster-colored shirt. His hands flew toward the wound, mouth gaping as if in the middle of a scream. Stumbling backward several steps, he fell onto the ground with a thud. His head lolled to one side, then went limp. His eyes remained open in utmost anger.

"Grandpa!" Shitou hit the nearby soldier with his fists and pushed him away. He rushed toward the old man. As he leaned down, he was attacked from behind. A soldier with a pockmarked face thrust his bayonet into the boy's back multiple times. Shitou collapsed on top of his grandpa. The young man with a ready smile stilled, blood oozing out of the stab wounds on his back.

"Grandpa! Shitou!" Little Fatty, the three-year-old boy, wobbled forward. His innocent voice was laced with fear.

"Come back!" people in the crowd shouted, warning the youngster. Several tried to grab him.

It was too late. Before the toddler reached his family, the soldier picked him up.

"No!"

The Japanese raised the child high above his head. Then, with a heartbreaking motion, he threw the toddler to the ground. The cry from the crowd was so loud that no one knew if the youngster had made a sound. His head was smashed on the hard surface. His Tiger-head shoes were not able to protect him.

Mutou broke into a frantic run. He didn't go far. With a wave of his arm, Sadao sent the German shepherd after him. In no time the dog tackled the teenager to the ground. Kicking and punching, he waged a fruitless struggle. The trained dog bit his stomach, ripped open his belly, and jerked out his intestines. Mutou's hair-raising screams mingled with the animal's satisfied growl, handfuls of candies scattered round him.

Chapter 53

━ ━ ━ ━ ━ ━ ━ ━

Jasmine had regained consciousness and watched in pure terror. "Murderer! Animal!" she shrilled. She felt as if her heart had shattered into a thousand pieces.

"Animal?" Sadao understood the word he'd been called. "You haven't seen anything yet, you stupid girl." His voice was pure ice, devoid of emotion. He waved his arm.

Two soldiers untied the rope from Jasmine's ankles, raised her bottom, and parted her legs. The man in charge lowered his pants.

"No! No! No!" Jasmine kicked and wiggled. But the two strong soldiers held her thighs and legs in their iron grip. With hands tied behind her back, she was pinned to the tree. Only her head was free to sway violently from side to side.

"Please, help me!" She turned to the interpreter who seemed to have a hard time watching. Blood, tears, and sweat dribbled on her cheek and bare chest. Her features dissolved into a mask of pure terror.

The interpreter averted direct eye contact with her. An empty detachment appeared on his flat face. He was powerless.

Once again, Sadao wasn't in a hurry. He stood between her legs, his penis erect. He gripped her bottom; his fingertips dug deep into her flesh. "One last time, where is the pilot?" Spittle flew from his mouth.

For a few seconds, Jasmine stared at him with a loathing and hatred that she'd never felt before. "Go to hell!" she spat and screwed her eyes shut.

He thrust deeply into her body. With frustration, fury, and lust, Sadao pounded her, relishing her cry, her shudder, and her fruitless struggle. When he was done, he grabbed her thigh, switching positions with one of the two men holding her leg. The soldier was inside her in no time.

One after another, the Japanese raped the young woman.

Each breath became difficult to take. Jasmine lost track of time. She left her battered body and floated upward. Looking down, she saw a naked girl tied to a tree, two men holding her legs apart for another man to rape her. Jasmine had no power to save her. She was a ghost.

She glanced down at the front yard. With heads lowered and shoulders sagging, the terror-stricken villagers stood docile. They—mostly old men, women, and children—had no means to help the girl. Four bloody bodies lay in front of them. Armed soldiers surrounded them. The Japanese kept one eye on the crowd and one eye on the girl, waiting impatiently to take their turn at her. *Keep floating upward. Leave this tormented place...*

Over the tree line, she flew into the big sky. Before long an aircraft with Tiger Teeth painted on its nose came into view. "Danny!" she exclaimed when she caught a glimpse of the handsome face. She flew alongside the fighter plane.

Jasmine lifted her right hand and laid it upon the window, hoping he would see her.

He didn't.

She pounded the window.

He couldn't hear her.

Nothing separated them except the thin layer of glass, yet she had no way of reaching him. She felt cold. The wind blew fiercely, pushing her away. She struggled to remain beside the aircraft.

Puffy clouds rushed toward them, swallowing the airplane. She whirled round, frantically searching for the aircraft. Instead, she spotted people hundreds of feet below. She glided toward them and found a girl and the pilot. Resting on their elbows, they were half-lying in a meadow carpeted with blue forget-me-nots. Brilliant smiles spread

215

across their youthful faces.

The pilot wove forget-me-nots into a garland, placing it onto the young woman's head. She had long shiny hair that hung all the way to her waist and a carmine red scarf around her neck. In the next moment, her short hair bounced off her shoulders, and the scarf changed color to pink.

Jasmine was happy for them. She yearned to be with them.

Then everything changed. Dark clouds rolled in, blocking the warm sunlight. A group of monstrous Japanese appeared from nowhere and overwhelmed the couple. They tied the pilot to a tree and tore his flight jacket to shreds. The man in charge whipped his Samurai sword across the American's face and chest.

Jasmine lunged forward. With open arms, she placed herself in front of the pilot. The blade cut through her invisible body. The piercing pain took away her breath. Yet she wasn't able to block the sword. It slashed his flesh, leaving bloody marks. No matter how she tried to stop the blade, it continued to torture the man she loved. His torment unhinged her. She screamed, kicked, and punched the attacker with unseen arms and legs.

Then, again, as fast as they'd come, the soldiers vanished, leaving the severely injured American behind. Where was the girl? Was she dragged away by the Japanese? Jasmine didn't know. She had no time to find out.

The pilot lay lifeless on the ground, his chest covered with bloody cuts. His white scarf was stained with bright red dots. Jasmine hovered above him. She longed to touch him, to gather him in her arms, to heal him. But what could a ghost do?

Leaning down, she placed soft kisses on his forehead. On his cheeks. Then on his lips.

"Danny, Danny, Danny!" Over and over again she whispered his name, even though she knew he couldn't hear her. "Don't leave me!"

Jasmine jerked awake. It was drizzling. Drops of rain fell on her face. She was still tied to the tree. One of the soldiers had just finished his turn.

"Danny? That's the name of the pilot, isn't it?" With his left hand clutching her leg, Sadao lifted her chin with his right index finger and thumb, forcing her to look at him. "I told you that you would tell me, sooner or later, one way or another. But for now"—he raised his hand, stopping the next man in line—"we have to go." It was getting late, and the rain might make their return too treacherous.

"Don't feel bad." Seeing the disappointment on his subordinate's face, Sadao offered, "You'll be the first one in line once we're back to the camp."

The jug-eared soldier curled the corners of his lips upward when he heard his superior's promise.

Jasmine blanched. She'd hoped they would kill her. The pain and humiliation was worse than death. But they wouldn't let her die. She was valuable. She was usable. She hadn't given up the information they needed.

Two soldiers took her down from the tree, and she slumped to the muddy ground stained with blood and body fluids. While she was on wet earth, they bound her arms behind her back. Sadao gave his order, and half a dozen Japanese went into the crowd and dragged several young women out. People fought for their loved ones, but the Japanese bayoneted whoever resisted.

The nightmare hadn't stopped there. Before they left, Sadao lifted a flattened hand to his throat and made a slashing gesture to the man with the machine gun. With a nod, the soldier opened fire, sending his tracers into the crowd. The startled and terrified villagers fell, one after another.

A few villagers ran away. But the soldiers caught up with them, thrusting bayonets into their bodies. Except for Jasmine and the other three girls, no one was left alive. Everyone—man, woman, child—was killed in a matter of minutes. The enchanted yard became a slaughter-house, and the timeless serenity of this faraway village was forever lost.

Chapter 54

▬ ▬ ▬ ▬ ▬ ▬ ▬ ▬

Jasmine watched the whole thing from the muddy ground. A wail traveled up her throat, yet no sound came out. Her throat was so hoarse from all her screams that she couldn't make any noise. Only the shrieks from the other girls echoed in her ears. Rivers of gut-wrenching tears poured down her twisted face.

When they left the village, she was half-dragged and half-carried by two soldiers. Blood, tears, sweat, along with raindrops, dripped from her cheeks, painting a horrifying picture on her bare chest. The pain was beyond words.

As soon as she gained a little strength, Jasmine tried to shake off the hands on her arms. Their dirty fingernails dug too deep into her flesh. The men sneered but didn't bother to fight her. They exchanged an amused glance and released her. Where could a naked, battered woman go when she was surrounded by two dozen Japanese soldiers?

The mountainous terrain was rugged and slippery. She dragged her feet, using all the strength left within her. Cold mountain wind and rain lashed down, numbing her body and mind. *I can't let them do this to me. I can't stand it anymore!*

But it wasn't up to her. She knew they would hurt her again. They needed the information only she knew. The American pilot was important to them. They wouldn't stop until they got what they wanted.

The prospect of going through torture and gang-rape again dragged her over the edge and into an abyss. *What can I do? How can I escape?* She didn't even have the means to kill herself. They wouldn't give her the opportunity to end her own life.

Jasmine pondered the questions as she trudged. Sadao was right about one thing: the likelihood of torture was as frightening as the torture itself.

No matter how much she did not want to admit it, she feared she might succumb. She'd already told them Danny's name. The information itself wasn't significant, but the implication was. *What will I say next?* An involuntary tremor rippled through her body.

No one could stand such cruelty and abuse. She was too weak to endure more pain. She would never forgive herself if she harmed Danny, even if she wasn't in a rational frame of mind. *It's only a matter of time before they drive me insane.*

Halfway to the Japanese camp, they passed a ridge. The rocky path was so narrow that they had to walk in single file. It was raining hard. Mist hovered over the mountainside, reducing visibility. Everyone kept their eyes on the muddy path. One slip might send a person tumbling down the steep slope.

Suddenly, the answer flashed before her. Without missing a beat, before anyone comprehended, Jasmine leaped toward the cliff. The interpreter grabbed her from behind. Using every last bit of strength and determination left within her, she kicked. As he ducked, she jerked away. He leaned forward. His fingers skimmed her wet arm, unable to hold her back.

In a breath, the young woman disappeared into the canopy of dark trees below. She had fulfilled what she'd said long ago: she wouldn't hesitate to give her life for the man she loved.

Chapter 55

▬ ▬ ▬ ▬ ▬ ▬ ▬ ▬

No mercy was shown at the camp. The Japanese tied the girls to trees then took turns raping them. Throughout the night, the soldiers were hooting, cheering, and drinking sake while they had their fun. All of them recalled the young woman they'd had early in the day. Her exceptional beauty was hard to forget.

Sadao missed the young woman most. From the moment he'd seen her, he'd wanted her to himself for the entire night, or if he was lucky, for many nights while they were in this out-of-the-way town.

The air smelled of alcohol and smoke. Sitting by the campfire, Sadao took a large gulp of sake from the bottle. He regretted cutting her cheek. Her gorgeous face would have been more pleasing to look at. In the heat of the moment, he was furious with her. Her willingness to sacrifice herself for the American enraged him. He understood then how much this Flying Tiger meant to her. The pilot was her life; he was larger than her life.

Sadao scrubbed a hand over his bleary eyes. He was jealous of this American fighter whom he'd never met. A Japanese soldier's life wasn't important to anyone. They were trained as machines to kill, to die for their emperor. That was part of the reason they treated their enemies so cruelly. If his life was insignificant, his enemy's life certainly was nothing to him. He wished his life meant something to someone. *If only I had a girl like that!*

He tipped the bottle to his lips, swallowing the burning sensation. Information about the pilot was crucial to him. He'd been ordered to bring the American back alive, and not to return until he'd found him. A Flying Tiger was invaluable to them.

He was close, but now he had to start again from scratch. Jasmine's resistance had hampered his task. What would his superiors say or do if he came away empty-handed? Sadao hated her guts. The setback was a bruise to his ego. It symbolized his sense of failure as a man and as an army officer.

His frustration flared to anger. He slammed the bottle of sake into the fire and with the back of his hand wiped the liquid from the corner of his mouth. He stood and walked toward his captives. His left hand grabbed a girl by her throat, and his right hand slapped her face. The girl made a goggling sound. Her eyes rolled back under the lids. Again and again, he hit her until her nose bled and her cheeks were swollen. One by one, he ravaged the girls with the cruelest form of violence. Spine-chilling wails from the tormented young women mingled with the soldiers' animal-like moans and groans, turning the camp into a living hell.

In the middle of the night, after all the soldiers had had enough, they offered one of the girls to the interpreter. Shaken and remorseful, the interpreter pretended to take her to the toilet but instead set her free. When he came back twenty minutes later without her, the soldiers kicked and punched him. They'd planned to keep the girls for more fun.

The girl had snuck out of the camp. With no clothes, she had nowhere to go but to return to the village. In the faint light she ran, stumbling and falling. By the time she reached her home, in addition to her split lips, broken nose, and bruised cheeks, her bare body was covered with mud and countless bloody cuts. She'd barely had time to put her clothes on when Birch Bai showed up in the village. With incoherent sentences, she managed to tell him the story.

Chapter 56

Tears rushed down Danny's face as he listened to the story. Now he understood why Birch said he'd had no choice when he threw the hand grenades toward his sister. The alternative was even worse than death.

He stared at the red scarf in his hand. A tidal wave of nostalgia washed over him. Once upon a time, Jasmine had used it to wrap his head with mashed forget-me-nots, saving his life. That was six weeks ago, but it seemed a lifetime away. In fact, it was a life away—the woman he loved had died a horrible death, and an unbridgeable space separated them forever.

The reality of her death hit home. Although he'd suspected it, he had doubts and harbored hopes. Now the thought that he would never see the graceful young lady again tore his heart apart.

Danny couldn't help but wish he'd told her how much he loved her. Jasmine would never feel the warmth of his hug again. She wouldn't taste the sweetness of his kisses. She would never know the pleasure of being a woman loved dearly by a man.

I should've gone down with my P-40. I shouldn't have bailed out. If I'd died, then the girls might still be alive! The exotic village would be as peaceful as it had been for thousands of years. The villagers would not have had trouble giving up a dead body, would they? The young women loved him; the boys worshiped him; the whole village had welcomed him with open arms. He was there to fight for them, to protect them. *For God's sake, look what I brought them!*

The war had taken a toll on him. He'd had enough. He'd seen too much blood and too much suffering. Before coming to China, he'd known there would be pain and loss. The agony of losing his best friend was unbearable. But he'd known the odds. They were soldiers.

Still, nothing had prepared him to face the death of so many innocent people. He hadn't expected to see an adorable girl being blown into pieces before his eyes. And never for a moment had he imagined that the graceful woman he fell in love with at first sight would die such an unmerciful death.

Danny was ready to go home to the peaceful life that he'd once lived in California. Many pilots had left when the American Volunteer Group broke up, their contract officially over. He'd come voluntarily, and he and Jack were among a handful of the Flying Tigers who had chosen to stay, to keep fighting. Now he longed to go home. No war. No killing. No pain of losing the ones he loved. No guilt or shame for not being able to protect them.

Then, as he envisioned his younger life, he painfully realized that he no longer had Jack. The war had taken his childhood friend from him. Its ugly claws had grabbed the beautiful woman he loved, the sweet girl he cared for, and the innocent villagers he'd befriended. Even if he walked away, his heart would be left in this remote part of China where Jasmine, Daisy, Shitou, Doctor Wang, and all the villagers once lived, and where they, along with Jack, would forever rest.

The fearless and high-spirited fighter pilot was beside himself with grief and despair. He sat transfixed. Those ugly claws that had taken his friends' lives were now squeezing the life out of him. An empty stare came to his brown eyes.

He dropped his elbows to his knees and covered his face with his hands. "Why?" he mumbled, trancelike. "Why didn't she just tell them? Why didn't they give me up? I wouldn't have blamed her. I wouldn't have blamed any of them. Let the Japs catch me. I'd rather die!"

He was a fighter. It was his job to face death. But not her! She wasn't a soldier. She was an innocent young woman.

"She would never give you up," Birch said. "She loved you. You know that, don't you?"

Danny nodded. *Of course I know!* As shy as she was, her love for him had been obvious.

"None of us would give you up. You fight the Japs. You risk your life for us."

"I'm a pilot. I get paid to do the job. No need to give up her life for mine—"

"Perhaps there are some things that are more important than our own lives..."

"Like what? Hell! What do I have?"

"You have wings. Don't forget you're a Flying Tiger!"

In a flash Danny recalled the conversation he'd had with Doctor Wang before being carried up the steep rock staircase. "You're a Flying Tiger with injured wings," the herbalist had said. "Take good care of those wings. Once they're healed, you can soar into the sky. Fight for all of us. We know you will. We believe in you!"

The late doctor's and Birch's simple, yet powerful words seemed to revive Danny. He was embarrassed for the momentary weakness he'd experienced. He was ashamed that he'd almost forgotten his promise—he was going to get well, to fly in the sky, to fight for them all!

In a single blinding moment, he knew what he was going to do next. He understood why he'd been saved time and again by people who had risked their own lives. There was no true peace in the world. Not until their enemies were defeated. Not until this awful war ended. He was more than a professional fighter. He was a Flying Tiger, a Tiger with great strength. He was a *Fei Hu*!

Now that his wings were about to heal, he must go back to fight, to fly once again into the sky just like the herbalist had wished. He wouldn't let Doctor Wang down. *I won't let Jasmine and Daisy down. I won't let any of my friends down.*

Now the war was personal—he would fight for his family, his loved ones, and for his friends now gone in sacrifice.

Chapter 57

Danny wrapped the red scarf around his neck. The long white scarf that Jasmine had given him was already there. In the warm sunlight, his grief and helplessness were replaced by fortitude.

He turned his gaze to Birch, who looked at him with kindness and concern. They were sitting by the river bank. Murky water flew tirelessly downstream, taking mud and twigs along with it as it disappeared around a big bend in the distance. Not long ago, Birch had carried him over the challenging river. In spite of the cool breeze, a sheen of perspiration clung to the Chinese man's face. This was the second time that Birch had helped him across treacherous terrain.

Danny felt gratitude as he stared at the young man who had lost both his sister and cousin over the past few days. Birch's forehead now bulged with black and blue bruises. His face was covered with abrasions. Dark blood splattered the front of his blue shirt and stained a large area under his left elbow. The Chinese had gone through hell to rescue him, to help him no matter how rudely he'd treated him. Not once had Birch blamed the American for his losses. Behind his bruised features, Danny discerned unimaginable suffering, along with unbendable courage.

Danny felt terrible that he had treated this dedicated and kind-hearted man in such an immature way. Opening his mouth, he tried to say something. But he stopped. No matter what he said, it wouldn't be enough to apologize for his bad behavior. No words would come close to the gratitude he felt and the debt he owed this fellow pilot. Nothing would erase the pain of losing his sister and cousin.

As he faltered, an idea rushed to his mind, and without a second thought, he blurted out, "Birch, we must swear to be brothers. If you will have me..." At least in this way, Birch's suffering would be his suffering; Birch's loss would be his loss. They would be bonded forever as brothers, and they could confront the unbearable pain together. Shared pain would be bearable pain.

Birch was caught off guard. Being a sworn brother of a Flying Tiger wasn't anything he'd expected. Danny Hardy was well known. He was one of the most decorated of heroes, Ace-of-Aces. His superb flying skill, unmatched bravery, and sheer determination had won the respect and admiration of the Chinese pilots.

"I've always wanted to have a brother," replied Birch. His dark eyes brightened with almost childish excitement. At that moment, he felt the presence of his sister and cousin; their spirits were all around them.

Sworn brotherhood was an ancient Chinese tradition and an honor. Only closest friends could enter into such a kinship and be considered each other's family member. Highly influenced and romanticized by a classic novel, *Romance of the Three Kingdoms*, this tight bond was an idealistic dream of many young men, often alluded to as the ultimate fraternal loyalty.

"How old are you, Birch?"

"Twenty-eight. I'm a Tiger."

Danny laughed. "Which month?"

"June."

"Then I have to call you *Big* Brother?"

"If I knew you'd be so concerned"—Birch scratched his head and smiled—"I would have asked Mother to keep me inside a little longer."

Danny was thrilled that his Chinese brother had a good sense of humor. "All right, I'll follow you." Ever since he'd read the classic novel, he craved to have sworn brothers and longed to have such an ultimate union. Jack and he had in fact performed this ritual when they were kids. But what could be better than carrying out this ceremony with a Chinese brother? He was ready to kneel on the ground as described in the book.

"Wait!" Birch stopped him. "No need." He motioned to Danny's injuries on his leg. "That's just formality. What's important is"—he pointed to the left of his chest—"in here. No need to worry about the superficial stuff."

"Well said, Big Brother."

Side by side the young men sat on a fallen log. Their right hands folded into fists; their left palms wrapped the right fists. Placing their clasped hands a few inches in front of their chests, they squared their shoulders and looked up at the sky.

"I, Birch Bai, in front of the heavens above—" Birch paused.

Danny followed: "I, Danny Hardy, in front of the heavens above—"

Exchanging an understanding glance, both men stated together, "We swear we will be brothers forever. We will share our joys and sorrows. We will go through life together, thick and thin. Though not born on the same day of the same month in the same year, we hope to die on the same day of the same month in the same year."

Danny turned and touched Birch's shoulder with his right hand. "Da Ge!" Warmness swelled around his heart as he said 'Big Brother' in Chinese.

"Hao Xiong Di—Good Brother!" Birch replied.

Danny grasped Birch's hands in his. His eyes glowed, luminous with hope and delight. Staring at Birch, he felt a sudden rush of exhilaration. He was happy he had the wisdom to make peace between them and thankful to form such a close bond with another incredible Tiger. It was ironic that just moments ago he couldn't wait to get away from this man. Now his life was connected to him forever, just like Jack, and Jasmine, and Daisy.

Birch pulled Danny to a standing position. "I don't know if it's possible, but I'm going to request a transfer to your squadron. I'd be honored if I could be your wingman."

"The honor will be mine."

Side by side, they stood to leave.

"Wait…" Birch grabbed Danny's arm as the taller man picked up two sticks. "Now that I'm your Big Brother, you have to listen to me, right?" One corner of his mouth pulled into an impish grin. "Hold on to me." He pointed to the stick in Danny's right hand, and then added, "Please…"

Danny threw the stick away, placing his hand on his brother's shoulder. "Well, we just did it in the Chinese way. May I add something, an American twist, so to speak?"

"Sure…"

"It would be an honor to die with you on the same day, believe me. But if you survive, promise me something: don't be sad. Don't think about death. Live to the fullest; for you, and for me. You hear me?"

"Will you do the same?"

"You bet. Not just for you, but also for Daisy, for Jasmine, and for my friend Jack."

Birch nodded.

"One day, when we all meet again in another world, in another life, I'll introduce you to Jack." Pride sparkled in Danny's eyes. He patted Birch on the back. "You'll like him. He's a Tiger." And in that other life, Birch and Daisy would be his brother and sister, and Jasmine would be the girl he would love with all his heart and soul. Danny was sure of that.

Chapter 58

As several months passed a legend was born. An indestructible fighter appeared in China's skies. The pilot, along with his wingman, repeatedly outfought the more versatile Japanese airplanes and destroyed a record number of enemy aircraft. This legend inspired the Allies and terrorized their enemies.

Many reports, either in Chinese or American newspapers, praised Danny Hardy as one of the most brilliant fighter pilots in history. He wasn't invincible though. He'd been injured a number of times. "It was his unmatched spirit that kept him going up again and again," said one newspaper. The unrivaled determination, combined with his superior fighting skill, made Danny Hardy 'untouchable,' proclaimed another paper.

Chiang Kai-shek, the leader of the Nationalists, stated: "Since the Flying Tigers first spread their wings in the skies above China, the enemy has learned to fear the intrepid spirit they have displayed in face of his superior numbers. They have become the symbol of the invincible strength of the forces now upholding the cause of justice and humanity. The Chinese people will preserve forever the memory of their glorious achievements."

When an American reporter asked for a picture, Danny wanted the photo taken with his wingman. Of course the reporter was more than happy to find out about this mysterious Chinese pilot.

"This is Birch Bai," Danny made the introduction.

"It's an honor to meet you." The reporter exchanged a handshake with the Chinese airman. "You and Danny have done an incredible job."

Birch gave a clipped nod. "I'm just doing my job, sir."

"It runs in the family," said Danny. "My brother can certainly fly and fight."

"Your...brother?" The reporter was bewildered.

"Big Brother."

The reporter still thought he'd heard it wrong.

Danny cracked a broader grin. "Birch is the best brother you could ever want." A lifetime ago, a cute young girl had told him that. And she was absolutely right.

Side by side, they stood in front of his fighter plane, fierce Tiger Teeth painted on the narrow nose of the craft. Danny wrapped his left arm around his wingman's shoulders, his right hand on his hip. Assuming a militant stance with feet apart and shoulders braced, Birch placed his left arm on the wing of the airplane.

They exchanged a thoughtful glance before turning toward the camera. Smiles spread on their youthful faces, but tears glistened in their eyes. Only they were familiar with the posture; only they knew the meaning behind the pose. They remembered the picture Jasmine had painted on the cave wall. But this time, Danny let Birch take the elder brother's position while he took Jack's spot.

"Excuse me," said the reporter. "This might be too personal. If you don't mind..." He looked at Danny's neck. "Why do you wear two scarves? Isn't red a little odd for a fighter pilot?"

"It's a gift—a gift of life," replied Danny, his hand touching the scarf. "Once upon a time it saved my life. It had my blood on it...and a girl's."

"Who is the girl? Where is she?" The reporter was intrigued. Any romance of a hero would capture the attention of his readers.

Danny pointed to the left of his chest. He didn't bother to elaborate and walked away with his wingman.

Even with a scar on the left side of his forehead, Danny looked as handsome as he had looked before his injury. His radiant smile had returned, yet somehow he was different. Some people spotted him staring at two red sachets in his hands. A faraway look flitted across his face as he sniffed the scented bags. Tears glittered while he placed a soft kiss on each sachet. Then carefully he stowed them in his breast pocket. Sheer determination took over once he put his hand over his chest, making sure they were tucked away safely, close to his heart.

No one knew how Danny and Birch had become sworn brothers. Everyone knew the Chinese pilot had gone to pick up the injured Flying Tiger in a remote region in Yunnan. They assumed that was the place they had forged such a tight bond. The brothers never told anyone about the young women's death, except for Birch's father.

Colonel Bai was devastated when he heard the tragic news. Both brothers knelt in front of him while he paced back and forth in their living room. Birch had tried to stop Danny from kneeling, for fear he would hurt his barely healed wounds, but Danny insisted. Bowing showed the ultimate reverence and repentance in China. Although he'd never meant to harm the girls, both young women had died because of him. Bowing was the least he could do for the grieving father.

Colonel Bai was distraught over his decision to send the girls to Yunnan more than a year ago, yet he circled his arms around the two young men. "Not your fault," he said with great fortitude. His voice trembled, tears welling in his sad eyes. He looked worn, as if he'd aged ten years in the short time.

Whom could he blame for the death of his beloved daughter and niece? He couldn't blame Danny. The Flying Tiger had risked his life, coming from a faraway land to help. He couldn't blame Birch. He knew how much his son had adored Daisy and Jasmine. *Not my fault, either.* He had to convince himself. He'd had only good intentions when he sent them away. How could he have predicted the tragic outcome?

The father pulled the young men up and embraced them again. He was shorter than the young warriors, but no less imposing. "I'm glad you brought back a brother," he addressed Birch and patted him on the back. Turning to Danny, he squeezed the Flying Tiger's shoulder. "Welcome, Son. Welcome to our family!"

Once again, Danny was glad that he and Birch had become sworn brothers. It helped the three men grieve the loss of their loved ones. The holes in their hearts wouldn't be filled so easily, but hand in hand they could encourage one another, and keep moving onward.

Epilogue

The tale of the invincible Flying Tiger spread quickly.

Yes, it was true that this larger-than-life hero had ferocious Tiger Teeth decorating the front of his aircraft. But then someone mentioned seeing a carmine red scarf tied to one side of the fuselage and two scarlet sachets to the other. Later, people swore they saw two goddesses flying along with the fighter plane. Each one supported a wing, lifting him into the sky, helping him fight, and protecting him from harm. The story became a hauntingly beautiful and enduring legend.

Real or unreal, people liked to repeat it. This tale soothed their tired spirits, boosted morale, and encouraged more people to join the fight. It was so widely spread that it reached a remote hunting cabin in the mountainous region of Yunnan. A middle-aged couple lived there.

One day the husband came home with the story. "Everyone in town is talking about this Flying Tiger. A red scarf was tied to one side of his plane and two sachets to the other. People say that he was saved by a couple of young women nearby. Oh, he has a Chinese wingman. The two pilots are sworn brothers." He kept a close eye on a girl sitting at their homemade table and helping his wife with sewing.

Four or five months earlier, they'd saved this young woman from beneath a cliff. Their hunting dog had spotted her first and barked nonstop for its masters. She lay naked in the tall grass, and her hands were tied behind her back. Her face and chest were covered with many cuts, and dried blood stained her cheeks and body. She appeared lifeless.

The couple carried her home and bathed her bruised body. They gently put her on a cot in the corner of their room and fed her medicinal herbs.

Even after she woke up, the young woman never spoke a word and had trouble walking for several months. She seemed like a ghost, only half a person. She could breathe, she could blink, she could feel, but she had no vigor. Her spirit was gone. One side of her face was smooth while the other side was etched with three long scars.

The kind couple nursed her. They didn't care that she couldn't speak, and they were never put off by her appearance. The couple lived alone in the deep woods. Their only son had gone to fight the war. They had no idea if he was alive or dead.

Several weeks later they heard about the massacre in the nearby village and about a young woman who had sacrificed everything to protect an American pilot. The couple realized their wounded girl was the heroine. From then on, they treated her with high regard. They never told anyone, though, for fear of her safety and their own.

After hearing the story of the Flying Tiger, the young woman heaved a sigh of relief. She stopped sewing and looked up. For the first time since her rescue, a smile crept over her face.

That night, instead of the nightmares, Jasmine dreamed of her brave Flying Tiger.

Danny is alive! He's safe. He can still fly! Jasmine had been worried about him but had had no way of getting information.

She suffered constantly: tightness in her chest and twitching in her cheek, stabbing pains in her head and heart, and a great despair that encompassed her spirit. Haunted by nightmares, she crept through autumn and crawled into winter. At times she felt like she was drowning. She had to keep reciting what Birch had told her: "If you die, you just let the Japs kill one more innocent person without even using their guns or knives. I know it's hard; it's very painful. Being alive can be harder than dying. You've got to be strong, Jasmine."

Now a ripple of excitement coursed through her. *How did Danny and Daisy get out of the cave? Where did they go from there? Did Uncle and Birch send someone to pick them up? How did they get in touch with Danny and Daisy, since both Doctor Wang and Shitou had been killed during the massacre? Was it Linzi who had found them?*

All these questions troubled her. But the man she loved was safe!

Danny has a sworn brother. But who is this wingman? And how did they become brothers? No matter who the Chinese pilot was, she was happy for both. She knew how important Jack had been to Danny. She wished her cousin Birch would be as lucky.

Once again, life seemed meaningful and hopeful.

But in the morning she woke with a start. Her stomach hurt as if someone had hit her. In fact, she felt a kick even after fully awake. *Oh, God! No! No! No!*

The dreadful reality jerked her upward, her heart fluttering in panic. She'd already suspected that she might be pregnant, but she'd been too afraid to admit it until now. Her period had not resumed after the torture. She assumed that it was because of her poor health. When she felt nauseous, she thought it was caused by grief. Her stomach swelled a bit. She prayed it was a sign of recovery.

Jasmine gasped audibly and immediately put a hand over her mouth. It was still dark. Through a small window, faint light snuck into the room where her cot was separated from the couple's by a homemade curtain. The only decoration nearby was a dried wreath made of for-get-me-nots that hung near her bed.

Whose baby? Sadao, the malicious Japanese officer? The pockmarked face that had stabbed Shitou to death? The one with the German shepherd that tore up Mutou? The one who machine-gunned everyone in the village? She shuddered at the thought.

What am I going to do?

She sat on the bed clutching the blanket to her body, waves of nausea washing over her. In the faint light of dawn, she got up and wrote a note on a piece of paper. She knew the couple was illiterate, but they would find someone to read it to them. She thanked them and apologized for leaving without saying goodbye. She didn't sign her name, though. As far as she was concerned, Jasmine Bai had already died. Japanese soldiers had killed her.

Grabbing the wreath, she tiptoed out of the cabin and gasped at the sudden assault of freezing air. A light flurry added itself to the carpet of snow on the ground. Jasmine bent her head against the wind and with a slight limp, started the long slog down the mountain.

———————

For centuries female purity had been upheld as a virtue greater than life. Any woman who could live through such humiliation without committing suicide was an affront to society. Jasmine had already struggled with unbearable shame during the past few months.

But a baby? An enemy's baby! She couldn't allow it to live. She had to find help. Perhaps she could reconnect with her uncle or her cousin. They might be able to help her.

It was a daring attempt. She'd heard from the couple that Japanese troops were still in town at the bottom of the mountain, which was the reason she would not ask them for help. She wouldn't allow anyone else to be hurt because of her.

The wind penetrated every layer of her clothes. The light flurry turned to a heavy snow. She could hardly see what was right in front of her as she staggered down the mountainside. Ankle-deep snow became knee-high. Soon she lost track of the footpath. She dragged her feet, inching forward through the dense forest. She hadn't ventured more than a few yards from the hut in months, and this strenuous walk left her breathless. Her limp became more pronounced.

It was almost twilight when she reached the top of a cliff. There was no way for her to climb down. The snow-covered forest seemed to stretch endlessly in the dim light. She sank to the ground. Her teeth chattered. Her entire body trembled with fatigue.

I'm sorry, Birch Ge, she apologized to her cousin. *I tried. Believe me, I tried.*

A single tear made its way down her cheek.

———————

Jasmine hated to leave Danny. There was nothing in the world she wanted more than to be with the brave Flying Tiger. She longed to hug him just like that night in the meadow. She'd thought he was dying and wanted to let him know that someone was with him. She could not let him leave this world without someone by his side.

Now, she was alone.

Once, his lips had grazed the back of her hand. She lifted that hand and placed a soft kiss on the spot that he'd kissed. *Be safe, Danny!* She shouted. *Be happy!* Tears of undying love blurred her vision. *Pay attention to Daisy. She's a sweet girl.* Blinking to clear the film of tears from her eyes, she pleaded for her cousin. She remembered seeing the infatuated gaze in her cousin's eyes when she left the cave. *Daisy loves you!* she said, wiping salty streaks and snow from her face.

She looked up. Snowflakes fell from the sky onto her face. A prideful smile came over her expression. Without her, there would have been one less Flying Tiger in China's skies. She was forever with him as he fought the enemy. She was part of his wing.

Jasmine lay curled upon the snowy ground and closed her eyes. In the fading light she looked calm, and for the first time in a long time she felt no pain. Nor did she feel sadness. She held the garland of for-get-me-nots tightly to her chest, just as she'd held Danny that night, and her forlorn figure disappeared in the darkness.

Interview with the Author

What led you to write this book?

Wings of a Flying Tiger is a work of fiction. But to me, a Chinese-American, it is also personal.

I was born and raised in China. My mother and grandma had lived in Nanking and escaped from the city days before the Nanking Massacre when the Japanese soldiers slaughtered 300,000 innocent Chinese and raped 20,000 women in six weeks. Both my mother's and father's families fled to Chungking, where Japanese frequently bombed the wartime capital. My father told me about the repulsive smell of burning flesh, and as a young child, he had nightmares about the raids for several years. A good friend's father drowned when Japanese attacked his boat; even unable to swim, he jumped into a river to avoid being blasted. A Japanese friend sincerely apologized for the atrocities her fellow countrymen had committed. She knew a former soldier who had forced naked Chinese women to march with them to bring up their morale.

China was an isolated country while I was growing up. We were told that the Americans were "devils" and the American soldiers were crude and cowardly. I didn't read anything about the Flying Tigers until I came to the U.S. I was touched once I learned the truth.

As a Chinese, I'm thankful for the Flying Tigers' bravery and sacrifice; without their help, the course of Chinese history might have been changed, my family might not have survived, and I might not have existed. As a U.S. citizen, I'm honored to write a book about the American heroes. It's a privilege. A duty.

The heroine in this novel was inspired by the women in my family. In the early and mid-twentieth century, education was rare for females in China. My grandma, Yuan Changyin, was the first Chinese woman to receive a master's degree in the UK. My aunt, Yang Jingyuan, earned her master's degree at the University of Michigan and translated *Peter Pan*, *Jane Eyre*, *Wuthering Heights*, and other classics into Chinese. My mother, Zhou Chang, grew up during the war. Later, she graduated from Saint Petersburg State University in Russia, became a professor at Wuhan University, and published four children's books after her retirement. Both my sister, Jin Yang, and I received our Doctoral degree at the University of Rochester, and my daughter, Jessie Xiong, is a medical student at the University of North Carolina. All these women were the reason I created a well-educated Jasmine Bai as the main character.

How did writing change your life?

Years ago I was a negative person in an unhappy marriage, and I tried hard to change the situation. One book I read claimed that if you kept writing down five positive things a day, in twenty-one days, you could change your negative thoughts.

So I jotted down five positive things a day. It started with words or simple phrases. In time, words became sentences; sentences turned into paragraphs; paragraphs grew into pages. All positive. I didn't change in twenty-one days. It took me two years. But the end result is remarkable. I'm no longer a negative person.

The side effects of this practice? I started writing short stories, then novels.

What frustrates you the most about the writing process?

Grammar!

Born and raised in China, I learned English as a foreign language in school. The learning was limited and sometimes even wrong. I came to the U.S. in my early twenties as a graduate student for a career in science.

My first English "teacher" in the U.S. was TV. I didn't even have the concept of the commercial. I thought accidentally I touched the remote control or there was something wrong with the TV when a program suddenly jumped to unrelated subjects. In China, at the time, there were two stations, broadcasting from 6pm to 10pm. There was no commercial.

I've always loved reading, but creative writing was a dangerous career in China. As famous writers, my grandmother and aunt were wrongfully accused as counter-revolutionary Rightists. I had to choose science—a safer path.

I learned fiction writing by reading lots of books. It took me many years. When I wrote my novels, I had to use two dictionaries—Chinese to English and English to Chinese. Even so, no matter how hard I tried, I still made grammatical mistakes. That frustrated me the most. Plenty of times I laughed and scolded myself for being so stubborn to embark on this journey that seemed almost impossible to succeed. Nowadays, so many people write; everyone has an advantage over me.

I wish I'd grown up speaking English. I wish I'd had proper education or training. Since I can't change the past, I just have to work harder.

Any advice for novice writers?

Writing a novel is hard. If you don't have a burning desire, don't start. But if you are passionate about it, don't let anything or anyone stop you. Skills can be learned. Passion comes from your heart. Follow your heart. The process alone is rewarding.

Start today. Keep writing! Don't give up. Persistence. Perseverance. Patience.

I'll share several useful Chinese proverbs with you:

"A journey of a thousand miles begins with a single step."

"Every step leaves its print."

"If you work hard enough, you can grind even an iron rod down to a needle."

Looking back, I'm amazed that I finished a novel (actually three—two have been accepted for publication; one isn't good enough to share with anyone), by writing down one word after another. If I can do it, anyone can.

What's next?

Another novel, *Will of a Tiger*, has been accepted for publication and will be published. It's a sequel of *Wings of a Flying Tiger*. Once again you will meet Danny, Jasmine, Birch, Daisy, Colonel Bai, Xiao Mei… From Yunnan to Chungking, then to Taiwan, the story ends in San Francisco, taking readers on an epic journey of survival, hardship, friendship, and love.

I'm also working on a story based on my grandmother. She was the first Chinese woman to receive a master's degree in the UK. Returning to China, she became a professor and a famous writer/playwright. However, in 1957, she was wrongfully accused as a counter-revolutionary Rightist. During Cultural Revolution, she was fired from her job and ordered to sweep streets. Later, she was kicked out of the house at the university and died alone in a small village. As the political atmosphere changed in China, she was once again a celebrated writer/scholar. She was called one of the most gifted female playwrights in *Writing Women in Modern China: An Anthology of Women's Literature from the Early Twentieth Century* published by Columbia University Press in 1998. There is a park opened in her name in her hometown. Her life was a mix of triumphs and tragedies. I'll try my best to write it down.

Acknowledgments

So many people have helped me along my journey to publication. It took a village to bring this book to life.

My deep appreciation to Anne Crosman, who volunteered to edit the manuscript. A retired journalist of thirty years, she was patient and thorough. Together we went through the manuscript word by word, line by line. Without her generous help, my dream for publication might not have come true.

Many thanks to Marywave Van Deren and Gary Jacobson for your guidance.

My gratitude to Wang Liya, Wu Xia, Phil Sullivan, and David Carrier for reading the manuscript.

Thank you, Yan Li, for encouraging me to keep writing.

I'm grateful to three writing groups led by Gary Every, Naxie Reiff/Rodger Christopherson, and Mary Ann Gove. Their feedback made my book better, and their praises kept me going. I'm thankful to Robin Harris, Megan Aronson, David Kanowsky, and Dana Best for reading the story. I would also like to thank Sedona Public Library and Cottonwood Public Library for their resources.

My sincere gratitude to David Ross and Kelly Huddleston at Open Books for taking a chance on me. They made my dream come true and their support means the world to me.

Many of the facts used in this novel came from two books: *Tex Hill:*

Flying Tiger and *The Rape of Nanking*. I thank the authors—Tex Hill/ Reagan Schaupp and Iris Zhang—for the invaluable resources. Their works inspired me and made my job much easier.

Finally I give thanks to my family. I'm eternally grateful to my mother Zhou Chang and father Yang Hongyuan for their love. My special thanks to my sister Jin Yang for being the first reader, my daughter Jessie Xiong for her love and encouragement, and my best friend Libby Vetter for her constant support.

Also by Iris Yang

WILL OF A TIGER

(Sequel to WINGS OF A FLYING TIGER)

In the summer of 1945, three years after Danny Hardy and Birch Bai became sworn brothers, both of their planes go down in Yunnan Province of China during one of many daring missions. They are captured, imprisoned, and tortured by the Japanese for information about the top secret atomic bomb. Days before the end of WWII, they are faced with another life-and-death situation.

From Yunnan to Chungking, to Taiwan, and finally to San Francisco, the story takes readers on an epic journey of hardship, friendship, and love.

Made in the USA
Middletown, DE
20 July 2019